INTO THE

SHADOWS

ANNEMARIE MUNRO

First edition printed and published in the United Kingdom 2023.

A CIP catalogue record of this book is available from the British Library.

ISBN: 978-1-7393052-0-8 (Hardcover)
ISBN: 978-1-7393052-1-5 (Hardcover KDP Amazon)
ISBN: 978-1-7393052-2-2 (Paperback)
Imprint: Independently published by Cold Moon Publishing
Typesetting design: Matthew J Bird

For further information about this book, please contact the author at: www.marinemoments.uk

Cold Moon Publishing

Dedication

My dad, Colin Patrick Munro, in memory.

CHAPTER 1

News headlines: October 1984
"Calls for cooler heads over the miners' strike"
(Independent)

Luke saw her as he scrambled over drunken bodies to reach the staircase. She was sitting on the top step, leaning into the wall to let others pass. She was just sitting there, surrounded by the noise, laughter, and the boom of a university house party in full swing. He grinned at her as he leapt past to reach the toilet door.

She called out to him, "If you need the loo, you're out of luck, there're two in there, in um, full swing of, 'lengthy sexual passion'. I am queueing."

At her words he retreated and sat beside her.

"Have you been here long?" he asked.

Clara shrugged, "Not too long, but I am kind of bursting, so no point re-joining the party until I've been." She blushed and glanced up at him from under her long fringe of dark blonde hair.

He smiled at her, his mop of unruly black hair falling across his blue eyes.

"Some of the other lads've gone outside into the bushes," she offered helpfully.

"What about you?"

She gave him an arched look, "I can wait."

"No, I've a better idea," Luke said, grabbing her hand and pulling her behind him back down the stairs. He had to let go of her as they came to the small living room to navigate people lounging across the floor or propped up against old sofas. The booming beat of Guns'n'Roses echoed from another room through an archway. Some students were dancing, but most were standing around chatting and laughing, waving beer bottles or wine glasses.

When he let go of her hand he said to her over his shoulder, "This way. Come with me." And she did. She was partly terrified, partly enthralled as she clambered after his slight figure. 'Oh my god!' she quailed, 'I can't believe this, after all my daydreams as I watched him lecture, marching back and forth in front of the blackboard.'

She followed Luke, climbing over legs, discarded bottles, and crisp bowls as he headed out of the door. Someone yelled out and Luke shouted back, "Loo's out of action, going to find a flowerbed." Much laughter. Three black-clad bodies peeled themselves off the floor and followed. Clara panicked, flowerbed! Was she expected to pee in a flowerbed? What should she do now? She hesitated, turning back, but Jake, Dale, and Joe were close behind her, and jostled her forward, sweeping her out of the door into the dark, orange 'street-lamped' night.

It was warm for late October but the sudden cold after being in a hot stuffy house made her gasp. She was only wearing jeans with a white T-shirt and a man's blue and white stripy shirt. Wrapping her arms around herself she followed Luke.

Luke was waiting for her, and she caught up with him along the tree-lined suburban street. The others were each at a tree, irrigating them noisily. Luke had grabbed his jacket, a plaid donkey jacket with fur lining, somewhere between the staircase and the front door. His hands were in his pockets, so he signalled with his elbow for them to proceed down the hill.

"There's a public toilet at the end of this road," he explained. Clara nodded to show she had heard him but was not sure what to say. They walked a few yards in silence, as yells from the tree waterers faded. They turned a bend in the road, and between the trees a full moon greeted them. It was hazy with a clear ring around it - like a halo. ·

"Full moon tonight," said Clara for something to say, and then, deciding it was obvious, added, "It's going to rain."

"Are those two statements related?" Luke checked out the serious face beside him. She shot him a piercing look. She felt nervous and her heart was loud in her ears.

"Kind of. The ring around the moon indicates it will rain soon, old sailors' warning, or so my father used to tell me - and before you ask, I don't know why, unless the halo effect is caused by rain clouds we can't see because it is dark: I dunno ..." She lost confidence.

But he was happy to keep the conversation going. "It's probably like other old sayings, such as when all the cows are lying down, it'll rain, no direct causal relationship, but a coincidental one. After all, it rains a lot doesn't it, and cows must get tired mustn't they?" She smiled at him as she started to relax, forgetting to be so nervous. His words stimulated more thoughts, and this distracted her from her shyness.

"Interesting. Lyell, a geologist in the early 1800s, claimed the scientific approach was hindered by the insistence of people attributing human feelings and thoughts to animals, rather than viewing them objectively - such as expecting cows to think like humans and be able to forecast rain. Do you think you could hypothesise instead, rather than being a barrier, this was an essential steppingstone? Linking reclining cows and rain is an example of cause and effect, which is a scientific process. And if that old wives' tale is older than 1800, my point would hold true, wouldn't it: 'Old wives' laid the foundation for the development of rational deduction?"

It was the most he had ever heard her speak. "Have you been studying the history of empiricism in geography with Tony by any chance?"

"Yes!" She leapt on ahead to elaborate on her ideas.

"And all these ideas came from the ring around the moon!" Luke exclaimed, teasing her. She snapped out of her train of thought, looking a little crestfallen at his response. "Look," he said, "I have had more beer than you, and my brain needs time to process what you have said." But he responded seriously to her hypothesis, adding his ideas to hers. As he spoke, he warmed to his theory, playing semantics with her. Clara caught up with his words, she softened, nodding as he spoke, encouraging him to elaborate.

Suddenly he stopped, bringing them both physically and mentally to a halt. He cut across their flights of academic fancy, pointing to a concrete bunker crouching in the dark to the side of the road. They had reached the public toilets. "Ooo, they look grim," said Clara.

"Yep," said Luke. "I'm going to pee in this shrub over here." He moved towards the hedge bordering the road, by a bench opposite the toilet block. "Go on, you'll be fine," he said as he turned his back.

Clara tentatively approached the building, crunching broken glass underfoot. The first doorway she came to she could smell rather than see. She instinctively veered away to find another option. The other side was no better. However, she was out of sight so pulled down her jeans and pants, and crouched by the wall, balancing precariously to direct the warm stream away from her trainers. Then she shook herself, stood up, and hitched her underwear and jeans back into place. She peered around the corner to see what Luke was doing. He was sitting on the bench waiting for her, so she made her way back over to him.

He made no move to stand as she approached. Instead, fishing into his pockets he withdrew a can of beer from each one. He held one out to her. She took it, pulled the top and it fizzled and burbled over her hand. Grinning, he opened his, leaning well away from the can with exaggerated care, "They might have got a little shaken on the walk down," he admitted.

She sucked up the spilled beer, taking another sip from the can, as she climbed onto the bench beside him. Looping her legs backwards, she leaned on the back of the bench. There was silence as they sipped their drinks. It was a calm moment. Clara looked over the hedge behind the bench. The land sloped away, and she could see the lights of the city centre. Luke faced towards the now silhouetted hulk of the toilet block. Houses tiered up the hill behind it. Distant city traffic hummed, and voices wafted across the night.

Luke took a glance at his companion beside him. Her face was pale in the moonlight, and her hair was escaping in tendrils from a long ponytail. She looked across, their eyes met, and she threw him a quick smile before turning once more out over the city. The intimacy of the look unnerved her, sending a warm shiver through her whole body. Out of the corner of her eye she noticed Luke fidgeting, perhaps also affected by the exchanged glance. He spoke in a sudden rush as if grabbing a random topic for discussion to diffuse the spark of sexual energy.

"So, what do you want to do after you graduate?" he said, tugging his fingers through his curls. The question poured water on the previous emotion, sounding very 'adult' and 'sensible'; a question a lecturer would ask. Yet, Clara was pleased with the new topic of conversation.

"It's hard to find out for sure, as in essence, I want to help people, save people. I know its vague but there is not much information to help with the details. I went to the careers section of the library, but it is a tiny room with a copy of the tabloids and a shelf of tatty leaflets - and not much else. I did find a pamphlet about an organisation called Voluntary Service Overseas. Volunteers are posted overseas in development work. This sounds positive - there are so many problems to help solve. I would like to be part of the solution to test the developmental theories I am reading about." She looked at him eagerly, seeking his view on the matter.

"Hmm," he started cautiously, "Sounds like a good experience, but isn't a career as such. Perhaps afterwards you could get into charity work back in the UK or take up lecturing in a university?" he suggested. But she clearly didn't think much of his answer, huffing in the dark at her end of the bench.

"I don't necessarily want to stay in the UK. After all the theory of a degree I would like some practical work at a grassroots level, giving poor people a voice. The theories we study originate from those who are not suffering, white men in suits, living in big houses protected by the high walls of academia. I like the emerging approaches, which are listening to and incorporating the ideas of the poor to find solutions."

"You rebel socialist!" He teased and earned a grin. "I'll try not to take the dig about white men lecturing in universities personally! It might be worth considering a master's first, to gain some authority in your area of expertise. Something to consider maybe. Come on, I'm getting cold and I'm hungry - pizza?"

Clara, untangling herself from the bench, was desperately trying to think what to do. 'Why is he asking me for a pizza? What does it mean? I ought to get back to the party. People saw us leave together and gossip is a favourite pastime.' But a fission of sexual attraction flared in her again. Dare she hope that the comment meant he wanted to be with her a little longer? She smiled to herself in the dark.

"I'll walk with you to the pizza takeaway and then head on home," she clarified, more to herself than Luke. He shrugged.

"Your call," he said. They fell into step together down the rest of the hill, and across the main road.

Soon they were squeezing inside the red and white checked 'Real Italian Pizza Place' wrapped in the mouth-watering aroma of baking dough. The takeaway was busy. Although Clara had intended to go home when Luke went in, as she stopped to say goodbye more people came to queue, shunting her into the small shop where there was no option but to wait while Luke placed his order.

"Sure, you don't want anything?" he asked.

"No, I'm fine." She answered, very conscious of being pushed and jostled up against Luke while he paid for and took the large pizza box. They turned, fighting their way past people struggling to push their way in. Then it became clear why the pushing and shoving had been quite so extreme: The moon had been right, and it was raining. The rain was lashing in straight sheets, thrashing down. Everyone was running - for shelter, for taxis. Luke and Clara hovered at this scene.

Clara surveyed the scene of scurrying drowned rats, and then up at Luke inquiringly. He took her hand, raised the pizza box above their heads to provide some degree of shelter, and tugged her out into the rain. They dashed along the precinct, to a blue door wedged innocuously between Woolworths and Russell and Bromley's shoe shop. He let go of her, thrust the pizza box into her arms to retrieve a key from his coat pocket, and opened the door. He hustled her in ahead of him, eager to get out of the downpour.

Slamming the door closed behind him, he put on a light, and they were in a small hallway. A couple of coats hung from wall hooks and a pair of muddy walking boots were cast off on the floor. To the right was a steep flight of stairs. Luke nudged her to go up. At the top, the room opened into a lounge. There was a small TV propped up on a milk crate, and a battered old sofa littered with what looked like a pile of assignment scripts. On the far wall was a large window flanked by bookshelves. To the left, an archway opened into an alcove revealing a fridge, sink, and cooker with yellow doored kitchen cupboards above. To the right were two more doors, both closed.

"Move the chessboard off that coffee table and put the pizza down - I'll get us a drink." Clara wandered across the room, ignoring the instructions, hugging the pizza to her while she went to examine the bookshelf. Luke saw her.

"Oh no you don't," he called. "Bring the pizza back here - let's eat it before you drown it." She dragged herself reluctantly away from the books and returned the pizza to the sofa. "You are soaked!" Luke exclaimed. She looked at him, standing there with a beer in each hand, raindrops dripping from his curly hair and moustache. She laughed.

"You, too!"

He put the cans by the pizza and tossed her a towel off a drying rack standing guard in front of a two-bar electric heater.

"Here you are, use this." She rubbed herself down, but her jeans were wet through, cold, and felt horrible. "Take them off, I'll put the heater on," Luke suggested, handing her one of his jumpers to put on instead. He disappeared into the bedroom to change himself. She peeled off her jeans and shirt, hung them on the drying rack, and put his jumper on instead. The jumper was soft, came down to her knees, and smelt of Luke to an overwhelming sense of intimacy, making her feel giddy. Panic flooded through her as she realised, she had gotten herself, in the blink of an eye, into such a situation. She thought she shouldn't be here but was also aware she wanted to be. She felt excited but afraid. 'Any minute now my nerves will get the better of me and I will turn into a crimson tongue-tied moron, and he will hate me,' she fretted.

Luke had changed into jogging bottoms and another t-shirt. He joined her as she sat on the sofa, curled like a cat, swamped in his jumper. He placed the pizza box between them and passed her a beer. As she had predicted she was at a loss for words, locked in behind a wall of self-consciousness, as if viewing the scene from a distance. This is what had prevented her from speaking to him before now. Being with him in a lecture with fifty other students was fine but having all his attention to herself terrified her. Her heart beat fast, deafening her. She wasn't hungry at all and had to wash the pizza down with beer. She knew he was saying something but had no idea what it was. Turning pink under his gaze she was desperate to calm herself.

She spotted the chessboard. Chess, she loved chess. Her mind rested on the pieces and started to trace the game. As a lullaby soothes a baby, the process of analytical thought soothed her nerves, distracting her. She forgot her beating heart and managed to step out of her prison of nerves back into the room. Luke was looking at her strangely, he had obviously been saying something deserving a reply. She shook her head and swallowed her pizza.

"Sorry, I wasn't listening - I was looking at the chess game. Who're you playing with?"

"Oh, just something to amuse me between marking assignments. Bryn, your favourite psychology tutor and I, play occasionally - Or I play against myself." Clara was surprised.

"How can you do that? Surely it must always be a stalemate as you would know what the other side's planning?" He laughed.

"It's not that planned, believe me! Sometimes I even forget whose turn it is and play the same side twice: I always win though, which is nice." She smiled at his joke.

"And, who's turn is it now, black or white?"

"Hmm ..." He surveyed the chessboard, frowning as he tried to remember. "I've only just started this one, white's turn I think." Clara giggled as if he had made another joke. He raised his eyebrows at her in query. She needed to explain.

"Well, one more move by white to checkmate, isn't it? It's going to be a very quick game! I used to get caught by that one all the time at school. I was desperate to be the first girl onto the chess ladder - so frustrating." She laughed at his only partial comprehension and slid off the sofa onto the floor, to reach the board. She moved the bishop forward two spaces and he understood. He grinned sheepishly, flopping back on the sofa.

"Girl, you cannot expect clear thought at this time of night!" But she clearly did.

"Can I borrow one of your books?"

"Which one and why? I guard my books, or I'd have none."

"Silent Spring. I've read about how influential it has been but haven't managed to read the actual book. What did you think of it?"

"Questions! Questions!" he moaned dramatically. But seeing how she seemed to unfurl as they chatted, he sat up and slid off the sofa onto the floor beside her. Forcing his befuddled brain to cooperate, he attempted to answer her question. They chatted for what seemed both ages and no time at all. Luke was delighted with her conversation, it betrayed wide reading and deep thinking about what she was being taught, very flattering for a lecturer. As they talked, she stretched her legs out and leaned back against the sofa. He joined her and they sat shoulder to shoulder throwing wild suggestions out into the room.

There was a natural lull in the conversation and Luke disappeared into the bathroom. Left alone, Clara wandered back over to the bookshelves. With her head on one side to easily read the titles along the spines, she did not hear Luke return, until she felt him - his breath on her neck, his presence right behind her. He was too close for her to turn without them bumping noses. Her brain swam, crashing about. She couldn't think of what to do, so she did what she wanted to do and turned to him.

He raised his hand and stroked her cheek. His fingers went to her neck, through her hair and he pulled her into a kiss. The kiss was velvet smooth. Soft lips caressed her own, lighting such a fire in her belly she thought if she looked down, she would see flames. He must have felt the same intensity, as he pulled her tighter to him. Their bodies pressed against each other, his tongue pushed between her teeth, making her legs buckle slightly.

He drew her back to the sofa, where they sat entangled, legs interlaced, half on, half off each other's lap. The kisses continued as his hands moved under the jumper and caressed her back. 'Oh god! oh god!' screamed her brain, 'What do I do? What do I do?' The inevitability of where this was now leading was clear, and she worried she was not doing things right. Doubt plagued her mind - how to move, what to touch - she felt awkward and clumsy.

The jumper came off as he peeled it over her head. She feared she would look flushed, but he was looking straight into her eyes, and she felt the rising panic abate. He released her bra strap and as it followed the jumper onto the floor, his head bent to kiss her breasts. She arched her back towards him, her fingers combing through his curls.

She tugged at his t-shirt, feeling unequal in her nakedness. With a grin and a flourish that was on the floor too. They explored, absorbed in a world of intoxicating touch. At some point, they unbalanced and toppled onto the floor. Luke, then led her through to the bedroom, the bed unmade and vaguely strewn with clothing. He pushed her gently back onto the folds of the duvet. Then, stripping off his bottoms, he stood naked before her in the dimness.

Clara's memories from that point were hazy. She remembered the rocking rhythms and riding on the wings of his passion, sensing more than directly experiencing a heightening of ecstasy. At one time she pulled him closer to her and he moaned, bucking under her grip. Gasping and with a final exclamation, he fell heavily on her, hugged her to him for a moment, then slid off sideways beside her. She felt exhausted, shaken, and unwilling to move. She was dimly aware of him leaving the room, a toilet flush, and then he slid back in beside her, throwing the covers over them. The grey morning dawned as they slept.

CHAPTER 2

Top UK chart hit: October 1984
Smooth Operator: Sade

Before she was even conscious of being awake, she was aware of a dull throbbing headache. She tried to swallow but her tongue stuck to her mouth. She half opened her eyes. She groaned, sat up, and groaned again. The bed was empty. She could hear faint clicks and clacks of cups. Then Luke was there, a cup of coffee in one hand and a bottle of paracetamol in the other. But Clara barely noticed what was in his hands and did not register as he placed them on the bedside table. He hesitated, then turned and left the room. No, she had seen his face and it had winded her like a kick to the stomach - she felt hot, cold, and very sick all at once. His face was blank, his eyelids hooded, his eyes cold, his mouth thin in a tight-lipped downturn. Obviously, he was not happy to wake up and find her there, the memories causing regret. She had his expression imprinted on her brain which played over and over tormenting her. In the silent flat she felt claustrophobic, unable to breathe. Her head hammered, waves of hot shame washed over her, and the chant, 'he regrets it, he regrets it,' was on an endless loop.

She stumbled out of bed. 'Where the hell are my clothes?' She peered out of the bedroom into the living room. It was empty and she could hear what sounded like a shower coming from the bathroom. She shot out, pulling on her clothes from the floor and the drying rack - memories, disembodied and floating out of sequence, besieged her. Hot tears fell unheeded as she tugged on her damp jeans. Dressed, she cast a look around the room. Her eyes rested on the chessboard. She checkmated the black king. She knew it was silly, but it felt good. After another listen to make sure the water was still running, she snatched a book from the bookshelf, sprinted down the stairs and out of the door, slamming it hard behind her.

She felt so hurt, so humiliated, crushed, a fool, and an idiot. She strode with no heed of direction, powered forwards by her raging emotions. It was cold and had only recently stopped raining. Her feet and the bottom of her jeans were soon soaked. She was down by the river, being lapped by super keen Sunday morning joggers, and dog walkers. She marched on, burning off some of her fury. Then she ran out of steam altogether and fell onto a bench, hugging her knees to her chest, ignoring the fact she was now soaked through. Allowing her feelings full reign she sobbed, her shoulders convulsing.

"Are you alright my dear?" A gentle voice cut through her misery. A hand rested on her shoulder, as light as a butterfly's touch. She looked up through her tangled hair to see a petite grey-haired lady looking concerned. Her terrier was sniffing around the bench, less concerned. Clara took a shuddery breath lowering her legs and gave the lady a watery smile.

"Yes, thanks. I'm okay - or will be - I just didn't realise how much I hate men!"

The lady smiled, "Man trouble? You and half of the global population. Take my word for it, things always look better after a good cup of tea. Go get yourself one of those and life won't seem so bad: After the rain comes the sun." She spread her hands towards the sky, which was indeed clearing to be a nice day after the night of rain. She called to her dog and disappeared along the path.

Clara sat back on the bench and took another breath as her tears dried. The old lady was right; she hated tea, but she longed for a hot coffee. She noticed a whole troop of runners making their way towards her, a bobbing flock of annoying cheerful neon pink and yellow lycra, colour-coordinated leg warmers, ponytails swinging - uh! She tried to look less deranged and hurried off in the direction of home.

At home, she retrieved her key out of her jeans pocket and crept into the hall. All was silent. The kitchen door stood open, no light, no noise: All good so far. She tiptoed up the stairs, pausing to listen every few steps - continued silence. She made it past Reeta and Judy's bedroom doors to the third floor and her attic room. She closed the door behind her with a sigh of relief.

She changed into her pyjamas, dressing gown, and slippers, feeling better all the time. Perhaps she could pretend it was all a dream? She was brushing out her hair when a face appeared around her door. Clara was startled at how close she had come to being found in the wrong clothes, on the wrong side of the door.

"You, okay?" said Reeta

"Um, yes, fine-ish," Clara hedged.

"We were worried about you. You disappeared from Jane's party and never came back. People were saying you left with

Luke - is that right? What's going on? You sure you're okay?" At Reeta's obvious concern Clara could not help the tears returning with vengeance. Her friend rushed to her, hugged her and then stepped back - "How bad is it? Coffee? Wine? Or so bad we have to raid the Bailey's?" Clara smiled weakly.

"Only 'coffee bad' - I'll come down with you." The kitchen was mortuary cold, as usual. They lit the gas fire, made coffee and toast, then sat on the benches at the kitchen table. As they were taking their first sips, Judy appeared, also wrapped up in layers of bedwear looking bleary-eyed.

"Hey, both. You're back then Clara, we were worried. Tell all." Waving her teaspoon she added, "Start away while I make myself a pot of tea." They both looked at Clara expectantly, waiting to hear, ready to offer advice and support. Clara suddenly realised the unforeseen cost of crossing unbidden lines as she had done last night. She didn't think sleeping with a lecturer was allowed so couldn't let anyone know about last night. She was going to have to lie to her friends.

"I did leave with Luke last night," she began. Both girls exchanged knowing glances and grinned. "No! It was nothing like that." Clara interjected, in earnest entreaty. "I left because he said he would walk me to the public loos, you know the ones at the bottom of the hill? Janet and Kev were bonking all night in Jane's bathroom." The other two nodded.

"They came out eventually when Jane went up and threatened to break the door down," Judy said. Clara nodded and then resumed her account.

"That was the best part of the evening." Clara confided, sticking as close to the truth as she could, "I had him to myself as we chatted down the hill." They grinned as Clara blushed,

21

remembering that segment of the night. "Anyway, the loos were all locked up and in a bad state, I couldn't go behind a bush on my period and all that. I couldn't tell him though, could I?" They nodded. "So, I told him I didn't feel too well. He walked me as far as Pete's Pizza Place at the end of the road - I came on home. Luke said he might go back to the party after he had bought his pizza so would tell you I had gone home - but I gather he didn't?" She realised she was holding her breath to see if her story sounded plausible.

"But what I don't understand then," said Reeta, Clara's toast held suspended between plate and mouth, waiting for Reeta to finish her sentence, "why the tears when I came up? Doesn't sound bad. What else happened?" It took Clara a second to think of a response, again she relied upon the truth as much as possible, and so was able to explain.

"I am so worried what will happen now. Everyone will think we went off together - I should have gone back to tell you I was going home, not leave it up to Luke. You know what the rumour machine is like. It will be all around uni already - Do you think Luke will be in trouble? He will never talk to me again!" She wasn't sure the story quite hung together, but the girls allowed the story to stand, and turned their attention to the problem at hand.

"Well," said Judy, pouring out her cup of tea, "I must admit the gossip was already churning last night. And to be honest, you do like him, and he likes you - his eyes follow you across a room … " Clara shook her head.

"No, he doesn't like me, not like that anyway!" They looked surprised at her bitter outburst, and she bit her lip realising it looked odd. "Well, he would have offered to walk me all the way home if he cared wouldn't he, not abandon me a mile from home in favour of a pizza?" she reasoned. The girls saw her hurt and feeling of rejection - truth shared out at last.

For the rest of the day, fear lay in the pit of Clara's stomach. She felt sick with worry, unable to concentrate on anything, even her ill-gotten book. Would anyone find out what really happened? Would she get thrown out of university? What would her parents say? She did not even appreciate the usual Sunday evening ritual of the BBC Poldark rerun on the black and white television in the kitchen. Instead of romanticising over Robin Ellis, imagined conversations flashed through her mind. Her father would be disappointed - a wound to pierce her heart more keenly than her mother's predictable tears about 'humiliation' and 'I knew you would not manage to survive on your own.' Clara would be fetched, packed up, and taken away; encircled back into their embrace of hostile reproach and scorn in rural isolation. She had worked so hard to persuade them she would be able to survive away at university. "But you are so shy and uncommunicative, no one will like you - you'll have no friends!" lamented her mother. "Stay home and we will sign you up to Open University. You can get a degree that way, then train locally to be a primary school teacher. You will make an excellent primary school teacher. You can talk to children," her mother had repeated the whole summer of her A Levels. 'And now I have proved her right!' thought Clara to herself.

Clara spent Monday hiding in the library to block out all other worries. She forgot about lunch, only breaking off when Mary, the librarian, dragged her out to lock up the building at eight pm. She had made good progress; had researched an outline of an essay for Bryn, her Psychology tutor, as well as planned an essay for an International Development module for her lecturer, Tony. Pleased, she heaved her bag over towards the Students Union Bar. She could hear Marillion's 'Kayleigh' pounding across the campus as she approached. Reeta worked behind the bar and Judy worked in the kitchen serving burgers and chips. Clara was starving but she didn't have much money on her - maybe a plate of chips and a blackcurrant and soda? She put her bag behind the bar, then fought her way around to the snack bar to buy some food.

Even though it was crowded, and smoky, she was aware of Luke's presence. He was over in the far corner behind the disco speakers, hanging out with Jed, Robin, and others she didn't know. It felt good to know he was near, but she didn't dare go over. Ignoring him she balanced herself near the bar to eat her chips. Returning her plate, she asked Judy when her shift was ending.

"Ten-ish, but we will stay open if we remain busy."

"Okay, I may wait, or go on ... I don't know yet." She was often left on her own when Reeta and Judy worked. Without these two friends to sit with, she didn't know many others well enough to be comfortable to join. She decided to go home: She could carry on with her essay. She collected her bag from the bar, pushed her way out into the cold night, heading towards the bike sheds.

"Clara!" Luke emerged out of the dark, pulling her from the path. They stood concealed from view behind a fence around the bins and barrels at the back of the bar. "Where the hell have you been? You missed my lecture this morning - they are not optional! Why weren't you there?"

Clara ridiculously, felt like smiling. Relieved. Even if he was scolding her, it was better than the blank face and silent stare from Sunday morning.

"I went to the library instead."

"You missed an important lecture," he retorted.

"I will copy Jorgi's notes, she has said I could," she answered, trying to annoy him.

"That's not the point!" he replied, clearly annoyed. "What were you up to in the library that was more important than my lecture?"

"Reading." He looked murderous; his eyes black with fury.

"Silent Spring, by any chance?" he hissed. "Give me my book back." Their eyes locked in silent combat. She reached down to her bag, removed the book, and placed it slowly into his outstretched hands. He snatched it and stuffed it into his jacket pocket.

They continued to glare at each other through the gloom. But suddenly a beam of light highlighted them as someone came out the back door to add empty beer bottles to a crate. They dodged behind a large industrial waste bin and huddled close. Clara could feel his breath ruffling her fringe. She wondered if he could hear her thumping heart. She was angry with him but also happy to be beside him again, confused in a tangle of emotions. As the door closed plunging them back into the dark, she blurted out.

"Everyone is gossiping about us, but I have told anyone who will listen, nothing happened."

Luke slumped back against the bin, facing her.

"Perhaps that's what should've happened," he said in a flat voice.

"Well, it's obviously what you were thinking - or wishing - the next morning!" came the sudden response; the bitterness and vehemence surprised Clara herself.

"What would you know about what I was thinking? You slammed your way out of the flat so fast, I didn't even have time to share my thoughts!" Luke snapped back, jumping forwards glaring at her.

"You had shared them! They were written all over your face."

"That was my very hungover, hope I am not going to chuck up face. I could barely focus, and I believe I even managed to make you a cup of coffee! If you had given me a chance, we could have resolved a few issues. We would certainly not be in a position of adding more fire to the rumour flames! But no, you had to flounce off, to goodness knows where, slamming the front door so hard you even broke the glass!" They were nose to nose, as he had leaned closer warming to his theme, releasing pent-up exasperation with her. There was silence for a moment, then Clara frowned.

"What glass? There isn't a window in your front door." She tried to picture it - "It's blue, wood, solid with a letter box, door handle ... no window." At her words, the tension snapped, and Luke forced a weak grin.

"Yeh, I know - got carried away. But if there had been a window, it would have shattered," he told her sternly. But the absurdity of what he was saying made them both laugh. In a softer tone, Luke said, "Sorry, I didn't mean to make you run away." She shrugged, beginning to see the whole experience from a different perspective.

"I'm sorry too - I take everything too seriously. Let's forget it." By 'let's forget it,' she meant 'forget the whole night', so they could turn back the clock to pick up from before, student and lecturer once more. The thought made her feel very sensible, but also bereft. She was sure it was just a silly drunken evening as far as he was concerned, and she was providing him with a way out. He didn't say anything, so she made to leave.

"I'd better go, I have to get a psyc. essay in by tomorrow which I haven't finished yet." But he caught her wrist drawing her to him. His hand cupped her chin, raising her face to his. He leaned in kissing her tenderly. She melted into his kiss but then struggled to withdraw.

"Does this not complicate things even further?" she asked. He smiled and pulled her back in for a fuller kiss, lips melting into lips, tongues pushing hungrily into each other's mouths, bodies locked. As they parted, he answered her.

"Or you could argue it simplifies it?" He raised his eyebrows, seeking her reaction. She nodded, not entirely sure what he meant, but the kiss seemed to indicate he was no longer regretting Saturday night.

"Will you come down to my place?"

"What? Now?"

"Look," he fumbled around in his coat pocket, "take my door key, you have your bike and will get there before me. I will go and finish my pint with the lads, then I will be with you. There's beer in the fridge, don't steal all my books, oh, and it's your move in chess. I started a new game; it's waiting for you." With a final kiss, he melted back into the night, leaving her clutching his key.

CHAPTER 3

News headlines: December 1984
36 of Britain and Ireland's top pop musicians gather in a Notting Hill studio to form Band Aid and record the song "Do They Know It's Christmas" to raise money for famine relief in Ethiopia.

Clara breathed a sigh of relief as the scenery sped past. The flat bleak levels of Somerset eventually gave rise to the soft chalk hills of the East. Then fields gave way to urban lives flicking past the window. Luke had invited her to spend a week in London with him at his sister's flat at the end of the Christmas holidays. It was an opportunity to have time together without having to hide and pretend they were not a couple. Clara had spent Christmas with her parents. When it had come time to go to London, Clara let her parents think she was off to spend the week with Reeta. Although pleased to see she was making friends, the IRA terrorist bomb attack in London at Christmas the previous year, made them nervous. It took a lot of convincing to persuade them to drop her off at the station on the day, in time for the 11.40 train to London Paddington.

Luke, hunched up inside his donkey jacket against the bitterly cold January weather, was there to meet her at Paddington. Arm in arm they plunged into the underground.

"How was your Christmas?" he asked her as they found a space on the crowded platform. Clara pulled a face. "That bad, eh?" he grinned, pulling her close.

"Oh, it was so boring. I walked the dogs so often they hid when they saw me coming. The Two Ronnies and Wogan on Christmas Day - compulsive viewing," she faked a yawn, "although I did get the new Howard Jones cassette album from my brother which I have listened to 100 times already. You'll like it - Oh, and my dad has taken up yoga; he took me along to some of his sessions."

"Yoga?"

"Well, yes, I enjoyed it actually - I may look for a group nearby at uni to go to this term. I find it calming." She glanced up to see Luke's reaction. He grinned as their eyes met, but he didn't seem to think it was an odd thing to do.

"Whatever floats your boat, honey. If I were ever to get down on the floor in a cross-legged position, I don't think I could ever get up again though, so count me out."

They pushed their way onto a train and swayed along the Northern Line to Clapham.

"Have you been at your sister's long?" Clara asked him as they emerged into a cold afternoon to walk across the common. She was trying to gain some insight into his Christmas.

"Not long. I went to see the parents briefly, then came here. You'll like Charlie, she's a laugh. She has the week off - on school holidays as she is a PE teacher, so we can all go and do touristy things together." Clara was rather daunted by this prospect, but it was worth it to be with Luke without having to hide it. They turned into the forecourt of a low block of art deco-style flats and Luke held the door for her as they went in.

"Don't mind her husband, Greg. He is alright really but can be a little gruff and curt."

Clara was amused to see Charlie had the same curly black hair as her brother, with tumbling locks disobeying all combs. Charlie was friendly but the girls had little in common, so Luke bridged the gap. Brother and sister were very close, and Clara was content listening to their sibling banter. The relationship between Clara and Greg however was less congenial.

On the first evening, Greg merely said a polite hello, then read his paper. The other three sat around the small Formica table in the kitchen chatting, mainly Luke and Charlie catching up on family gossip. Yet Clara had a distinct impression Greg was not reading the paper but instead listening to their conversation. She thought it was weird, why not put the paper down and join in? All she saw of him most of the week was a spray of rusty strands on top of his head, and his fat fingers around the paper. His left thumb nail sported a very vivid, painful-looking bruise as if he had shut it in a car door. If he had been more friendly, she may have conjured up the nerves to ask about it and express her condolences for such a nasty injury.

One evening, after an exhausting day of art galleries, they were all gathered in the small living room. Greg had been home when they arrived back and he put his paper down for two minutes to chat, asking after their day. Charlie then went to make tea and although she declined Clara's offer of help when Luke offered, she said he could earn his keep and peel the potatoes. Left alone with Greg, Clara thought she had better say something, so she asked Greg what he did for a job. Greg had gone back behind his paper just answering her curtly from behind a page.

"In Government."

"Clear as mud. Glad I bothered to ask," She retorted, stung by Greg's rudeness and self-importance.

Greg put his paper back down to reconsider the flushed face eyeing him from the sofa.

"Oh, she does have a voice then: A smart-arse sarcastic one - the lowest form of wit and hubris typical of hot-housed university fodder." She ignored him after a quick darting glance and returned her attention to the book in her lap. He levered himself up to get himself a drink. He waved a bottle of whisky in her direction.

"No thanks."

"So, what is Clever-Clogs studying at that world-famous - 'not' - university of yours?"

"Psych, Socio-politics, and Development Studies," she replied in a sharp tone, irritated.

"So, employed to do nothing useful at all then. What are you planning to do with such an odd assortment of dangerous snippets of knowledge?" he asked as if he didn't really want to know.

"Probably work in Government like you if I am employed to do nothing useful." Clara flushed deeper at her words. They were more cutting than she had intended, but he riled her. Greg did not seem insulted, but more interested in her than previously, and he eyed her curiously over his whisky glass.

"Be careful what you wish for young lady," he replied before disappearing back behind the newspaper once more.

On their last day, Luke said he would like to go to the Imperial War Museum. Clara and Charlotte skimmed the displays, taking a general holistic impression of the war history.

Luke was left behind digesting each display and reading all the information in full. They went for a coffee while they waited for Luke to re-join them. Clara was curious.

"How did you meet Greg?"

"At one of my parents' house parties. They live in an embarrassingly large pile of stones in Kent, the family home they sink all their time and money into - organising charity balls for endless 'good causes. Hasn't Luke revealed his wealthy roots?" she inquired.

"No, he has kept that well-hidden, hiding his tracks as an articulate socialist!"

"Yeah well, us kids see it as a burden and spend more of our time ignoring the old parents. Although we do contribute sometimes to their good causes - homeless puppies, etcetera. Well Greg and I do, Luke not so much. Better make sure you have a ball gown hidden away for when he is ready to share you with the rest of the family."

Clara realised how little she knew of Luke. Was it her fault? Had she not been interested enough to ask? But no, she remembered one night, resting in bed together they had asked the, 'how many brothers and sisters do you have?' kind of questions. He had said he had one sister and his parents lived in Kent. He had chosen not to share much when he had the opportunity. She couldn't think it was of particular concern though. She had done the same, abbreviating details of her own home to, 'one elder brother, parents in Somerset.'

"Luke has never introduced me to one of his girlfriends before," Charlie told Clara. "I can see he likes you a lot." Clara smiled, warmed by her words.

"He tells me you are one of his students. Is that allowed?"

"No, apparently not. It makes things, um, difficult. This week has been lovely though, thank you for letting us stay."

"Mmm, I hope it is the right thing."

Clara wasn't sure how to respond, but Luke showed up at that moment, accusing them both of being uncultured ignoramuses. A debate ensued on whether there was such a word, or not.

It was as they were walking along the Thames it happened. They battled against the bitter January wind whistling up the river, regretting their decision to walk along Southbank, rather than go home.

"Don't remember seeing so many cops along here before," remarked Luke, pulling his collar up higher against the wind.

"Yes, more here than we have seen all day," Clara added.

"Probably due to the IRA threat …" replied Charlie, "Although why here rather than anywhere else I can't think."

"Last year the bomb went off in Harrods, didn't it? Is it near here?" asked Clara

"No, Harrods is in Knightsbridge, across to the West, about an hour's walk away- Oh look! That's clever. To hold so still on a day like this, he deserves a medal, not just a few pennies in a hat!" exclaimed Charlotte, leading Luke and Clara over towards a street artist braving the icy air - a man pretending to be a gold statue. There was also a multi-coloured acrobat careering around with spinning batons and a maniacal laugh.

Set back from the street artists in the shadow, hunched over to shoulder the wind, were a couple of homeless men, grey and faded like the pavement on which they sat. Clara's attention was caught, not by the acrobat, but by these grey hunched men: There was something about them. They didn't portray the lethargic hopelessness of resigned, poverty-induced lassitude she had seen others around London exude. These two seemed like coiled springs, with the pent-up energy of a ticking bomb. Their faces were hidden in the hoods of their jackets. Yet, her eyes lingered on them.

His hands gave him away - she knew those hands, pudgy fingers, the bruise on his thumb showing clearly. If the men were there just to observe, their body language would not be so 'charged' and on edge. She was instantly alert to the wider environment, feeling protective towards Charlotte and Luke. She looked around but the others were still engaged in the entertainment. She felt danger; it prickled along her skin making her shiver. Every instinct was screaming at her to get away.

The gold statue suddenly jumped off his dais, startling a small crowd who applauded and showered coins into his hat. He bowed, but is eyes were sweeping across the crowd as if looking for someone, his hands balled into fists, as if ready to pounce. His stance galvanised Clara into action. With one last glance at the shrouded figures, Clara pushed against Luke and Charlotte.

"Can we move somewhere quieter? I don't know what's wrong, but I feel faint." She dropped to her knees, pulling on Luke. Luke and Charlotte tore their eyes away from the gold man and acrobat. Between them they held Clara as she clung to them.

The acrobat was now twirling his batons with ferocity right in front of them. He tossed them high as he peddled his unicycle under their spinning, capturing the crowd's attention away from the gold man. Clara caught the acrobat's eye.

"Which way?" she mouthed, as much to herself as to him. But he pirouetted with a flourish and pointed his batons to the left behind him, where she spotted a narrow alleyway leading to the back of some shops. She dragged Luke and Charlotte that way. Not a moment too soon. As they made it to a bench, they heard shouting and screams on the riverfront behind them. Sirens wailed as people streamed past them, out of the way of whatever was going on. Luke and Charlie made Clara put her head between her knees until she convinced them she felt better. They then let the crowd sweep them along, away from the Thames, and the chaos.

"What do you think that was all about?" asked Clara.

"Probably arresting someone," said Charlie, "who knows - IRA related maybe as we said earlier." She shrugged and led the way into the underground. Luke put an arm around Clara's shoulders giving her a small smile.

"Forget it honey, we will probably never know, and don't need to - at least we missed getting caught up in it and I suggest we get you home."

Luke and Clara had agreed to take Charlie and Greg out for a meal to thank them for their hospitality on the last evening. They had booked a restaurant across The Common. Greg phoned before they left to say he would be late, but for them to go on without him. They walked, wrapped up warmly, linking arms pretending to be dancing along the yellow brick road to the Land of Oz. This set the tone for a rather silly and hilarious evening. Greg didn't show up, and Clara wondered if this worried Charlie. But Charlie shrugged.

"He often has to work late."

Greg was there when they arrived home though. He was coming back down the stairs as they piled into the building.

"Need a smoke. Busy day," he said to Charlie, kissing her and waving an unlit cigarette in his hand. "Clara, would you mind bringing me down a whisky - two fingers, no water? Cheers." Without waiting for an answer, he went out onto the front steps of the building.

"Here," Clara said, holding the whisky out to him as he leaned against the low wall dividing the art deco block of flats from the main street. He produced a hip flask from his breast pocket and took a swig from it.

"That's yours," he said, "I have mine here." She made a face. "Go on, down in one," he ordered. So, she closed her eyes gulping it down as if it was medicine. It hit the back of her throat with a bitter blast, making her eyes water. However, the spreading warmth seeping through her veins after she swallowed, she had to admit, was a pleasant defence against the freezing cold.

She placed the empty glass on the wall and shoved both hands into her pockets. She assumed the meeting wasn't over. Greg did not speak for some moments, dragging hard on his cigarette, inhaling deeply before letting the smoke out slowly. He looked across at her serious profile standing still and patient beside him. Her name and details had been fed into the headquarters computers. 'Female, born 1964, student, no record,' - a nobody.

"Of all the places for you three to be today, you had to be there, didn't you?" Greg said.

"As far as I was aware, we didn't know we weren't supposed to be there."

"Charlie said you were going to the Imperial War Museum."

"We did, then decided to walk along the river."

"Who decided?" Greg barked. Clara shot him a sideways look before once more addressing the street.

"Why? Do you think one of us designed to be there? I assure you; it was accidental. For the record, you made a rubbish homeless man."

"Why?"

She considered for a moment.

"It was not your appearance; it was your stance. You gave off a feeling of energy, of being 'wired.' Homeless men are generally apathetic, sunken in depression with a sense of hopelessness."

"It couldn't have been that obvious. No one else noticed. But you noticed. You ignored the acrobat."

"Your hand was showing."

"God! My hand? What the hell!" He threw the stub into the gutter spinning to face her, the strain of the day etched in his scowl and in the roughness of his voice. She stood firm under his stare, breathing slightly deeper to steady her as she had learned from her yoga practice. She knew what she knew, and she wasn't afraid. She was more curious than anything. She was calm in the face of his frustration but remained alert. She sensed someone else quite close although she couldn't see anyone. But Greg was still a towering column of questions and she realised he was demanding an answer. She sighed, annoyed with him.

"Your hand was clean, no dirt under your nails. You have nice hands; they are all I have seen of you most of the week as you've held the newspaper in front of your face. And you have a bruised nail on your thumb," she explained, adopting the tone he used when speaking to her, distant and disinterested. He took out his hip flask, took a gulp, and handed it to her. Again, the flash of flame and the appreciative warmth.

"What and who else did you see?"

"Not sure I know what you mean. The pavement was crowded. You attracted my attention. I realised it was you. I sensed your energy and was afraid for Charlie and Luke. So, I pretended to feel ill to encourage them to come away. The acrobat told me to go through the alleyway behind - so we made our escape. That's it. All hell broke loose, and we were swept along, and came home." While she spoke, the atmosphere changed. Greg had frozen and out of the dark a tall man materialised - long black coat, nondescript features, medium height, short dark hair, medium nose, average mouth; almost as if designed to be easily forgotten. He stepped between Clara and Greg with authority, taking over the questioning. Clara was forced to take a step back, and she looked over his shoulder to Greg, who was staring intently at her.

"The acrobat?" the stranger asked.

"The acrobat what?"

"You said, 'the acrobat told you which way to go.' What do you mean?" Clara ran again through her memory of events checking herself. Did it happen as she thought? 'Stranger' sounded as if he would not tolerate any mistakes.

"Well," she said, trying to remain undaunted by him, focusing only on her memories. "I was trying to pull Charlie and Luke away. But I wasn't sure which way was away from pending danger. I caught the eye of the acrobat. I was distracted, pretending to faint. But I kind of mouthed or shouted out - not sure now - 'which way?' and he looked right at me, twirled his batons to point behind him to the alleyway. It may have been a coincidence, but that is why I went where I did." She waited to see what would happen next. Greg was pacing back and forth, running his fingers through his hair distractedly. 'Stranger' turned his back on Clara, facing Greg. There seemed to be some kind of silent debate going on and it no longer appeared to involve her, so she took a step back. Greg reached out a hand onto her arm to hold her.

"Clara, thanks for telling us this. It helps. Please keep this conversation to yourself - national security?" Both were looking at her.

"Yes. Sure. No problem. Can I go in now, it's freezing out here?"

"Yes, go in - can you tell Charlie I have to go back to work? I will see her tomorrow." With a glance at 'stranger', who nodded at her, and a final glance at Greg, who, she was almost certain, gave her a faint wink, she gratefully retreated from the strange gathering.

CHAPTER 4

February 1985

The Boomtown Rats are playing at The Gaumont while at the cinema Eddie Murphy is starring in Beverly Hills Cops.

"He knows Luke! He knows about us!" sobbed Clara as she stumbled up the stairs to his flat.

"Calm down for goodness' sake. Who knows what?"

"Bryn. He saw us. This morning when you passed by and touched the small of my back making me jump, and we caught each other's eye - Bryn saw us. He knows!"

"Don't be daft, he couldn't know from such a tiny action, he would have no idea. You are being over-sensitive. Look, the kettle has just boiled, make yourself a coffee then come and see what you think of this article."

The doorbell to the flat rang shrilly. Luke went down to the front door, and Clara was not surprised to hear Bryn's voice. She heard Luke tell Bryn it was not convenient for him to come in. Clara leaned over the banisters to address them both.

"Let him in Luke. He knows I am here. I told you; our body language gave us away."

"Clara!" He disagreed, claiming if she hadn't 'butted in' Bryn would never have known.

"I knew the instant I saw you both together. Other things fell in place too." Bryn interrupted their argument, coming up the stairs behind Luke. He was angry and sad - his voice tore at Clara's heart. She gathered her bag and coat.

"I am going to go. You two need to talk."

"Oh no you're not," interjected Luke.

"Yes," she argued, "You two are friends and you need to sort this out. I know how awful it is to have secrets from friends, I live with it too remember - you have to make up." She was thinking sadly of her friends she had had to keep silent to about Luke and went to leave.

"I'll give you a lift home Clara." Bryn turned to follow her. "And then I'll come back," he said over his shoulder to Luke.

"No, it's okay, I have my bike."

"No, it's late."

"Bryn, I'm okay. I don't want a lift."

"I don't care what you want. We'll put your bike in the boot of the car. I insist on giving you a lift home." Reluctantly she let him do as he said, hoisting her bike into the boot of his Morris Marina and securing it with a bungee cord. She dreaded the next conversation. But once in the car, he was grimly silent until he requested directions. By car, it was only a five minutes' drive. He pulled up outside the house, cut the engine, and turned towards her. She knew better than to do anything other than meet the terrible gaze - she felt his waves of disappointment and disapproval keenly.

"How long?" he asked sharply. She thought back.

"Since October," she admitted. He sat back exasperated, banging his hands on the steering wheel, making her jump. He leapt out of the car slamming the door. After a moment, she clamoured out too, feeling shaky. Bryn was leaning against the car, and Clara went to stand beside him. It was cold and she had a sudden flashback of standing in the dark and cold with Greg: What was it about having to have conversations in the freezing bloody cold? (At least Greg had had whisky.). The silence lengthened so Clara moved towards the boot of the car.

"Can I get my bike now? It's cold out here, can we talk about this tomorrow?" she tried. He did help her to get the bike out, but then stood holding on to it, so she was still stuck, waiting for him to release it to her.

"Are you aware it is against university rules for you two to be in a relationship? You can't continue. It has to stop now."

"Why? We're not hurting anyone. No one knows, how can it matter?" Clara was frightened.

"It hurts you - and Luke: He would lose his job, don't you care?"

"Of course, I care. But no one knows."

"I know."

"You would get him fired?"

"Yes, it's wrong. It is a betrayal of trust, and he has abused his position."

"You would fire him because he has betrayed your trust?"

"No! Your trust!" Clara could not believe what she was hearing.

"What are you talking about? It was my decision as much as his - I love being with him, you can't take him away from me now. He doesn't even teach me anymore so there is no conflict of interest. Bryn, please!" He rested the bike against the fence of the house pulling Clara towards the low wall bordering a neighbouring property.

"Sit down and calm down." He sat beside her. "Look, can you seriously, truthfully tell me you have always felt free to say to Luke, 'stop', or 'I don't want to.' - can you say with 100% confidence there was no time, part of you was not worried or frightened because he was your lecturer and what would he think if you did not comply? It is essentially an unequal situation - you can see, can't you?"

"No, not really," she retorted stubbornly. "It is equal because we both lose if it gets out. I can see how it could be in some circumstances, but this is not a casual thing. I feel safe with Luke, he's kind. We have rows sometimes, we get fed up with hiding and being cooped up sometimes, but I want to be with him. I don't see why you are making such a fuss."

"How would you react if someone you were responsible for was doing something that could cause them harm and damage their prospects. What would you do, stay silent and let it happen? Or warn them?"

"How is going out with Luke damaging my 'prospects'?"

"Luke is older, introducing you to a wide range of people, places, and experiences. You are missing out on meeting your peers, enjoying a social life you only get at university, and sharing new experiences with those of your own age - all things to regret later."

"Luke is only five years older, that's not much – we are not together all the time. I still go out with my friends and he with his. I am miserable when I have to lie to my friends about where I am and who I am with - it isolates me. That's why you should be talking to Luke, not me - you two need to be friends again."

"This isn't about Luke - it's about you at the moment." There was a pause, then Bryn changed tack.

"Has Luke ever asked you to do something you don't want to?"

"What? No! Of course not. What are you suggesting? That Luke tells me what to do, and I blindly obey? Our relationship is not like that. I am not like that!"

"But you have to admit you are young and inexperienced. Are you not willing to consider the advice given?"

"Do you not think Luke is trustworthy or able to give good advice? I have you and Tony too." He smiled despite himself. There was silence for a moment.

"Bryn?"

"Hmm?"

"Please don't be so angry about it."

"The student I am mentoring and feel responsible for, as any tutor would, I find is sleeping with another lecturer, who happens to also be a good friend of mine - or so I thought - placing me in an impossible position. I don't believe what you are doing is right. It's as simple as that, Clara."

"Well, you will have to do what you think is right and let the chips fall where they may," she said bravely, "However, I would rather move to a new university and continue seeing Luke, than not see him, and stay here if that is what it takes. But I would rather stay here and carry on working with you," she ended softly. Bryn leaned towards her and bumped her with his shoulder in an endearing touch, then stood up.

"You are the most annoying creature! Go inside, get warm and I will catch up with you later." He waved his car keys in her direction before getting in the car and driving away. Clara wheeled her bike into the house, not entirely sure whether she had managed to rescue the situation or not.

Clara slept fitfully, dreaming she was on a sinking boat. Luke was trying to get her to safety onto a wooden raft, but the waves were too high. He kept disappearing behind a wall of water every time she reached out.

The next morning after a politics seminar, Clara walked over to the study block with Tony to collect a new book he had for her. Afterwards, she tentatively knocked on Luke's study door. She so rarely went to see him at university she didn't think anyone would particularly comment. She heard him call out to come in, so she slipped inside. He was surprised to see her, meeting her mid-room with a hug. Then he returned to his desk chair while she curled up in the armchair.

"You alright?" she asked anxiously. He looked tired and tense.

"Bit hungover if the truth is known," he said ruefully, "We had a session ..."

"And?"

"And what?"

"Luke! Bryn said he was going to report you and get you fired, or we had to split up - how did he leave it with you?"

"Yeah, well he said all that - and some more. Then we demolished a bottle of vodka, so we rather lost the plot," he caught her eye and hastily went on, "Okay, okay, we made up, we're friends again, he's not going to fire me - today anyway - we can carry on as we are for now." She looked at him closely.

"What are you not telling me?"

"No, honest, that is it in a nutshell. You must keep doing well in your studies, blah, blah - all else is good. 'Don't worry faint heart,'" he quipped, quoting a phrase from The Magic Roundabout to lighten the mood.

"Hmm," she said, only partially happy with his answer, but relaxing slightly. Luke could see he had not done a good job of reassuring her.

"Look, this should convince you all is okay; Bryn has invited us, as a couple, to one of his dinner parties, Saturday week - there you go, proof - all friends again."

"Dinner party?"

"Yes, he has them periodically. His wife works at a refugee centre in Birmingham and lectures at the university occasionally on counselling courses. Bryn, when he is not lecturing, works as a counsellor for various charities and organisations - they know lots of interesting people. His dinner parties are great events." Clara wasn't sure she wanted to go, meeting all those strangers - wouldn't they want to know who she was? Judge her for being with Luke? Was this Bryn's way of making them suffer - what would she say by way of conversation? Luke read her thoughts - it wasn't difficult as she sat there pale and frowning, biting her bottom lip.

"Trust me, it will be a good afternoon and it is a sign of friendship, not punishment." At his words, she relaxed further and although still nervous and worried, she was more certain Luke was not about to vanish from her life.

She unfurled and stretched back into standing, "I'll see you later?" she asked him.

"Yeah, I'm too hungover to go out tonight, come round later and we will have a quiet night in?" She smiled at him in a way that prompted him to leap up and grab her before she reached the door. He encompassed her with his arms and kissed her hungrily before letting her leave. Once the door closed behind her though he went back to his desk with a heavy heart, to continue going through the Educational Supplement, seeking new research posts in UK Universities.

The Saturday of Bryn's dinner party dawned fine, with a keen breeze. Clara had no idea what to wear and Luke was no help, shrugging when she asked.

"Well, what do others wear when you have been before? Smart? Casual? Jeans? Dresses?"

Again, a shrug. In the end, she settled for one of her long flowing skirts, white shirt, cardigan, and flat ballet shoes. Feeling self-conscious and nervous she made her way to the train station to meet Luke. When they spilled out of the train at Bromsgrove, a taxi took them to Bryn's house. Clara thought was the loveliest house she had ever seen.

Located along a narrow country lane, hidden from the road by tall hedges, a wrought iron gate let them through up to the front door of a big red brick house called,' Swallow's Swoop'. Steep, red-tiled roofs backed up against each other adorned with twisted chimneys. Yet, the full magic was revealed once you went into the living room. Along the back of the house, long windows, floor to ceiling, looked out beyond a veranda, to a garden sweeping down one side of a gentle valley. Beyond the tumble of flowerbeds, patios, vegetable patches, a walnut tree, lawns, and a pond complete with bridge, the eye naturally swept up the slopes on the other side of the valley, across a field to a straggly copse of trees, messy with crows' nests.

Clara did not have a chance to appreciate these charms at the time, as she was introduced to a gathering of people. There were twelve people in all. Clara was the youngest and felt 'studenty' in her outfit. The other women were clad in soft turtlenecks,

Laura Ashley skirts, and silky scarves. She thought they all looked very professional. The men wore casual trousers, and some had blazers. Bryn greeted her warmly, kissed her on the cheek, and introduced her to Linda, his wife. She was a petite lady with dark hair and a tiny waist tied with a wide black belt over a flared orange skirt. She had laughing eyes. Bryn handed Clara a Martini and soda as he introduced her to everyone else as a student studying at university. Linda waved a plate of creamy mushroom stuffed vol au vents under her nose.

Juggling the flaky pastry morsel and glass she hovered. While eating she listened to conversations nearby. A group of three men were discussing the possibility of a June election. Another group was chatting about the concept of 'interdependence' as a growing number of countries were being linked through trade and finance. Now, this was interesting! They realised she was listening and welcomed her to the conversation, making room for her. She smiled to acknowledge their inclusion and listened further before getting brave enough to chip in, adding to the debate. She mentioned the role of the state in protecting national interests and the impact this had on the international movement of capital.

So, the afternoon proved more pleasurable than she had imagined: A succession of interesting conversations, interspersed with French onion soup, chicken Kiev, vegetables, and individual chocolate mousse, completed by coffee in tiny cups - black and bitter.

As people started to leave, she looked around for Luke, but he was outside on the veranda deep in conversation with someone who had been introduced to her as Alec, a researcher at Birmingham University. Clara caught Linda's eye and asked if she wanted any help with the washing up. This offer was readily accepted so she went through to the kitchen and started to fill the sink with hot water. Linda said she would be with her directly she had shown her guests out.

Clara made a start on the mountain of plates. Suddenly a door from the garden opened and a smaller, older version of Linda appeared with a young child in each hand. Dark hair, and big eyes, they looked at Clara with open mouths.

"Are you The Help?" The lady asked.

"Well in a way, I suppose, I am 'helping'."

"Good. This is Jenny and Ewan. I'll leave them with you. Tell Linda I will see her tomorrow." She left. The two children stood staring at her.

"Want to help?" Clara asked them.

When Linda reappeared half an hour later, she found most of the washing up done amidst lots of soap bubbles, chatter, and laughter. Her two children were industriously washing up and drying, towels tied around their waists. Clara was acting as a quality monitor as they showed her how clean or how dry their plate, cup, or bowl were.

"You two look as if you are having fun!" Linda exclaimed, "Where did you come from?"

"Nanny brought us back early as she said we were being 'frustring'"

"Frustrating?"

"That's it."

"Mummy, what's a Help? Is Clara a Help? Is she going to live here with us?" Linda looked appalled.

"Oh no, I am so sorry, did my mother think you were 'The Help' - how embarrassing! I do apologise. I did tell her I was getting one, but I wasn't really. I don't think I need one."

"You don't," piped up Jenny, "Clara says we are the help. Look how good we have been!" She spun the plate she was drying in the air. Clara grabbed it and placed it onto the pile. Linda filled the kettle for a pot of tea.

"Tea?"

"We want to show Clara the garden," the children cried, tugging on her hands. Clara didn't relish being dragged around the garden.

"Let me have a cup of tea first, then I will see, okay?" They zoomed off out of the kitchen door. "We should be going," Clara said to Linda, "I should find Luke."

"Don't worry, he is still trying to charm a job out of Alec. I wouldn't worry for a while - enjoy a cup of tea first, you deserve one after all your hard work." Linda chatted as she threw some tea bags into a fat blue and yellow teapot.

"Charm a job out of him?" repeated Clara "Luke has a job already you know." Linda busied herself with making the tea, pouring milk, and adding sugar. Her voice, when she replied, was light and casual.

"I overheard them. Alec is looking for researchers on his latest project for which he has secured funding. It keeps you alive and, on your toes, working on different projects from time to time you know. What do you want to do when you finish your degree?"

"I'm not sure. I am learning about so many problems in the world. I'd like to make a difference, in some way try to improve something. But how exactly is eluding me."

"Don't force it. You have time. You need to learn about yourself first, know your strengths and weaknesses to see where you would best fit."

"Or find out what I would like to do and then work to make my weaknesses strong to fit?"

"Good point, your view is less deterministic than mine - make your future. There's a lot to choose from."

"Yes, that's the trouble," admitted Clara, smiling.

They caught the last train back - just. Bryn gave them a lift to the station, and they made a mad dash as the guard was blowing his whistle. They tumbled ungracefully into an empty carriage. Since there was no one else around Clara snuggled up close to Luke as the train gathered speed. Although it had been an interesting and somewhat enjoyable day on one level, unformed thoughts, fears, and emotions were now lurking since her conversation with Linda. She felt on edge. She had a sudden memory of her dream, trying to reach for Luke and the wall of water coming between them. He kissed the top of her head, lost in his thoughts. The clack of the train lulled them. But then Clara heaved herself out of her comfort zone and faced Luke in the yellowing British Rail light.

"Luke? Linda said you were talking to Alec about a research job - would this be as well as lecturing?"

"Don't know. I don't have it yet, but there is at least a chance - exciting!" He looked at her, eyes shining. "So useful, these social engagements. You find out about opportunities you wouldn't hear of otherwise."

"That's not right, surely? What happens if you don't know 'the right' people? They should advertise jobs for everyone equally." But Luke was cross.

"Not at all, you - Joe Bloggs, everyone - have to realise this is just how the world works and learn to network to create these connections. If we'd stayed in the flat all day it would have been nice, but it doesn't get us anywhere in the grand scheme of things. We have to get out and meet people, create links and opportunities."

"I didn't know you were even looking for another job, you didn't say we needed to be 'networking.'"

"Well, you always have to keep your eye open to new opportunities." He wasn't looking at her now but addressing something over her left shoulder. "I don't want to be a lecturer in a non-researching university forever. I have been thinking lately of doing my Ph.D. If I was awarded this research post, I could lecture as well as work towards my research. I might even get tenure, that would be great!"

"How come you have never mentioned any of this before? You have always said a Ph.D. was a pointless slog, and you enjoyed the lecturing side of your job rather than doing other people's research - why the sudden switch?"

"It's not a sudden switch. I just didn't know what opportunities were out there."

'What about me? How do I fit in?' She wanted to ask, feeling alone, but couldn't quite summon the courage, afraid of the answer.

"Stop chewing your lip and looking so worried," he said, pulling her back to him. "Things will sort themselves out, you'll see. We are both trying to work out what we want to do and be - we'll do it together alright?" She was only partially mollified, but remained silent and instead soaked up his embrace, watching the lights of the city take shape. She alighted as the station materialised. Luke would get off at the next one. She waved as he slid off along the track into the night.

She spotted the car as soon as she emerged from the station building - a long black car parked in the small semi-circle in front of the station. This was not a salubrious end of the city and the smart car - black though it may be - stuck out like a sore thumb. She turned away from it and walked along the road towards her home. She was surprised when the car glided along the road and pulled beside her. She was more than a little put out to be manhandled into the back seat.

CHAPTER 5

Top UK chart hit: February 1985
I Know Him So Well: Barbara Dixon & Elaine Paige

In the back seat of the car, she came eye to nose with a white-shirted, black-tied, tall individual whom she recognised immediately. Her man handler climbed in behind her. She glanced back at him as she rearranged herself into a more stable sitting position. He was a square-looking 'thug': No neck, misshapen nose, tiny eyes peering from a jowly face. He looked as if he had refused to wear his suit, but some giant had picked him up and shoved it into him forcibly. Clara glared at him and then turned her attention back to the other passenger.

"Do you know me?" he asked.

"No. Unless you are a full-time street performer who just happens to kidnap young women in your spare time," she snapped. He inclined his head to indicate the answer was in fact, a yes, she had recognised him. The car was speeding up as it made for the city by-pass towards the motorway. "Where are we going? - I'd rather go home."

"Oh, just for a chat - then I'll take you home."

'At least it was warmer than a freezing street corner,' Clara thought. She was detecting a slight twang to his words, American? Australian? - she couldn't quite decide. She remembered the effect on Greg and the 'stranger' when she had mentioned the acrobat. Now here he was. She glanced to the front of the car - one seat was empty, and the other was the driver - a small man, also clad in a black suit. She didn't recognise him. She waited.

"I would like to know what you know about me," he asked her. She glanced at him.

"You go 'undercover', if that is what you were doing, more convincingly than others I could mention - juggling and unicycle - impressive." He made an impatient movement and 'Ugly' on the other side of her shifted uneasily. She sighed. "Honestly, I have no idea what games you are all playing, or why I suddenly seem to be getting tangled up with you - it is all coincidental, I assure you."

"Try again, Buttercup - I'm not convinced."

"Why not? How about you ask me some more specific questions if you want specific answers?" Her confidence was ebbing, and she was feeling a little frightened as she had no other answers. What on earth was going on? Who did he think she was? She could feel a flush rising in her cheeks as her heart started to hammer. She desperately tried to breathe some calm into them as she waited for his next question. She forced her shoulders to relax, her hands to rest open and calm in her lap. Her breathing slowed as in her mind's eye she started to empty her crowding anxious thoughts, as her yoga training taught her.

"Who told you what to do on The Embankment? How are you linked to The Operation?" His voice now laced with menace made her concentrate on her response. She quelled her invading fearful thoughts and focussed on his questions only.

"Please, believe me, it was entirely accidental. I could see the increased police presence, uniforms multiplying all around, as well as others who all seemed to be communicating through tense waiting poses. I just thought it would be a good idea to get my boyfriend and his sister out of the area. That's when I caught your eye. I followed where you pointed, but afterwards, I thought I'd been mistaken about you pointing towards the alleyway. Maybe you had just been waving your batons around. If you hadn't shown up tonight, I would have always thought you were the acrobat you were when I last saw you." She looked at his profile to see how he was going to take her words. He glanced at her smiling wryly.

"I think you should know what I know about you. Then I will have a truthful version, please. You are an above-average university student, who recently fell into the welcome arms of Mr. Marsdon, son of the tycoon of Marsdon Corporation - connections running straight into National and International economic, social, and political networks. You then spend a week in the company of the Marsdon children and an MI6 operator, where you find yourself calmly protecting said heirs of fortune from a potentially violent conclusion to a long-planned Operation. Then you report my presence to your superiors, single-handedly upsetting Anglo-American relations over said Operation." He sat back watching to see how she received this information. Her face remained impassive, her fingers resting in her lap, even breathing.

"So, if you know who I am - can I ask who you are?" she asked, as she tried to drown out the growing clamour of fears and suspicions. At his words, everything she thought she knew shifted. She felt sick.

"You can know me as Harry," he replied. "Now, who told you what to do, who briefed you that day? - The truth this time please."

"I appreciate you have all created your theories, weaving me into your experiences, but honestly (she stressed the word slowly) I am an accidental interference. I did not know about Luke's connections; he never talks of his parents. I just acted by gut reaction, sensing danger and wanting to get them away from it. Charlie's husband asked me the same questions you are if that helps. He got excited when I told them about you telling me where to escape - I didn't mean to upset diplomatic relations. But presumably, you were not exactly playing by the rules, otherwise, my mention of you would not have had such an impact." She spread her hands emphatically. "I don't know what else to say: I am not interested in working for any of you. Your research must show since Christmas I have just been here studying for my degree?"

"It shows you have spent the afternoon in the company of a wide range of operatives and officers known to us, so try again Buttercup."

"What? Oh, come on! My psychology lecturer was just trying to prove he had forgiven me for sleeping with another lecturer - while all along trying to link Luke to some mate of his who can get him a new job away from me," she explained. Until she said it, it had not been clear to her. Now her suspicions were out in the air, she saw what was going on. Although maybe that was not all that was going on.

"You need to wise up, don't you? You're being manipulated and played with and are attracting attention, which will not be to your benefit if you don't want to work for us. You need to make up your mind about who you are." It sounded like good-intentioned advice. She felt vaguely she was indeed being stupid and naive - she would have to think it all through later. "What will you do when you graduate?" he asked unexpectedly.

"Lots of people have asked me lately. I would like to make a positive impact, but not sure how yet."

"Be careful who you tell - otherwise other people will be defining 'making a positive impact' for you. The world is full of people with good intentions."

"I intend to make decisions for myself, I'm not that stupid!" She suddenly felt angry, stirred by deep fears.

"I suggest you start applying your intelligence then!" he snapped back, "We can do without any more dumb blondes floundering across our operations."

"That's not fair! If you think I am being manipulated, go after those doing the manipulating, not me!" The car was beginning to feel claustrophobic to her and she wanted to get out into the cold air.

"I prefer to get the dumb blonde to wise up," he replied coolly. "If you decide you want to work in this line of business, give me a call. We could do with some intelligent operators who stay calm under pressure: Incidental or not, everyone was impressed with your conduct. But you have been noticed, which is not so good for you while you remain naive. You are as they say, 'easy pickings,' - don't be so susceptible to paternal attention." His words stung.

"You came to warn me? Give me advice - more paternal attention?"

"Warn, warn off, tell you to get onboard or get the hell out of it - take your pick."

"If you don't mind, I will take the 'get the hell out of it' option: Can I go home now please?"

"Sure kid," grunted 'Thug' as he swung the door open. She realised they were back in Francis Road, outside her house. As she was shuffling along the seat to get out, Harry caught hold of her arm.

"Your instinct will tell you to keep this little chat we have had to yourself. And if you do decide you want - or 'need' (he stressed the word oddly) to renew our acquaintance, go to the US Embassy, explain you need to report a lost cousin who went to America in August, and would like help to trace him - your lost cousin's name is, Harry Winfield. Remember." She nodded as his arm tightened on hers. He let her go. "See you later, Clara Day."

"Um, okay, bye," she mumbled as she stumbled out onto the pavement. 'Thug' grunted and the door slammed shut as the black car glided away. Swearing under her breath, she scrabbled in her bag for her door keys.

Once in her bedroom, she threw her bag onto the bed and marched restlessly around in circles. The chilled room was a relief after the stuffy car. She had not just felt suffocated by the heat of the car but by all these people closing in on her, shaking her trust and faith in who was who. She stripped off all her clothes with angry brusqueness and stood naked, in the centre of the room, arms spread wide, outstretched. This was her, alone, on her own, in her own space, right now: She felt the cold ripple of her skin leaving a wave of goose pimples, her nipples hardening. She breathed deeply, breathing in through the nose and out through the mouth, steadying her heart rate to slow her stampede of thoughts. The cold felt good and regulating her breathing also gave her the sense of control she craved.

Then she climbed into bed and lay on her back: Was she a puppet? Had she been like a lump of wood as the people around her - her parents, Luke, Bryn, Greg, and Acrobat-man-Harry all pulled strings? Was nothing as it seemed at all? The ground seemed to crumble away underneath her, and she imagined herself left suspended, floating in space - alone and adrift. Was it bad to be a puppet? Or good? Were people seeing her strengths and using her for good reason? Would unknowing good be better than knowing inactivity?

The news covering the growing desperation of people in Sub-Saharan Africa affected by the drought was growing. Breakfast the next morning was accompanied by harrowing images of starving children. Clara gazed without seeing into her coffee mug. She knew enough to understand it was the poor people who were dying first; the rurally isolated, the voiceless faceless majority. The reasons for this were hideously complicated. She kept coming back time and time again to this point, mulling over her role in life. These are the people she wanted to reach out to directly, the ones she wanted to communicate with, learn from, and help. She wanted to save these lives, to give them a chance to bring about changes for themselves. Watching the skeletal wretches on their haunches staring blankly into the BBC cameras under the scorching sun, she determined to make her career helping these people.

"That's a daft idea," said Luke when she told him about her career ideas, "not much more detailed than your usual mantra of wanting to have a 'positive impact'. So, you save a rural, marginalised person's life, what then? Their life may be worse, they may not be in a fit state or know how to make their lives better."

"What are you saying? Some lives are worth more than others?" she lashed back, eyes shining with passion.

"No," he said, "it's just, for you, rather lame - you don't want to be a medic, your strength is in academia - how can you save lives and work with these people? What are you imagining - flying in on a helicopter, holding the head of a starving baby while you give it the food you have brought, and then flying home?" As that was more or less as far as her inexperience had envisaged, she was even angrier at him.

"Of course not! But ..." she floundered "... there must be lots of people working behind the scenes to help the medics, organisers getting the food supplies and medicines to the right place..."

"Then you need to work for the United Nations - and you will need military training - can't see you doing what you are ordered to do somehow." He laughed, trying to jolly her into a better mood.

"I want to be the one giving the orders. I would be good at organising and coordinating lots of comings and goings. It would be like a complicated game of chess."

"You can't do that until you have first worked your way up through the ranks. And anyway, you're a woman, so can't do any of this anyway, think again," he advised.

"Harumph." She threw herself onto the sofa sulking while he worked on planning a lecture for the next day. But she then interrupted him again. "I could work for an Aid Agency or volunteer with VSO."

"We've had this discussion before. They won't pay much, you know. What about the ODA?"

"What's that?"

"The Government Office - Overseas Development Aid"

"Isn't that just a desk job?"

"Maybe, but there is nothing wrong with a desk job. You can help people while remaining safe yourself.

"I could ask Greg, he will know about jobs with the Government."

"Mmm."

She tapped on the door and opened it as she was expected for her tutorial. Bryn was striding around the room looking agitated.

"What's the matter?" she asked.

"Oh, Clara. Nothing. Well, I am trying to solve a family crisis," He collapsed into a chair, "Linda's mum has broken her leg, she can't have the kids for the weekend as planned - Linda and I are supposed to be presenting at a conference." While he talked, Clara filled two cups with water from a recently boiled kettle onto some dried mint leaves and handed it silently to him. "Thanks. Have you done babysitting before? Would you consider helping me out?"

She sipped her tea. "Well, depends." He studied her closely, sensing something different about her: A new steel edge to her voice.

"Go on. I'm listening. Depends on what?"

"Is this a genuine request?"

"Explain please Clara."

"Well do you genuinely have to go to a conference? Or is it a trick to engineer me to be somewhere, to meet someone? Like, for instance, inviting us to a dinner party so my boyfriend - who you don't want to be with me - 'casually' meets someone who, 'coincidentally' is looking for a researcher in Luke's exact field of expertise. Just asking." She stared at him challengingly.

"That's some crazy conspiracy theory. When did you develop paranoia?"

"Is that your answer to my question, or deflection?" She continued to challenge, not backing down, a new fire in her belly from somewhere.

"Where is all this coming from? You are blaming me for Luke chatting with Alec? It is not the first time they have met. If you had attended other dinner parties, you would realise they are often the same people. I don't have an endless supply of friends. Why are you lashing out at me? This is between you and Luke." But she wasn't happy. Now she was the one pacing around the room.

"I don't intend to lash out at you. I sometimes feel … well, there are lots of connections, patterns, oh, I don't know - 'meanings' and 'intentions' floating about, affecting me in ways I don't always fully understand, and I feel out of control … oh, it doesn't matter. I can't explain."

"Are you, in a roundabout way, telling me you have cause to distrust me?"

"No! - well, maybe - Can anyone trust anyone else really, ever? We all have individual agendas, reasons that may coincide or cross with others …" She petered out, coming to rest like a ruffled canary on the arm of a chair.

"Are you being asked by anyone to do anything you don't want to?" he asked gravely. Clara slid off the arm. Why did Harry and Greg immediately spring to mind? Neither of them had asked her to do anything she didn't want to, but how had Harry known where to find her? She sighed deeply. She wanted to ask Bryn which of his friends were Secret Operators and Officers - was Bryn himself or Linda? She so desperately wanted to trust Bryn.

"I'm sorry," she said into the long silence, "Of course, I will babysit Jenny and Ewan."

"Now who is deflecting?" Bryn responded softly, but with a firmness letting her know a further response from her was required.

"No, I am not being coerced into anything I don't want to," she said. He sighed with a small smile and replied.

"Thank you. I will collect you from the station, then drop you home Sunday, okay?"

"Yeah, fine."

"Right, now," said Bryn, changing the subject and pace of the conversation, "What did you make of the essay question I gave you?"

Luke was pleased to hear she was babysitting at the weekend.

"Good," he said, kissing her, reaching past her for his plate of beans on toast. They took their tea to the table, clearing a space amongst the papers and opened books. "I need to go and meet Alec on Thursday about this research opportunity. I was thinking of staying up for the weekend so was going to ask you to join me there. But if you are busy, I will just kip on my cousin, Christian's floor, rather than seek us a free room." He tucked into his food.

"Will you know after you meet with Alec on Thursday whether you have the job?"

"Maybe," he answered with a mouth full of beans.

"If you get the job, can I transfer to Birmingham University for my final year so we can still be together?"

"Don't be daft. Then I would be back to square one again, 'sleeping with a student!" he snapped back instantly. He realised what he had said but it was too late.

"I knew it! This is all Bryn's doing. He was going to get you fired! He is only allowing our relationship to continue if you find another job elsewhere. Why didn't you tell me? Why all the cloak and dagger stuff?" She pushed her plate away angrily and leapt up, leaning on the table. " I don't appreciate being lied to! No secrets!" So angry, she grabbed her coat and dashed for the door to get outside.

CHAPTER 6

Top UK chart hit: March 1985
Human Racing: Nick Kershaw

Luke caught up with her before she reached the top of the stairs.

"Wait! You know storming off mid-argument solves nothing - come on, we need to talk this through."

"Can we go outside to talk then? I need some fresh air."

He snatched up his coat, cigarettes, and keys and followed her. In silence, they made their way down towards the river. They strolled side by side along the footpath meandering opposite the cathedral, then away from the city, out across the flat fields. Eventually Luke broke the silence.

"Bryn is responsible as a professional counsellor for the emotional well-being of students. What we did and his knowledge of it, you must see, Clara, has put him in an untenable position. It would be like having a friend who was a policeman who then discovered we were dealing drugs." She started to say something, but he laid a hand on her arm. "Hold on, I know in our heads what we are doing is not on a level with drug dealing - but the principles are similar, and Bryn is still in a difficult position isn't he?" He took her silence as agreement, albeit a grudging one. "That night he came back after taking you home, he was in a right state, totally torn. He is a real friend, who cares for you too Clara. He is a good soul. But I couldn't give you up." He squeezed her hand. "So, finally we agreed I would look for a new job, and in the meantime, he would turn a blind eye to us. I have until the end of the summer term to find something."

"So, he throws dinner parties and matches you with potential employers," she said bitterly.

"Maybe. But can't you see he is trying to help? He doesn't want to have to report me in the summer term. He doesn't want to alienate you. He is trying to help all three of us."

"Mmm, except you two were in on the scheme, while I was left out. I am not a baby!"

"You are many things - a baby is not one of them," he teased gently. She shot him a warning glance; she was not ready to forgive yet.

"I don't like being manipulated, duped. I don't like my trust in people, shaken. Life is complicated enough as it is. I wanted you and Bryn to be the two people in my life I could trust."

"Love and trust go hand in hand, Clara," he said softly. Suddenly the birds sounded louder, and their footsteps crunched along the path with deafening clarity.

"Well, maybe ... So, no more secrets?"

"I only kept it from you to protect you. I didn't want to worry you at first - I was worried enough for both of us. I wasn't sure I could handle your anger over it all: You are not exactly being supportive, are you?"

"But I didn't know the whole story, did I? You didn't - neither of you - trust me with the whole story."

"I apologise, Clara." Brief silence apart from the loud crunching of footsteps along the towpath. "Where do we go from here?" he asked her.

"Do you want this new job? Why don't we reconsider who leaves? Why does it have to be you? I could get a transfer."

"Do you want to do that?"

"I would if it works better for both of us. I am happy here but am equally happy to consider other options."

"Actually," said Luke slowly, "I would like this research opportunity. Before you came along, I was quite content. I was also being lazy, kind of resting after completing my master's, and getting to grips with lecturing. I was enjoying feeling confident in what I did for a while. But you challenge me, Clara - daily. You have made me want to take up the reins again and push myself further." He nudged her with his elbow, "I have to run to keep up with you." Again, an attempt to lighten the mood but she was still not there.

"About the job Luke, stop deflecting," she said severely, frowning. "What is it exactly and how does it fit in with your long-term plans?"

"God! You sound like Charlie! The job is to be part of a research team investigating the expansion of urban landscape into rural landscape in North-eastern Europe, and its impact on the agricultural industry. There are three years of funding. At the same time, I can be doing some lecturing - which pays more. Also, I can do my, or at least start, my Ph.D. In the long run I would like the security at uni, for research and lecturing - this is a real opportunity to achieve this goal. It's what I have always wanted, but didn't think it was possible, until now."

"Everything is possible with the right connections!" she snapped, but then regretted it immediately and attempted to make amends. "Sorry. I did mean it, but it is not appropriate at the moment." She turned to him, forcing them to stop walking, "Thank you for telling me. It's just …" she faltered, tears springing to her eyes. She swept them away impatiently.

"It's just?" he echoed, tilting her chin upwards towards him and kissing her. "We can make this work. If you want it to?" he said.

"Of course, I want to, otherwise I wouldn't be so worried about all this!" Did he have to be so exasperating?

They were far out of the city. At this point a five-barred gate gave a glimpse of a field of tall grasses, glittering slightly in the March dusk. Impulsively Clara climbed the gate and ran into the field, luxuriating in being out under a huge open expanse of sky, stripping off her coat, letting it fall. Opening her arms wide she spun around, as she did as a child, going faster and faster, so the whole world spun. She tripped and fell with a loud laugh, lying on her back as the starry sky continued to rotate above her.

"You are quite mad, you know?" said Luke breathlessly as he knelt over her, having finally caught up with her.

"Yep!" she agreed.

Before he knew it, she had pulled off her jumper, lying back before him. She rarely wore a bra as she had such small hillocks of breasts, she never thought it worthwhile. So now she lay bare, with her breasts pert domes; the nipples standing upright in the cold air. Her body was fluorescent white, her nipples dark, winking at him.

"God ..." he murmured, "you are the most surprising and erotic creature." He sat back on his heels, throwing her long, wide skirt up and over her. It flew up over her nose, making her giggle. She left it where it fell, now lying mysteriously draped like an exotic dancer. He leaned in and sank his fingers between her exposed legs, into the curls, pulling her lips apart. With slow, deliberate movements he stroked her lovingly, causing her to wriggle and squirm. She moaned softly. With one hand he tugged at his trousers and as she rose towards him arching her back, he entered her, collapsing shortly afterwards on top of her, the smell of crushed grass and dew fall adding to the intoxication of spent sex.

After a few moments, Clara heaved him off her, rolling on top of him instead. With one arm he reached her discarded clothes and covered her bare back as they lay cocooned for a few moments, until neither of them could ignore any longer the creeping dampness of the ground. Reclothed they walked hand in hand, back the way they had come.

Monday, between lectures, Clara spotted Luke in the distance and knew immediately he had been successful in his job hunting. She noted his body language which, unintentional as he didn't know she could see him, betrayed how happy he was - she sighed: Life was about to shift again.

"Come up with me at the weekend - meet everyone? I will show you my new place - come, and see?" he cajoled when they were together later, eager and excited to include her. She had several essay deadlines on the horizon as it was three weeks until Easter break, but she didn't want to appear unsupportive.

"Alright. Be good to see it all," she agreed.

"Great. Because obviously, you will be there a lot too, when you are up at weekends. And I've saved the best news: There is work for you as a temp researcher on my project. I know you hate going home in the holidays, but if you have a 'respectable' job instead, your parents won't make you. We can spend all holidays together." He watched her, waiting for her reaction, his eyes shining. She was very happy.

"It's too short notice for Easter, I've already accepted four weeks of boring, but well-paid work on the checkout at Sainsbury's. Be perfect for the summer though."

"Even better. Give me the Easter period to find my feet - then you can join me in the summer."

They toasted Luke's new job with marmite sandwiches and a bottle of Blue Nun. Then alternated between sex and chatting about a new future straddling two universities, laying markers for future careers and research topics.

"As you work as a researcher all summer you might find an idea for your dissertation next year," Luke pointed out.

"I will have complete access to the library," added Clara excitedly. He laughed, caressing her shoulders and neck.

"Then," his mind raced on, "you could apply to do your master's at Birmingham. The fact you are already working there should count for something and if you get your First, that would be definite."

"Master's? I am still not sure I want to do one."

"You had thought as far as a career rescuing starving orphans from their plight in Africa - was that before or after your master's?"

"What do I need a master's for? How will it help me help others?"

"I thought we both agreed education and research provided a depth of knowledge and expertise to provide authority. Won't you need authority to boss around UN troops?"

"Don't tease. You said I couldn't join the UN as a woman."

"Be the first then kiddo." He was carried away by the euphoria of his success and feeling generous towards her crazy notions.

"You're drunk," she replied dismissively.

Birmingham University had its own train station and Luke was there to meet her. Clara received a cursory glimpse of the campus, with Luke waving an arm vaguely at a block here, and a hall there, as they made their way directly to the flat.

"I can show you more later. I'm trying to get you to the flat as fast as possible," he admitted with a grin when she complained about the poor quality of the guided tour. She forgave him with a blow of a kiss, and they hurried to a tall building of residential apartments circled by trimmed lawns. Much later they went to one of the university bars where Alec was with others on the research team. Then they progressed to a different bar to meet Christian, Luke's cousin.

Clara had heard of Christian. He was at the university studying for a master's, but she hadn't met him before. It would be true to say they didn't hit it off. She thought he was a privileged, superior snob with an oversized male ego and dubious sexist views. He seemed to think she was an annoyingly argumentative, jumped-up nobody who thought she was entitled to have a voice just because she slept with a lecturer. Neither of them gave the other an inch and Luke grew tired of their battles and dragged Clara away.

"Can't you pretend to agree with him for once, or ignore him?" he complained, putting an arm around her shoulders as they returned to the flat.

"No. Can't."

"You have to try and get on with people - when you get a job and work as a team you can't go head-on with everyone you know."

"Stop lecturing me. I will get on with whom I choose. But I will not back down or accept sexist views from someone who is only right because they think they are!"

"He is a well-respected master's post-grad. heading for a First you know?"

"A worthy opponent then!" she snapped.

"For someone who is essentially shy and does not like confrontation you have a knack for picking sharks rather than minnows," he observed.

"I don't pick fights for the sake of it! How am I going to follow my career dreams if every way is blocked to me? According to Mr. High and Mighty, I can't work for the UN, the British Council or get into high levels of charity organisations because a) I am a woman, b) don't have a first-class degree at a Red Brick University - nor was I born with a silver teaspoon in my mouth! I will just have to break in some other way," she complained, thinking back over her argument with Christian. "It is so frustrating to be locked out! How dare he try to justify it! He deserved everything he got - and more. And-" she added, turning to face Luke, "Don't ask me not to fight with him when the fight was about unequal struggles of power - a worthy fight." She stood glaring at him, hands on her hips. He reached for her hand.

"Clara, please! He was ragging you. As soon as you let your political leanings show, he was messing with you. Don't allow yourself to get spun along so easily."

"Now I hate him even more," she grumbled but allowed Luke to take her hand. She replayed the scene with Christian in her head as they walked. She realised that yes, he had been baiting her, but so had she, him. She had been testing out ideas and rationalisations aloud she had read and written about. She suspected that although Christian may not hold the views he had expressed as vehemently as he had suggested, he was definitely in a stronger position than her. He was male, with a first from a red brick University and if he was Luke's cousin, he had a silver teaspoon stuck in his throat. She looked sideways at Luke.

"How is he related to you then?"

"Oh, my father's brother's son. Growing up, we spent quite a few summer holidays together after his father died. He is the 'golden' child - I'm the less successful one: Although now lecturing and researching here has redeemed me somewhat." Luke smiled at her as she took his hand once more. He had shared more about his family than ever before. He usually found a way to change the subject - as he did now. "Let's go into the Slug and Lettuce for final orders before calling it a night?"

CHAPTER 7

News headlines: May 1985
39 have died and 400 have been injured during crowd riots
Heysel Stadium football match in Brussels, Belgium:
Liverpool fans have been blamed.

Clara poked her head around the door and Tony looked up from his desk, pipe in his mouth. He was marking scripts.

"Clara, please tell me you have come to interrupt me. These first-year scripts are depressing." She smiled, wandering in through the layers of tobacco smoke. Sun from the window was highlighting the smoke trails, pretty silver garlands breaking and twisting as she wafted through them. She took up her usual position in one of the armchairs. Tony swung round in his chair, reached out a long leg and pushed the door closed with a bang.

"Out with it, what's up?" She shrugged, her eyes scanning the books littering the room searching for treasure to discover.

"I dunno - I thought you may be able to give me something new to think about. I'm sorry, but revision for exams is boring." She waited to see if he would be angry at this confession.

"No one to distract you during the week anymore, eh?" he said, shocking her. She felt herself go pink and shifted under his unwavering gaze. She decided to ignore the comment, aware at the same time her flush had answered it already. She grabbed a question lurking in the back of her mind.

"Tony? Would you say language is a facet of identity and you can never fully work with a cultural group effectively until you can speak their language?"

"Absolutely."

"Can you speak Gaelic? I thought you might with all your research into the Shetland Islands. I thought you could teach me if you knew?"

"I would if I could, but they don't speak Gaelic there. The main historic influence is from Norway - you would be better off learning Norwegian. The Danes were the colonising power for many years, complicating things further. But don't look to me - all I can say is 'Meo logum skal land bagga' which is Danish, the Island's motto - "By law shall land be built.'"

"So, language is colonial imperialism, repression by a conquering force?"

"Yes, also, look at our language in this country. When the French conquered, it became the language of power and influence. The Anglo-Saxon language was considered rough and crude, associated with the poor and those to be ruled over. All our existing swear words are only seen as socially unacceptable in formal situations because their root is Anglo Saxon. 'Faeces' is the Latin/French, 'shit' - the Anglo Saxon: Same meaning, one acceptable in polite company, the other not."

"I have been reading Noam Chomsky, who says by studying a culture's language, you can learn more about the society. For example, the Inuit People of the Polar North, have twenty-five words for 'snow', demonstrating the importance of snow in their lives. They have to be able to distinguish between 'slush', 'clear', and 'dense' types, to know whether they can cross frozen wastelands safely, or build igloos to last. But I was thinking, turning the argument on its head; it would stand to reason that unless you learnt these twenty-five words for snow, you wouldn't be able to identify them. It would then be hard to relate closely to these people and understand their needs and requirements."

"So, what you are saying is, if you learn people's language you can be accepted and build relationships on an equal footing?"

"Yes," said Clara, "I think so. What do you think?"

"I think you are quite right - is this your thesis for your dissertation next year?"

"It might be, it is organically growing."

"It is problematic though, how do people learn so many languages? If it was easy, we would know lots of them: Perhaps you could argue that is why we have so many entrenched differences and misunderstandings, culture to culture?"

"I read that our education system makes it more difficult to learn languages than is necessary. There are more effective ways I thought I would test. I will create a method based on sound only; no written word, no learning of grammar with lists of verbs by rote; it slows down the process and is a 'constructive' process rather than a fluid puzzle. My idea is to match sounds to meaning, paying attention to inflections, accents, and 'sound'. At first, I wasn't sure how I was going to gain access to different language speakers, but then my housemate invited me out for a pizza, and I knew!"

Tony chuckled with dawning comprehension. "So, the languages you try to learn will be closely related to the foreign restaurants here in Worcester, or those around Birmingham University?" He surmised. She nodded with a grin. "Sounds as if you are onto something, certainly. If you are bored with revision, put in some time exploring these ideas - if you were to sit your exams tomorrow you would pass, wouldn't you? So, get stuck into this, is my advice - do I have anything here to help you?" He waved his arm towards his shelves.

"Really?" she asked, eyes shining. Fifteen minutes later she had extracted three or four books, leaflets, and articles related to cultural identity and language. "Can I borrow these?"

"Of course, I look forward to hearing your critique of them as usual. I expect a multilingual discourse mind you," he joked as she slipped out of the door.

Clara was addicted. The links between language and culture fascinated her. Whole new worlds revealed themselves to her from where they had existed right under her nose. An Italian and Turkish restaurant along the high street in her university city welcomed her visits. In an Indian restaurant called The Blue Tiger in Birmingham she befriended a girl her age called, Saanvi. Clara revised her school French and German by buying tapes from WHSmith's. Then she thought of taping the conversations in the restaurant to listen to later, and her whole world became a colourful kaleidoscope of sound. It filled her mind with a buzz she loved; she practised and practised - after all, there was nothing else to do. The time she had spent with Luke was exchanged for hours of listening and absorbing new ways of expressing the world. When she returned each week to her Italian and Turkish friends they clapped their hands with delight at her rapid advancements, which only inspired her further. Firm friendships were forged, especially between Clara and Saanvi.

CHAPTER 8

News headlines: August 1985
Madonna weds Sean Penn on her 27th birthday.

It was August and the market was busy. Clara and Saanvi couldn't chat as they elbowed their way through the crowds, heaving baskets of vegetables to take back to the Blue Tiger restaurant. Once on the pavements, it was clearer. They ambled shoulder to shoulder, savouring some time together in the sunshine, before getting back to shred and chop all their purchases in the restaurant kitchen.

"So, is the summer temp job with Luke at the uni. as boring as usual?" asked Saanvi with a grin. Clara rolled her eyes and pulled a face making her friend laugh.

"Oh, it is so boring, Saanvi! I thought 'researcher' sounded interesting, finding out new facts and learning. But no, it's no better than being a general dogsbody. I spend most of my time making tea and photocopying." She stopped to switch the baskets from one hand to the other to ease her back. "And it never seems to stop. Alec, the project manager, to my mind has a screw loose. He is quite fanatical about scrutinising these maps of Central Europe - looks like a load of grainy blobs to me. But they will discuss for them hours. Do you know the other evening they took thirty-eight minutes, I timed it I was so bored, to decide if they were looking at a haystack or not!"

Saanvi laughed so much she had to put down her bags. Clara had been talking in Hindi but having never needed to use the word 'haystack' before had substituted it for what she thought was 'grass pile', but instead had said 'cake pile'.

"I never have time to be bored, always something needs doing," said Saanvi once more collecting the bags and forcing a pace as she remembered the endless list of jobs she still had to do today.

"I'll help," replied Clara, striding along beside her. She loved the steamy busyness of the kitchen with the women industriously prepping vegetables and spice mixes, gossiping and chatting amongst themselves. The men stood around pretending to be important, waving about knives and lighting the charcoal under the tandoori ovens, braying importantly over their heads. Clara would zone in and out of each stream of conversation, male and female, which floated around the kitchen like separate ribbons, only occasionally touching each other. The separateness between the men and women was so clear she could almost see the lines drawn in the air. It felt more honest than her own culture, where the lines were equally drawn but disguised and blurred.

"But Luke lets you out to be with me when you are not being a researcher, which is good of him." Saanvi pointed out as Clara continued to complain about her summer.

"'Let's me!' I am free to come and go as I like, Saanvi." She protested, horrified at the idea she needed permission from Luke to do anything.

"Ah, yes, your liberated society!" exclaimed Saanvi astutely. A summer with Clara had been educational. "It seems to me, if Luke didn't want you to come, he would make it difficult for you to do so - the same thing."

Clara scowled and they walked on for a moment in silence. "He doesn't like me coming." admitted Clara. "We had a huge fight about it in the first place. Do you remember when we first met, Luke and I were out for a meal and Naveed invited me on a tour of the kitchen? Well, Luke was mad about it because I abandoned him to a meal on his own while we were chatting. It was his fault, he could have come too, but wouldn't … anyway, he laid into my language learning, was furious about it. Called it 'dangerous' and told me I must keep it a secret from everyone. How insane! How can learning languages be dangerous for goodness' sake?"

"Didn't he explain?" asked Saanvi frowning.

"Not really, I tried to get him to, but he just said I would get headhunted to do translation work and I would be extremely bored - hardly dangerous - can't be much more boring than being a researcher!" Saanvi smiled at the attempt to lighten the mood but was worried Luke did not support Clara.

"It can cause all kinds of problems when a man does not support his lady."

"I don't need his support!" Clara retorted, "I would like it," she admitted, "But it won't stop me," she added determinedly. Then with a mischievous grin, she told Saanvi, "I am learning Russian at work at the moment, right under his nose! That'll teach him! He says I should just write about the importance of learning languages to unlock cultural understanding, rather than actually learning them - but where is the fun in that?"

"Clara! Russian! Why? How?"

"Simeon, who was from Tallinn, in the Balkan region of the USSR is on the same project. I pestered him into teaching me. We take many coffee breaks where we can chat in Russian and he's even recorded a series of fairy tales and nursery rhymes for me to listen to, as well as key phrases. I have taped conversations too which I listen to while doing all the photocopying and other boring admin tasks. Makes the time pass a quicker."

They had reached the restaurant and turned along the narrow alley beside the front entrance, past a shed used for storing fats and oils, into the kitchen. Immediately they were swallowed up by a wave of warmth and aromas, transported to the exotic world of Pakistan. The girls deposited their baskets, and the women came to sort through what they had managed to buy. Saanvi was told to grab some lunch from their small kitchen upstairs, before resuming prepping salads for the evening's business. Clara offered to stay and help.

"You can stay longer?" asked Saanvi in surprise.

"Yes, if it's ok. Luke is away for the weekend with his cousin, Christian."

"Oh! And I imagine you didn't want to go with him?" she said laughing. She had heard all about Clara's views on Christian's shortcomings.

"Exactly," replied Clara, "we needed a break from each other to be honest. The summer has not turned out as idyllic as we had both imagined. I think we both had different expectations. Luke has been so tied up with this project which I have found boring, and he has criticised my language learning at every turn. We have rubbed each other up the wrong way all summer. I think he went to Christian's to get away from me, as he knew I wouldn't want to go. I love him, Saanvi, but is that enough to live happily with someone? " She confided as they sat down to a heaped plate of curry dished up for them by the ancient grandmother.

Saanvi reached a hand across to her friend and smiled.

"Love is always enough, it is all we have at the end of the day. It will all work out, you'll see." She reassured Clara.

Suddenly from downstairs came a slamming of doors, raised voices, and a stampede on the stairs. The kitchen filled with the family, ushered all into the room by Jorwain, Saanvi's uncle. He was waving a scroll of papers, wild-eyed and crying out for all to pay attention at once. The girls leapt away from the table but were then crammed up against the kitchen counters as the men shoved their way in. They gathered around the table, hastily cleared by the grandmother. Clara was curious, but Saanvi elbowed her to get out of the room. However, there was no space to move, so they stayed still and quiet, ignored by the men. They were all fixated on the papers Jorwain laid on the table as he gesticulated and continued to cry out with manic energy.

"The race is on my brothers! We shall prove our claim to Siachen! These are the plans - look, this will be the base camp. I am flying out tomorrow to play our part. I will tour family and contacts to raise the funds needed for the climbing equipment. The better the equipment, the faster our team can climb this time of year to beat India to the top They have no idea we are re-attempting the climb, and by the time they do, we will be at the summit! This is a life and death matter. Allah will be on our side. We will win back our lands!" There was much applause and hollering at Jorwain's words.

"Look here!" continued Jorwain, "Here on the map is the glacier, and here the historic boundaries of Pakistan before those traitors India stole it from us. Win back the glacier, win back our lands for future generations - this is more than a fight for our lives and livelihood, it is for the future of our family. This is our origin, our homeland, stolen from us - now we take it back!"

"Naveed. Here, take the map and stick it to the wall, so we can be reminded every day what we are working for - our homeland back!" The men once more streamed from the room, some back to work, and Jorwain to pack for his flight. Naveed was left rummaging in the kitchen drawers for some cello tape. Saanvi tentatively stepped forward, reaching for a roll on a shelf near her, and handed it to him. The map was dutifully fixed to the wall, and the girls were left alone.

Clara raised her eyebrows at her friend and Saanvi smiled.

"It is great news, Clara! Come and see, I will show you." As she was speaking, she led the way over to the map on the wall which was a relief map of the Northern boundaries of Pakistan with India, a mountainous band of dark browns and purples. A red felt tip pen circle identified the Siachen Glacier region.

"Here," explained Saanvi pointing to the area inside the red circle, "This is our ancestral home, but India and Pakistan have been fighting over it for as long as I can remember. Since 1981 we became, officially Pakistani citizens. It is confusing, as I grew up thinking of myself as Kashmiri. I grew up in a region called Gilgit-Baltistan in a town called Silbu." She reached for an envelope propped up behind a large black telephone. She took out some photographs showing wide streets, brightly coloured vehicles against a backdrop of surging snow spike-topped mountains and rocky outcrops interspersed with turf and wildflowers. "Here, look, this pretty pink rose flower grows near all our homes, it is the 'Sia' plant, and its bark is used in 'payo cha', umm, 'butter tea'. Do you understand?"

"I am not sure I quite understood everything Jorwain was saying; how will climbing the glacier win back the land?" asked Clara.

Saanvi frowned, "Not sure actually. Let's go down to the kitchens and see if the aunts know."

But the aunts hushed their questions when they went down to start prepping the salads in the kitchen.

"Those are the affairs of men. You are just children, stop your questions. You will be sensible to pretend you heard nothing in the kitchen, you shouldn't have been there. Nothing good will come of you wagging your tongues. Be aware of the danger of knowing things you shouldn't."

Luke returned Sunday evening to find the flat in darkness. Clara returned about 1 am, creeping in, expecting Luke, if he was home, to be asleep. But he was sitting up getting papers sorted for Monday. Or so he told her. In reality, he had been waiting up for her. He didn't need to ask where she had been as she smelt of spices and was clutching a large bag of hot rice dishes and a pile of poppadoms.

Clara dished up the food despite the late hour and brought it to the table, sharing it with Luke. They made small talk over the meal asking after each other's weekend. But since neither of them wanted to share too much for fear of igniting new fuses, their comments were limited. There was a strained silence while Clara played idly with the salt pot. Luke finally cleared his throat laying his hand on hers and the salt pot.

"I've missed you," he said.

"You've only been gone two days," she pointed out.

"No, I mean, I've missed you - the Clara you usually are, not the one of the past few weeks. I'm not saying it's your fault, it's mine - I'm making a hash of apologising - too wrapped up in my new job. Can we rewind to the beginning of the summer, and start again?" She had opened and closed her mouth like a goldfish during his short speech, attempting to interrupt but now he'd finished, she wasn't sure what to say.

"Sure, we can," she said, trying to sound more cheerful than she felt. "But can we make some space for 'us' beyond the research? I am feeling, well a little 'smothered.' The project is not my area of interest ..." she ventured cautiously, not wanting to precipitate another row between them, but trying to find a little wriggle room. "I have interests of my own too," she added even more hesitantly. He looked irritated by her words but didn't object.

"Let's try," he replied.

With a will on both sides to be more considerate of each other, Clara managed some changes to break the boredom. Luke turned a blind eye to some rather long lunch breaks Clara took so she could be with her new friends at The Blue Tiger. She taped those conversations and alternated between Russian, Hindi, and Urdu during the afternoons and evening project sessions, her Walkman permanently glued to her ears. Most of her wages was spent on batteries. However, the tensions between them remained as a dull throb in the background, muffling their joy in living with each other.

As they left work for the flat on the final evening of her research post for the summer Luke grinned at her, dancing on the balls of his feet alongside her, clearly excited.

"What's up?" she asked, laughing at his sparkling eyes and mischievous look. She hadn't seen him looking so happy for a long time.

"Hurry up," he replied as he opened the flat door, "Pack your stuff and come with me, I have a surprise for you."

"What? Now? How do I know what to pack or how much if I don't know where we are going?"

"I was hoping you will come with me to Greece."

"To help you with your project? I didn't know you were going there - how come? Are we leaving now?" She tried to keep up with the turn of events.

"No work - a holiday. I thought we deserved one - come on, we have a flight to catch.

"Greece!"

"Can you speak any Greek?" She was immediately on tenterhooks.

"Um, no." she ventured.

"Good, I expect you would like to learn Greek?" he said smugly, looking pleased with himself.

"Why the change? What's going on?"

"It is a surprise for you. I am owed a break. I like Greece, thought I could show you around - might even teach you a word or two myself," he said laughing.

She stood staring at him, unable immediately to take in what he was saying.

"Are you coming or not?"

Clara had never flown before. It felt decadent and exciting. Once there, a taxi took them to a white-washed villa, with a small wrap-around tiled patio opening straight onto the beach. Along a beach path, other white buildings clambered up the hillside, evolving into a small town. Somewhere a church bell was ringing, drifting on the hot air, blending with the gentle hush of waves along the shore. It was delightful. The small villa was basic but charming. They found a generous basket of fruit, cheeses, vegetables, and olives on the kitchen table.

"How did you find such a lovely place?" she asked, as she brought fruit, olives, and bread out to Luke, who was opening a bottle of wine on the small terrace.

"It belonged to my uncle, now, since his death, his son, Christian - anyone in the family can book it, except we usually all want it the same week if we want it at all ... I asked and it was free, so thought for once I would take my turn. Glad you like it." She was standing before him, tray in hand, her hair loose, so slight and pale, that bite of the lip at the mention of Christian.

"Let's let the wine breathe," he said huskily, grabbing the tray from her, and putting it on the table, to pull her by the hand to the bedroom. There was a large double bed under a huge window - no glass only shutters, which they threw open to let the sky, and sounds of the sea into the room as they made love.

During the day after a lazy breakfast and strong coffee while looking out to sea, Luke worked on papers he had brought with him, following the shade around the villa. Clara paddled along the shore and then up into the town to spend most of the day talking to anyone who would talk back. By late afternoon they would have a lazy siesta, luxuriating in long drawn-out sex, nothing for them to rush off for. Then they would shower, and dress to go into the town for an evening meal in the bars.

Looking back later Clara identified their Greek holiday as an oasis of heaven. It was a perfect time, when things looked so rosy and positive between them, more delightful for coming after such a gruelling summer. She left Greece looking forward to her final year at university and sinking her teeth into her dissertation, spending the weekends in Birmingham seeing Saanvi and staying with Luke. She did not see the storm clouds gathering on the horizon.

CHAPTER 9

News headlines: October 1985
Russian party leader Gorbachev visits Paris on his first visit abroad

"Come up this weekend, there is a fundraising fancy dress party - be a laugh?" Luke's voice came down the phone line.

"I am not sure, it will be for students, not staff, won't it?" she replied hesitantly. Clara was thinking of his devoted student followers who swarmed him in pubs, wanting him to discuss his lectures with them. There was an uncomfortable silence as her words spelled out the problem in greater clarity than she intended.

"Oh, come on! It is raising money for famine relief; you can't say no to that can you?" She could hear his triumph through the long-distance crackles.

Clara found a white shirt, a red full skirt with a wide black belt, and a long red cape which equipped her for a Little Red Riding Hood. Feeling a little more prepared and therefore more confident about it, she went up to Birmingham, to see Saanvi at The Blue Tiger before heading over to the university. She found Luke as usual in the bar, pontificating on some theory or other to a group of young students. She tried to catch his eye but although she was sure he knew she was there; he could not be distracted. A student with a shock of red curls sniggered at her and pointedly asked Luke a question, receiving a ready response. Clara retreated to the bar to get a drink, annoyed at the rebuff, and stared moodily into the depths of her beer. Then who should appear at her elbow but Christian.

"What's hacking you off then?" he smirked as he placed his order. He glanced around towards Luke, "Oh I see, unable to prise him from his fan club, eh? Now, now, share and share alike." He grinned at her, and she glared back.

"Get lost Christian. Go back to your privileged playpen and play politics."

"Ho! Is that the best you can do? Pathetic tonight, aren't you? No wonder you can't attract his attention, he mistook you for a dumb fresher." She was tired, frustrated at Luke and gloomy about the weekend ahead. Christian always knew how to press her buttons to make her snap. His smirk goaded her.

"You bastard!" she hissed, throwing the rest of her drink into his face. She turned on her heel.

"You bitch!" he spluttered in outrage. Thumping his pint down on the bar, he raced after her. People turned in their direction. Luke, sensing trouble, pulled his attention away from the host of upturned faces to witness his cousin slamming his girlfriend into the wall. They were screaming at each other, nose to nose. He rushed over, pulling them apart and dragging Clara outside.

"What the hell is going on?" he yelled at her.

"What are you shouting at me for? Your cousin just threw me against the wall - bastard!" Christian had melted away but not before Luke had seen his dripping hair.

"Why was he dripping wet?"

"Coz he's a complete tosser!" She stamped ahead of him towards the flat. He caught her arm and spun her around to face him.

"Is there something going on between the two of you I should know about?" he asked seriously.

"What? Are you mad? Yes, I usually throw drinks into the faces of people I like!" They started walking again.

"Sometimes people who act as if they hate each other, fancy each other," said Luke following her.

"You've been spending too much time with Bryn and his psycho-babble," she said crossly. "Christian was extremely rude and annoying as usual, he had it coming to him."

"You shouldn't go around making people so mad."

"By 'people', you mean, Christian. Why are you so afraid of him? What can he do? Really, Luke, you worry too much. He was rude, he should take the consequences."

"As long as you can."

"Don't worry about me. At least I managed to attract your attention finally. If Christian and I hadn't fought, you would still be there with your adoring fans."

"Don't be silly."

"Don't be silly yourself - I mean it," she said sharply; was he unaware of his adoring trendy permed ginger-headed fan? In silence, they walked the rest of the way home.

Good humour was restored the next day as Bryn, Lin and the kids were in Birmingham for the day, and they all met up to go around the aquarium in the afternoon. It was a rush when they finally arrived back to the flat to get ready for the evening's fancy dress party. They tripped over each other with much hilarity as they dressed. Luke had a gorilla costume, which encompassed him from head to toe in fur. He had a hairy top, attached to hairy trousers by a concealed zip, topped with a fierce-looking head.

"You should have hired a wolf costume to go with my Red Riding Hood" Clara pointed out, helping him into the legs part of the suit.

The venue was one of the sports halls on campus, decked out in balloons and posters about the need to continue to raise money for the starving in Ethiopia. A bar was set up in one corner, a band on a low platform at the other, and a dance floor marked out in the middle with a scattering of chairs and tables around the edges. Other smaller rooms opened off from the main hall with more chairs and tables. Everything was in full swing by the time they arrived, the room was crowded, smoky, and loud. They fought their way to the bar and screamed at the barman to make him hear their order. For the first drink, they stood together, then danced to the U2 tribute band. But Luke's costume made him so hot so quickly he pulled the head off after the first few songs and they made an escape to one of the side rooms.

As soon as they had sat down students, dressed in various Madonna-esque garb which Clara considered verged on the pornographic, encircled them. In contrast, she felt prudish in her shin-length skirt and modest shirt with cape. The looks she received from the Madonna-look-alikes suggested they shared her view of herself. She sat by him, half-heartedly joining the banter. The evening dragged on.

Later, feeling ignored by Luke whilst at the same time, a baby for feeling that way, she pushed her way through the crowded dance floor towards the toilets, weaving unsteadily. The alcohol she had steadily consumed all evening was having its desired effect, and the world was rather more distant than usual. She was concentrating on finding her way when she felt someone grab her. Turning she saw Luke had caught her up, one of his gorilla claws on her arm. For some reason, he had replaced his gorilla head. 'Perhaps he is trying to evade his fan club for two minutes,' she thought, pleased.

He steered her to a quiet corridor and through a door into a small store cupboard where gym mats and redundant sports equipment were stored. It was pitch black. The noise of the party was reduced to a dull throb of sound. She was startled, but at the same time relieved to have him to herself, pleasurably surprised at his sudden switch to uncharacteristic spontaneity. As she tripped over the clutter on the floor she fell into his big hairy arms. Giggling she nestled against him. It was quite tricky having sex in a small pitch-black cupboard with a gorilla, but they managed it somehow.

"Take your head off, you daft bugger and let me kiss you." She laughed at him, but he growled and rather indistinctly through his mask said,

"Let's do it differently shall we?" Luke discarded his glove to be able to feel her. He released her cape ties, running his fingers down her cheek, and neck, as he undid her shirt buttons, hungrily seeking her breasts. She moaned softly, a warm glow creeping over her. As she fell against the piled sports mats, he came behind her. Hands to her thighs, moving higher, circling with restrained intensity, then probing between her legs, fingers dancing as if playing the oboe or clarinet, driving her to an intensity she had never known - was she going to die in a cupboard? Then he was in her, entering from behind. They came together in a flood of sensations leaving Clara breathless and disoriented. She gasped for breath, trying to summon the energy and coordination to turn around into their customary post-sex hug. A beam of light fell across her face, then was as instantly gone, lunging her into an even darker blackness as the door clicked closed.

"Luke?" But even as she said his name, she knew she was alone in the cupboard.

It is amazing how quickly one can go from hot to stone cold, how rapidly drunken half-thoughts can crystallise into sober clarity in mere moments. 'No, not possible' she whispered to herself as she felt around for her cape and rearranged her clothing. She tentatively retraced her steps to the main hall. The crowds had started to thin out at this late hour so she could see across to the bar. Her stomach heaved violently, even before her eyes could communicate with her brain. There leaning at the bar were two gorillas, heads off on the bar beside them, chatting, a pint of beer in each of their hands. She stood there, unable to make her feet move. Aware of her gaze both Luke and Christian turned to look at her. As if released by their attention, she turned and fled, making it outside to the nearest shrubbery before being sick. She flopped down on the pavement trying to recover, retching over and over as waves of revulsion hit her again and again. Luke appeared, looming above her.

"What's up? Too much grog?" She shook her head weakly.

"Can we go home?" she asked.

"You can go on ahead if you like, I'll be along later."

"But please Luke! I want you to come with me. I don't feel too good."

"What's happened?" he said, crouching down beside her.

"I can't explain here," she stuttered through ragged breath, shivering as she felt the cold evening creep into her bones, "It's Christian - " she began.

"- No. I'm not listening if you two have been fighting again." he said crossly, standing up, "I am fed up with the two of you - I am not going to listen. Why can't you stay away from him for even one evening!" He stomped back inside.

"Sod!" she muttered to herself. Forcing one leg in front of the other shaky leg she made it back to the flat. Once at the door of their flat she searched around for her door key only to remember she didn't have it on her, as she had no pockets. Luke had said he would carry it. All emotional and physical energy spent she crumpled down by the door letting the tears flow freely.

"Clara?"

"Go away. Leave me alone." She knew he was still there. "Or, go and get my door key from Luke if you want to be useful." She tried to make him leave.

"Can't, he's snogging that redhead fresher," he replied coolly, not moving.

With an effort she wiped her eyes on her cape, pulled herself back to standing and turned to face him. 'There are not sufficient words in the English language to express how I feel!' she thought to herself. Then she realised she had at her disposal other more expressive languages to rescue her. She proceeded to release her pent-up feelings at Christian in a torrent of Italian. She wasn't entirely sure she was making grammatical sense, but the general essence of her emotions was evident.

"Giurare contro di me in italiano non lo rende migliore, sai?" (Swearing at me in Italian, doesn't make it any better you know?) Christian replied calmly.

"Mi fa sentire meglio però." (It makes me feel better though)

"Look, come into my flat while we wait for Luke with the key, you can't stand here all night," he offered.

"No. I would rather stand out here all night. What you did tonight is unforgivable - it's rape!" she spat at him, anger flaring again. She had switched back to English and the ugly English word 'rape' hung in the air like acrid smoke. Christian looked a little contrite and spoke softly.

"Sorry, I didn't mean for that to happen …"

"Yes? Try that on someone else! You think I am that dumb?" she challenged. "You planned it. It was not a coincidence you were both dressed the same - you planned it!"

"Yes," he admitted, "then again, no," he added, "The shared costumes were because I borrowed them from a mate's stag do for us both - don't ask me why they were going to stag in gorilla outfits … Anyway, I was planning on locking you into the cupboard for a few hours to get you back for the public humiliating drowning you gave me the other evening."

"So stupid! You thought locking me in a random cupboard was a payback? I don't believe you. I think you deliberately set out to humiliate me in the most awful way - "

"-Stop it, Clara. I didn't plan to do what we did this evening. Honest. But you tripped and fell against me and -"

"Oh, so it's my fault, is it? Typical, bloody typical!"

"Just listen, will you!" he raised his voice, getting angry and stepping towards her. "When you fell against me and hugged me with that sexy giggle, I decided not to lock you in after all. I was about to reveal who I was, but then you were so delightful I couldn't. And then I couldn't stop; I didn't mean it to go so far, but god, Clara, for all your apparent innocent and virginal naivety act, you are amazing. You are a total contradiction, aren't you; not what you appear at all, are you?" She stared at him coldly.

"If that's your defence I recommend you don't go into law." It was all too much to deal with. She just wanted to sleep, run away from it all. "Please go away now," she begged.

"Fine!" He turned on his heel and marched off. She heard him stomping down the stairs and slamming the outside door. 'Bloody hell' she thought, 'I have upset my 'rapist' and am left feeling guilty about it!' She curled up on the doorstep and waited.

Sometime later she was dimly aware of gentle arms lifting her, carrying her, laying her down, and covering her with a duvet. She was too sleepy to rouse herself, and she floated back to sleep shortly afterwards. She woke the next time with the sun streaming in through a window, straight into the inside of her skull which seemed to be on fire. As she struggled to focus, she saw two men looming over her. 'Back to the nightmare', she thought.

"What are you doing here?" asked Luke.

"I dunno," she answered looking around to see where she was - she had no idea.

"I put her here last night. She was locked out, and you were eating the face off the redhead, so I put your girlfriend into my bed - you have a problem with that?" Christian replied. They were squaring up to each other. Clara sighed and lay back down, burying her head under the covers to block out the light and their voices. At this moment in time, she hated them equally.

"Go away, both of you," she called from underneath the duvet.

She fell asleep again and woke much later; the sun had slid around and was no longer in her eyes. She sat up, feeling much better physically. The green luminous hands in the clock face beside the bed showed it to be four pm. She eased herself out of bed, still dressed as a crumpled Red Riding Hood. She wandered through the adjoining door into a living room. Christian was sprawled fast asleep along the length of the sofa in there, The Times sliding onto the floor from his grasp. She let herself quietly out of the flat. The door to her flat opposite was unlocked she discovered with relief, and she slid inside.

Luke was slumped on their sofa, a mirror image of the flat opposite. She smiled a small smile as she noticed he too was dozing in the same sprawling manner under a spread and falling broadsheet - the Independent newspaper. She went through to the bathroom and stripped off to have a shower. The hot water was reviving. She could feel some of the sticky confusion washing away, but she knew the memories of last night and the accompanying waves of remorse, would fade slower. She felt violated and invaded, robbed of choice and free will, suffocating. But she also felt the sense of some responsibility; a small voice of doubt was questioning herself; did she not know at any time it was Christian and not Luke? Could she not have stopped it? Did she have to keep it locked inside as a secret, and how did that affect her relationship with Luke when they had promised 'no secrets'? How should she behave towards Christian? How did she feel about him? What was it about him that made her want to argue his every point? Was Luke right - was she attracted to him, so had brought last night on herself? The questions danced with the droplets of water running down her body and into the vortex spin of the plug hole.

Once clean, smelling of shampoo and dressed, she went through to the inert body under the newspaper. He heaved himself upright trying to shake off the late afternoon somnolence.

"Okay?" he asked.

"Yeah sure," she heard herself say in a chipper tone. He eyed her closely and ran his hands through his hair: She fidgeted under his gaze.

"How did you end up in Christian's bed last night?" he asked as if he didn't want to, but it came unbidden to his lips.

"He told you, I was locked out." She went to fetch a couple of paracetamol and a glass of water to take the final remnants of her hangover away. He followed her into the kitchen. Again, he spoke in a wooden manner as if forcing himself to ask questions he didn't want to know the answers to.

"Is there anything going on between you and Chris I should know?" She faced him squarely.

"That's rich when you spent all evening wrapped up in the arms of Gingernut!" She lashed out, angry and scared in equal measure.

"It's not true, I wasn't at all - "

"But Christian said -"

"Christian, Christian, Christian!" he shouted at her, "He is ribbing you as usual, yet you take him seriously every time!

101

What's the matter with you? I was not with Claudia last night. I can prove it as I spent all evening with a group of students." He slammed his hand down on the table with frustration. "I swear, Clara, if you ever mention Christian's name, talk about or to him, I will never speak to you again!" He swung round and grabbed his cigarettes and his jacket. She thought he was going to storm out on her, but he stopped with his hand on the door handle. He sighed deeply, energy seeming to drain from him. Hunched, he turned back to her. "Come on, my most annoying girlfriend in the whole wide world, I'm starving, and you must be too. I'll treat you to an Indian if you don't make me go to The Blue Tiger and insist on speaking in foreign tongues all evening?" Wordlessly she put on her shoes and coat, and followed him out of the door.

They caught a train into the city centre, choosing an Indian restaurant near the Bull Ring neither of them had been to before. It was quiet on a Sunday evening. They were shown to a table by the window. It was cosy with soft red carpets, walls heavily papered in embossed roses, and red covers on the tables with big gold serviettes flowering out of the tops of the wine glasses. As they looked at the menu to make their choices, Clara could hear the waiters talking in the background. Despite herself she burst out laughing. Luke looked startled and rose an eyebrow in enquiry.

"Sorry," she said hastily, "I couldn't help hearing what they were saying, it made me laugh that's all," she explained, returning her attention to the menu. But Luke had put his menu down.

"You can't leave it like that, you have to tell me now, I'm curious."

"They were trying to guess who we were to each other. They decided we were brother and sister!"

"Why did they think that?"

"Well, because we were bickering when we came in - a rough translation anyway." One of the waiters came over to get their drinks order. Clara resisting temptation kept quiet while Luke ordered two beers. But when he returned and smiled at her as he placed the beer down, she thanked him, without thinking in Urdu. He was startled but completed the formal phrase equivalent to 'you're welcome.' Then much to Clara's relief, he left them to consider their food order. As he retreated, Clara lent towards Luke.

"Sorry. It slipped out. I won't say anything else!"

"Relax and help decide what we are having will you?"

Their orders came and they tucked in, both realising how hungry they were, working out they had not eaten since the lunch at the aquarium the day before. Mid meal the waiter came over to check they were all alright with their food. As they assured him everything was delicious, he turned to Clara.

"Kaysay rakhnna aap aalim Urdu?" (How come you speak Urdu?)" With a worried glance at Luke, she hastily replied in the same language.

"Mayn hun talib-e-ilm aor yay juz ka mayra mutalia karna. Magar, mayra dost kartaa naheen maanind kehna zabaan anjaani taraf oos ko." (I am a student, and it is part of my studies. But my boyfriend doesn't like it when I speak languages he doesn't know,) He raised his eyebrow.

"Boyfriend?"

"Yes," replied Clara, "not brother," she said mischievously. After a startled look he laughed loudly, throwing back his head and slapping Luke on the shoulder.

"Good for you mate," he laughed, "You have a right one here!" He waved his hand at Clara.

Left alone again Clara breathed a sigh of relief, making a mental note never to come to another Indian restaurant with Luke if he was going to hold her to promises not to speak the local languages. Luke, satiated and picking at remnants of naan bread, was not cross.

"You sound quite fluent in the language you were just speaking - what language was it?"

"I am no way near being fluent but what I do say sounds like a local, startling people. But as far as my research has indicated, it is the fastest way to gain links to people and build trust to enable meaningful dialogue. I learn through listening and memorising them like songs." She eyed Luke cautiously. He smiled at her.

"It has not been the best of weekends, has it?" he said.

"Well, with us, it seems as if it is all good or disastrous," she replied, smiling at him. He kissed her hand.

"I love you, Clara."

Caught off guard, she flushed deeply, the words opening the floodgates of remorse, and a sense of grief rather than joy - did she deserve this love after last night? Was she worthy of it? Tears sprang to her eyes. Luke looked on with confusion. She brushed them away briskly, smiling at him.

"I don't know where they came from. I'm just tired, I guess. You took me by surprise. I certainly love you, but I am not always confident we can make it work." He smiled and took her hand once more.

'Maybe', she thought, almost too scared to dare hope, 'maybe, I can lock away last night, pretend it never happened, just concentrate on being with this lovely, and kind man.'

"I hoped you loved me, but I wasn't sure. We do seem to make life difficult for ourselves, don't we? Shall we persevere? See where it leads us? " Luke attracted the waiter's attention and ordered coffees. When it came and they were alone again, he took a sip, then leaned back in his chair. "Tell me about your dissertation, how is it coming along?" She sighed.

"It is at that stage where I have lots of ideas, and half-developed theories. But not yet sure if I will have a meaningful conclusion. Am I making sense?"

"Of course, perfectly - been there, got the t-shirt, remember?" She nodded in acknowledgment.

"I just have to keep going at this stage: Leaps of faith and all that!"

"Go get your First - you deserve it."

"I will miss the people I have enjoyed getting to know so well during my research when I do finish. I have made some real friends, especially Saanvi," she added wistfully.

"Tell me," he asked, spreading his hands to invite her to share.

"She is my age and married to Aarif, the youngest chef, and they arrived in the country about two years ago to join the family here. They are great teachers. I have learnt so much, not just about the language, but also about India and Pakistan. Saanvi showed me photos of the part of the Northern Indian border region they come from, in Kashmir, neighbouring the Siachen Glacier – so beautiful.

I have taped many of the conversations, especially when I was first getting to grips with the language. I documented, in diary form, the comings and goings of the family, applying cultural analysis on family dynamics. There are the usual family tensions, especially around Jorwain. He organises the ordering of supplies and the importation of rice and spices, which he also supplies to other restaurants. I think he is a schizophrenic, or something, as sometimes he is nice as pie with smiling eyes and other times, I wouldn't want to be alone in the same room with him. Everyone is afraid of him in that mood: Wild looking with small but 'dead' eyes. Fascinating. He rants and raves about everything. He is a leader of some kind in a movement for his region to become part of Pakistan again, but never seems to leave the restaurant, so not sure how he manages this. Perhaps he is delusional. He has appealed to the British Government to intervene to act as intermediaries between India and Pakistan to agree on boundaries and the ownership of the Siachen Glacier in particular."

"And are you saying you have gained access to these people and their lives because you have learnt their language?" Luke appeared interested in what she was saying.

"Yes, mainly. You also need to make an empathetic connection. I mimic body language and adapt my voice and accent to match theirs. I have analysed accents in Northern India and Pakistan - language is politically sensitive in this country and region. I can hear distinctions between them, crossing to and fro from Urdu and Hindi. I change my accent and voice to whom I am speaking, it elicits a more positive response."

"Is your whole work based on this family?"

"No, I have also included reference to others - Italian, Turkish, Greek, and some Russian."

"Russian?" He frowned at her. She grinned at him.

"Simeon. We were research partners in the summer. We met for a few conversational sessions during the lunch hours." He tried to give her a severe look, but failed and smiled instead, shaking his head. "Can I ask why you are interested now but not before? You have hated my work." Clara asked, surprised by his sustained interest.

"Yeah, it's a valid question," said Luke, "Let's just say a mutual friend of ours gave me a pep talk and made me see being so unsupportive was not 'conducive to a successful relationship'," he explained.

"Bryn?" He nodded.

"I'm sorry, I was afraid I suppose I was losing you to a place I could not follow, on subjects I could no longer support you on. I have always seen you as a student, with me as your advisor. So, our mutual counsellor friend tells me that I need to start seeing you more as a partner and an expert in your own right. So, I thought I should start putting good sense into practice."

That night, they made love so tenderly it brought tears to Clara's eyes again. They fell unnoticed in the dark. Guilt and confusion churned in the pit of her stomach. Memories of being with Christian came unbidden as she lay with Luke. As Luke caressed her, she drew on reserves of personal strength and forced Christian out of her head. She surprised Luke by asserting gentle authority over their lovemaking, climbing on top to enjoy a sense of unity as far removed from the violation she felt the night before as she could.

Clara dreamed she was on a beach, her back against a high cliff. A wall of water in the form of a huge wave was heading towards her. She knew there was a way out because the beach had been full of people two minutes ago and now, they had gone - but she couldn't see where. Now it was just her, stuck between a wall of cliff and water. She woke suddenly, thrashing about in the covers, dripping in sweat.

"You, okay?" muttered Luke sleepily.

"Bad dream."

"Come here." He reached out an arm and pulled her into his warm body, spooning her close and falling asleep after kissing her ear, breathing softly across her cheek. She relaxed into his embrace feeling the stress and internal turmoil start to subside. If she had Luke at her back, she would be safe.

CHAPTER 10

Top UK chart hit: October 1985
St Elmo's Fire: John Parr

B ut the next afternoon as the train clattered and swayed across the barren and bleak countryside at the end of Autumn, waves of shame and anger washed over Clara as if they had been waiting for Luke to vanish to a pinprick on the horizon to spring. Memories and emotions leapt like a pouncing tiger. The harder she tried to shut her mind to the stuffy cupboard with Christian, the more it invaded. Anger bubbled like molten lava through cracks in the ground. 'How dare he take without asking! He is a thief!' She tried her yoga breathing, which helped, but the memories of his touch seemed branded into her mind.

In a state of emotional turmoil, she arrived back in her room at university. Instead of doing any of the work, she went in search of her friends. She found them sipping drinks in The Union Bar, chatting about the latest gossip. She joined them, feeling as if a hundred years had passed since they last met. She felt separated from them by an invisible barrier but soothed by their company.

"A penny for them," said Reeta as they wandered back home at the end of the evening. The offer hung there tantalising her, but she panicked. She couldn't afford to lose her friend and she was afraid on telling, she would be judged. How could someone not know who they were having sex with? How could she not have known it wasn't Luke? She smiled and linked arms.

"Nothing I can't handle, just not been the best of weekends." The moment to share was gone.

"What's the matter?" asked Bryn when he next caught up with her crossing the quad the following morning. He regarded her bitten bottom lip, and black rings under her eyes with concern.

"Nothing, why?" she asked him, as they fell into step together.

"Coming up for a coffee?" he asked lightly.

"Um, I was going to see Tony about something."

"Coffee first." It didn't seem like a question anymore, so she did a mental shrug and followed into his office. "The kids are still talking about Saturday, you know - they love your company".

She smiled, accepting her mug of mint tea ('Coffee' was a general term for Bryn as he always gave her peppermint tea regardless of what she asked for.). She sat down in her favourite chair by the window, looking out, today on the bare twigs of late autumn. He sat opposite her in what she noticed with apprehension, was what she called 'his counselling pose': His fingers steepled, face with a neutral expression, eyes soft. She preferred him in 'lecturer pose' - seated leaning forward, hands waving around as they debated theoretical nonsense.

"Your body language is of someone struggling under a huge burden," he said, letting the invitation to share drift across the space between them. Much to her annoyance, in response to his tone, she felt tears springing to her eyes and knew he noticed. She wracked her brain for an answer to make him go away.

"Oh, it's the build-up of pressure with getting my dissertation fully researched - feeling it all a bit at the moment," she said hopefully.

"Everything alright between you and Luke? You know I care about both of you, don't you?" She smiled at this.

"Yes, so I hear - Luke is suddenly interested in my work," she said.

"But?" he asked astutely.

"No 'but' as such. He showed an interest, which is nice, but I know it still annoys him below the surface. He told me he loves me, which was nice too." She went pink, thinking she was saying things all wrong: Why was she blurting that out?

"And?" he nudged her, keeping still and passive. She shrugged.

"And what? Oh, well I love him too obviously. Is that what you mean?"

"You know full well it isn't what I mean." he scolded her gently. There was a taut silence, fingers twisted in her lap. Her voice, when she found it, was hesitant.

"Things have switched gears. I think I ought to be happy, but I feel rather unqualified, unequal to the situation somehow. Is that normal? It's scary, relationships, aren't they?" She had stood up while speaking, half turning away from Bryn to stare out into the trees. Her eyes followed the flailing of tatty leaves as they were ripped from the branches by the wind.

"Have you talked to Luke about this?"

"No, we didn't have time; snatched weekends."

"Perhaps when you have finished here and have more time, you can explore and unpack this together, as it is different for every couple. Sorry, I know it isn't what you wanted me to say. But the most important thing in every relationship is to talk, keep all communication channels open at all times - no secrets." That was really not what Clara wanted to hear. Should she tell Luke about Christian then? But he always sided with Christian against her; he wouldn't listen. 'He wouldn't believe me, and Christian would lie, so his word against mine', she thought, as she flopped back down into the chair.

"Clara," Bryn leaned towards her, although she seemed to be a hundred miles away. He was acutely aware the conversation they had just had, had been a total smokescreen, a diversion from what was going on. He was being locked out. "What is going on? Let me help you," he said softly.

"Nothing Bryn," she replied, getting up to go, " I am fine, just been a tiring weekend, lots of work to do - when it's all over, you will see, the sun will shine again. I know I will feel much better when I'm more confident with my dissertation." At the door, she turned. "Bryn? I want to manage on my own for now. Will you be here for me, even when I leave university?"

"Yes, of course I will be - you know that don't you?"

"Life has twists and turns, and I admit I have encountered a few unexpected problems to overcome recently. At the moment I want to learn to cope my way." Clara came a little way back into the room, "But," said Clara, "I promise you - I will come to you when I need you, if you promise you will be here for me."

"Call when you need me." He told her firmly. Then with an apologetic glance, she did leave, closing the door on Bryn's concerned face.

She found it hard to settle into her work. The conversation with Bryn rattled around her head. She felt she didn't deserve Luke's love because there was no way she could talk to him about what happened between her and Christian at the weekend. On the other hand, was what Bryn said true? Surely love could withstand secrets. Everyone had secrets. Hadn't she been told to keep secrets following her conversations with both Greg and then Harry? Weren't others also keeping secrets - who were the people Harry referred to at the dinner party? Was Bryn who he appeared to be?

Luke suggested they met in London for a change and as she was sure she would not meet Christian there, she agreed. When she arrived at Greg and Charlie's, Luke was already there and the arrangement for the evening was shared with her: Greg had tickets to an opera at the Albert Hall. Clara was excited. She had never been to an opera before - it sounded glamorous! Greg and Luke looked smart in suits, and Charlotte was out of her usual tracksuit for once, in a skirt and jacket. Clara had not brought anything, but Charlotte had anticipated that. She had borrowed a dress from a 'skinny bean of a friend.' Consequently, Clara felt pretty in a blue round-neck, short-sleeved dress, dropping straight down from the bodice down to her knees.

It was an evening of revelation for Clara. They hailed a taxi from the flat to South Kensington, which Clara thought was a huge extravagance, but Greg paid the large taxi fare without a murmur. The Albert Hall, which reminded Clara of an ornate biscuit tin her mother stored freshly baked flapjacks in, towered above them, in a stylish pink and white stonework. They blended in with the flow of people through the foyer, to a bar where they ordered drinks. Then they found their box, and nestled into cosy red seats, separated from neighbours by red curtains - the stage laid out before them. Clara was enthralled. Charlotte and Luke became increasingly tipsy throughout the performance of La Traviata, sitting at the back of the box, and taking turns to take trips to the bar. They cast only occasional glances down to the stage. Clara however, barely sipped her first drink, absorbed, from the opening notes to the final heart-wrenching song.

Clara had never concentrated on classical music before and hadn't been sure she would like the sound or be able to follow the story. But as the first notes fluttered overhead it was as if they fell like magic rain onto her, dissolving emotional walls and barriers she had been busy building. The extravagance and over-the-top drama keyed into feelings bubbling under the surface. During the high strains of the love song between Tosca and Violetta, she rode the rollercoaster of the story, bathing in the emotional accord. All the stress of the past few weeks seemed to fly up on the chords of the drama and evaporate amongst the bubble ceiling of the venue.

Italian, she decided, was the perfect language to soar on the wings of the notes of love, love denied, and love regained in death as Violetta's tragic story unfolded. By the end Clara felt elated, almost as drunk as the other two, feeling lightheaded but strangely at peace. Without having consciously been thinking of anything other than the story, by the end she felt something had changed inside her. There had been a crystallising of focus and direction of energy. She was resolved to never forgive Christian for what he did and what he stood for. Christian was someone you kept close and trusted not one iota. She would, however, one day get even with him. And if it took her entire lifetime, she would make sure he would learn the lesson for underestimating the abilities of women. This conviction struck her with force.

They gathered up their coats and bags as the applause faded, Clara taking longer than necessary with her coat, trying to regain a level of composure to reface the world. Charlie and Luke raced ahead into the crowd seething as a mass towards the exit. But Clara noticed with some alarm, Greg was silently waiting for her. How long had he been watching her she wondered? As she drew level with him, he gave her a small smile, holding eye contact for a moment, and then put his arm about her to guide her through the throng.

"Good emotional outlet, isn't it? You need to remember what works for you when you need it," he told her as they swept along to join the other two, who were stamping their feet and blowing on their hands as they waited.

Back at the flat Charlotte made coffee and Greg passed around the whisky.

"What did you think of the performance Clara?" Greg asked her as he poured a generous serving of whisky into her glass.

"Oh, loved it!" she said enthusiastically. Luke and Charlotte rolled their eyes comedically laughing.

"What?" asked Clara, "Am I not supposed to enjoy it?"

"You can say so if you didn't like it, we won't mind. I find the actual opera boring but thought it might cheer you up – you have been down lately," said Luke.

"All somewhat unintelligible and, well, 'noisy' to my mind," said Charlotte. "But Greg loves them, and I like the Albert Hall, so I was happy to go along."

"Oh," said Clara rather deflated. She felt wrong-footed and not too pleased to be paired with Greg on something.

"Did you gather the story? Do you want me to clarify anything?" asked Greg helpfully.

"No, I understood the story thanks. Isn't Italian the perfect language for opera? So true!"

"Do you speak Italian then?" he asked casually.

"Fairly well, yes. Enough to follow the opera."

"Do you speak any other languages?"

"Ye- " Clara started to say, but Luke suddenly spilled his whisky, and it splashed over himself as well as getting some on her dress. Worried, as the dress wasn't hers, there was lots of rushing to the kitchen and sponging down. Luke then suggested they should change out of the sponge-wet clothes. As soon as the bedroom door closed Luke pulled Clara close.

"Clara!" Luke whispered, "For goodness' sake don't tell Greg you are multilingual! I have told you before, don't tell people!"

"Why not?"

"Just don't."

"Why? You can't say that."

"Look," he pulled her down to sit on the bed, "You know he said he works in the Government? He also sometimes says he works in the Foreign Office, but it is not his real job. He works in a secret arm of the Government - no one knows what he does exactly, we aren't allowed to ask." He looked at her for a reaction and she feigned surprise.

"Does he? So?"

"I don't want him trying to recruit you into that outfit - you won't like it. Don't give him any reason to consider you. Your insistence on acquiring multilingual skills may give him ideas."

"Well, I don't want to and will tell him if he asks - I am not sure why you are making such a fuss."

"Mmm, stay away and quiet, you don't understand how these things work."

"What things? What do you know about it?" But Luke was busy pulling a jersey over his pyjamas and didn't reply. Once clad in pyjamas, they wandered back out to finish their coffee. The conversation did not return to opera.

Clara came face to face with Christian as she left Luke's flat to return to her university one Sunday evening. He was emerging from his flat opposite at the same time. She hesitated, but he had seen her and greeted her pleasantly enough. She had no choice but to fall into step with him because they both had to go down the stairs to get out of the building.

"Where are you going?" he asked.

"Station," she answered shortly.

"So am I, we can walk together," he commented. She did not answer, and they continued side by side.

"I hear you have a liking for opera," he said conversationally after a while.

"Playing games again, are we?"

"An observation. I like opera too - saw Madame Butterfly last week. You'd like that one especially. I don't think Luke likes opera though, you will have to get into Greg's good books to see another one - or mine." Silence. "How's your dissertation going?

I'm at the point where I feel I am going around in circles and not getting anywhere. You?" he continued in a cheerful tone. She nodded still silent. "What next for you? Here for a master's, and then a lifetime of research and lecturing with Boyfriend?" Despite herself, Clara glanced up at his face in profile. He continued to look straight ahead, but the arrow had made its hit as he had intended, and she struggled not to respond.

"Maybe," she managed after a minute of internal struggle, trying to sound nonchalant. "What about yourself?" She didn't want to know but was trying to deflect attention from herself. But he was not to be diverted.

"I wouldn't have thought you would be happy to settle for such a parochial existence," he commented. She could not resist any longer, ('You weak and feeble individual,' she scolded herself).

"And what may I ask is 'parochial' about global research?"

"Oh!" he said triumphantly, seeing he had managed to goad her into conversation, "Madam thinks she is going to be part of 'global' research - how important, how significant - that will save the world!" he mocked.

"Better than taking up a career in banking, or whatever you rich toffs do to amuse yourself; actively upholding the world's inequalities!" she fired back at him.

"You do realise, my love," he said, changing tack, "if you were (heaven help us all!) to end up marrying Luke, you would also be joining the rich elite 'toffs' as you call them - and if I remember correctly, you didn't object to being whisked off to a romantic Greek island villa for a week either. Methinks the pretty lady is confused about life in general."

"Piss off Christian." But they continued to walk together. She had no alternative as she had a train to catch, and so presumably did he; she prayed it was not the same one.

"Does Luke ever talk about his family to you?" She didn't reply. He continued, "They are influential people. Luke fell out with his parents as their political views did not match his own - as you may imagine. Recently however he has made moves to make up with them. If he does and ends up introducing you, Luke's father will be interested in your skill set. You are bright, quick, and have an aptitude for languages. You will have many opportunities for work at your fingertips through their connections. Life could be more exciting than being a research assistant in a middle England university, answering daft fresher questions. Doesn't that attract you?" They had reached the station, and she stopped to go to her platform, as he was, to her immense relief, going the opposite direction.

"I didn't say I would be a researcher, that was your assumption. But whatever I do, I will do it off my own back and not through special connections and nepotism. I don't want to be part of the problem; I want to play a part in the solutions." He stood before her, blocking her way.

"Clara, two things - first, have you considered you may have to be a part of the problem, to gain the power required to fix any of the world's problems? Secondly, you are already a beneficiary of connections you are making, no one can act alone. Recognise where the connections are, and how they can meet your needs and take some reign over them. Alright?" The 'Alright' was delivered softly, intimately, with personal concern. She found herself feeling arousal at his presence, his body standing so close to her, almost whispering in her ear.

'Perhaps anyone would feel the same with him breathing in my ear, and it is a normal reaction. I just have to stand back outside his physical influence', she thought with panic. She tried it, and nearly fell backwards down the steps to the platform. He grabbed her by the arms pulling her to safety. She wrenched herself free, as angry with herself, as with him.

"I can look after myself," she said fiercely. The fact he had saved her from falling and so the statement was not exactly appropriate for the given moment made her smile rather ruefully at the words as they were voiced. She glanced up at him from under her fringe. He stared at her solemnly for a moment, then said roughly,

"God Clara, I want to shake you and kiss you in equal measure!" And he spun on his heel and marched off towards his platform.

CHAPTER 11

News headlines: March 1986
In South Africa anti-apartheid campaigners cease school boycotts by black pupils.

It was a dark, wet evening, and Clara was walking from The Blue Tiger to the flat on campus. The wind kept changing direction, so the umbrella was useless, soaking her. She was freezing as well by the time she reached the front door, having ditched the umbrella altogether by then. Her fingers were numb and she could not fit the key into the lock. She stood for ages trying to get the door open. She was so intent on her activity, her vision blurred by a dripping fringe, she jumped when a hand took the key from her, and opened the door, nudging her inside. He disappeared into the bathroom, as she dropped her rucksack to the floor and peeled off her coat. He returned with a towel which he threw at her. She dried her face and hair.

"Christian, stop being weird and nice, for God's sake!" she snapped at him, perturbed by his presence. "Thank you, but please go and rescue some other drowning maiden in distress." But he settled into the sofa, his feet on the coffee table.

"Christian, please go away. I am going to go back out to find Luke."

"He is in his usual bar, quite content without you. It is still pouring with rain so you may as well stay here in the dry - or do you have a compulsion to go and check up on him?" he said in his usual mocking tone, not moving. She turned her back on him and went to make a jam sandwich, realising how hungry she was.

"Do you want one?" she offered, waving a knife at him. He wrinkled his nose; presumably, jam sandwiches were beneath him. Seeing no alternative, she went to sit opposite him in an armchair. He considered her for a few moments, while she finished her food.

"Can you dance?" he asked, as if it was a question burning him for years. She was puzzled.

"Dance - what kind of dance do you mean?"

"Waltz, foxtrot, that kind." She couldn't for the life of her see where this was going. She shrugged.

"Not a skill I find to be in high demand," she started to say, but then added as a long-lost memory floated back before her eyes, "but my parents made me go to ballroom classes as a child, so I could probably remember them if I needed to -" Christian leapt up at her words, pushing the sofa and the table back to clear a space.

"Christian! Stop! What are you doing?" cried Clara, horrified, "Leave the furniture alone. I am not dancing here, and not with you -" But Christian snatched her into a dance hold and twirled her around the room in a waltz to his untuneful, "One, two, three, one, two, three!" Despite herself, Clara laughed at the ridiculousness of it. They crashed into the table, making Christian swear and break the dance hold to rub a leg.

"Mmm," observed Christian, "not enough space - but you dance well," as if she were passing some test. Clara rearranged the furniture back to where it was before. "Will you come over to my place for a minute?" he asked, watching her remake the room.

"Why?"

"If you want to know why, come over." He saw her hesitate, then back away as if about to decline. "Oh, come on. Two minutes, that's all I ask - I promise to behave as a perfect gentleman. Please. I wish to talk to you where you are not on tenterhooks, expecting Luke to walk in at any moment."

Clara was scared, scared of herself more than anything else. She acknowledged part of her was tempted, curious to know what Chris wanted to say and how it was linked to the bizarre ballroom dancing fiasco. She hesitated.

"We have at least an hour before he will drag himself away from the pub. I just want to talk to you - nothing else, I swear." Everything was screaming at her to refuse, walk away, and go out in the rain to find Luke. Instead, she heard herself agreeing to give him five minutes of her time. They went across the hall to his flat. He waved her to the table in his small kitchen while he fetched a bottle of wine and two glasses. He took a seat opposite and they clinked glasses. As they took a sip, he switched to Russian and in a rather clipped accent, he said, "Yesli vy poymete, chto ya proshu, vy sdelayete mne rabotu?" (If you understand what I am saying to you will you do a job for me?) She took a second sip.

"Niet."

"Why not?"

"I don't trust you and I don't like you."

"Well, a good thing - about time. I don't trust you either by the way - because I never trust anyone. So, will you do it? I will pay you."

"No Christian. I don't want to work with you. My Russian isn't that good anyway."

"I would have thought," he remarked, "you would jump at the chance to earn some money. To be able to support yourself financially would buy you freedom from your suffocating parents. We all want that don't we, independence; to follow our dreams? How are you going to afford to do a Master's?" She laughed without humour, ignoring the accurate quip about her parents.

"I would need to do more than a night of translating work to earn that much!"

"I'd pay you £1,000 for an evening's work."

"Shit, Christian! What the hell do you want me to do for that?"

"So, now you are interested then?"

"No, I'm not. Sorry I didn't intend to mislead; just curious."

"Curiosity is extremely dangerous, Clara," he pronounced before adding more lightly, "All you have to do is come to a party with me, listen to the Russian being spoken around you, and then tell me what they were saying later that night. That's it. Done. A grand in your pocket."

"I can't see why you need me - you also speak Russian."

"I can't be everywhere at once and would appreciate a second opinion. One evening. I don't know anyone else who speaks Russian - and dances the waltz." He caught her eye and she flashed a brief smile. But she was getting up to go.

"I can't Christian. Luke has forbidden me to talk to you anymore. We can't get on - unless you want me to do something for you, as this evening - it won't last. Let's leave it okay? I just want to be with Luke."

"This is purely a business relationship." But she left him twiddling his wine glass, to find Luke was still not home.

The strange conversation with Christian buzzed around in her mind all weekend. She felt there was a different dimension to the world, usually hidden from view, as if by a veil. She was getting glimpses of it now and then; taunted, tempted, and enticed through a slow reveal. Greg was behind the veil, as was Harry. Who else .... Luke? She considered it. No, she concluded. He seemed to be inadvertently dipping her into the 'other world' but be mainly ignorant of it - unless she blundered too close, as in the warning he gave her the other week about Greg and the hiding of her languages. But that didn't stop him from telling Christian all about her and her language skills (Didn't he suspect Christian at all? Even she had detected Christian's 'double life' approach to things, and Luke had grown up with him,) No, she decided Luke was throwing her to them at every turn but was oblivious or deliberately turning a blind eye to it.

Sunday, before leaving to return for another week of fighting with her dissertation, Luke and Clara went to the Slug and Lettuce for a burger and chips on their way to the train station. Halfway through their meal Christian materialised.

"Not staying," he said quickly as they both scowled at him. "Just wanted to let you know, Luke, there is a friendly football kickaround on Wednesday if you fancy joining us?" Luke shook his head and said he wasn't free. Christian shrugged good-naturedly and turned to leave, but bumped into Clara's chair, knocking her backpack to the floor. Solicitously, he bent down to help her pick it up muttering into her ear as he did so, "The Emperor Hotel, Shaftesbury Avenue, Room 212 - will you remember that?"

"What?" By way of an answer, Clara saw him slip an envelope into her rucksack as he rehung it. Then he loped off with his hands in his pockets.

As the train gathered speed, heading South, she rummaged into her bag to retrieve the envelope pushed into the folds of her weekend luggage. There was a train ticket for 11 am Saturday from Shrub Hill Station to London Paddington and another envelope stuffed with £10 and £20 notes. On the outside of the envelope, it said, 'half now, half after, C'. She tucked the ticket into her purse, the money into her bag. Then she sat back, letting her mind go empty, breathing deeply. The dark reflected her in the window: She was a shadow of a passenger on a train, hurtling along with no substance, no past, no future. By the time she alighted at the station, she felt resolved and calm but focussed: She would do it, just this once, to see for herself. Then tell Luke all about it afterwards, so there would be no more secrets between them. That was the plan.

Paddington was busy as she tried to navigate the tube to get to Shaftesbury Avenue. Once there she used her A-Z to find the Emperor Hotel. Taking a deep breath, she strode confidently inside and made for the lift, knocking on the door of 212 before opening it. Christian was lying on the bed, arms behind his head watching football on the TV as she entered. He grinned at her and sat up.

"Well done kiddo," he said. "Have you eaten? Let's go grab some food." Without waiting for her to utter a sound, he marched her back out, along the corridor, and down the lift. He steered her through a maze of twists and turns until finally sweeping her ahead of him into a small independent cafe, pertaining to be French. There were hanging plastic onions, bikes suspended artfully around the walls, and bunches of dusty lavender on the tables. They ordered lasagne with garlic bread and a bottle of white wine.

"Very French," commented Clara with a sardonic twist of her lips. Once their first hunger pangs had subsided Christian asked what Clara wanted to know about the evening's plans. She considered while chewing her garlic bread.

"What is the context, so I can focus on meaning - Business? Social? Political?"

"Mixture of all three. I am there as my uncle's business associate to chat up some Russian businessmen to try and broker a deal for the importation of Vodka. The venue is like a civil servant's social club where all sorts of people go based around Whitehall; Government staff entertaining their clients, visitors, or business associates. Lots of webs and paths interconnecting and crossing each other."

So, what and who am I concentrating on?"

"Essentially, you concentrate on the businessmen with our party - you are my muse for the evening. You play your delightful shy act and cling to me while listening attentively to private Russian conversations, discussing amongst themselves the English conversations they are having with us."

"So, this is about 'checking' the robustness of a business deal?"

"Mainly, yes." He held her glance for a moment or two and she nodded.

"One more for now," she said, as they finished their meal and washed down the last of the wine, "What on earth do I wear?"

"Ah, glad you asked," he said, rising to go and pay the bill. Ushering her out, he steered her by the elbow towards the pavement, hailed a taxi and they sped off. "We are going to sort what you wear tonight, now." She thought for a moment they were heading for Selfridges as they stopped outside. But he took her along a lane behind the department store. They went into a tiny clothing shop, space enough only for a comfortable chair, and a changing room behind a display window. They were clearly expected and as Christian took a seat, a sparrow-like lady introduced herself as, Em, and took Clara behind the curtain. After looking her up and down with darting looks, her head on one side, Em came back with a dress.

Clara would wear a silky green dress, with a boat neck falling in soft folds of layers of dark and pale shades of green, pulled in at the waist, and then tumbling to the ground. It was simple, understated, but elegant. Em twisted Clara's hair with fluttering movements, stuck some pins in, and sprayed it. A few tendrils cascaded down each side displaying a tall sweep of the neck. Em tweeted her approval in a high-pitched song. She then added shoes, and a matching bag, gave her strict instructions on how to repair the hair if it came loose, and showed her how to put her stockings on to avoid laddering them. Feeling processed as a product, Clara reappeared from behind the curtain back in her clothes, clutching a large dress bag. But catching sight of herself in the mirror with her hair still pinned up, looking so elegant and 'someone else', she imagined for the first time the reality of the evening ahead and felt nervous. Christian noticed. After thanking Em and emerging from the shop, he pulled her close.

"Feeling nervous?" She nodded. Looking up at him she voiced her main fear.

"What if my Russian isn't good enough and I don't understand anything they are saying? It's not my strongest language, and unlike the others, I have never 'immersed' in it before …"

"Come on, we need a coffee."

Christian led her into a dimly lit street by the river, where a curtained door opened into a smoky, dark cave of a room, long and narrow. A hush in the general conversation greeted their entrance, but levels of chatter resumed as they made their way to a table. A large waiter squeezed himself between the tables carrying a tray of small cups and a tall silver coffee pot. He raised his eyebrows. Christian nodded and a thick black stream of liquid poured into the cups, the aroma so bitter and acrid the fumes alone made Clara cough. The waiter smirked as he went off to refill at another table. Christian smiled at her.

"Listen around you," he whispered to her and sat back in his chair with his coffee cup poised before him. She tuned in. It was a tiny space, crowded, with all men she noticed: And Russian was the language being spoken. At first, she panicked, hearing only it was Russian, a ribbon of static. She forced herself to breathe slowly, spin her mind into neutral, and relax. The language fell like rain into her mind. The sounds gradually took shape, words, then phrases, as the lives of the people around her sprang to life. A son was arguing with his father over his university aspirations. Two colleagues were complaining about their boss. Two other businessmen were discussing the purchase of a building. At the extent of her hearing, a huddled group of four caught her attention as the accents around the table were markedly different, she could swear one, or even two of them were English Russian speakers. Their conversation was disjointed, she caught words such as 'catch', 'hunt', and 'dispose'. It was also the body language, the visceral energy behind the words attracting her. She glanced over to Christian, but he was zoning out, patiently letting her listen. She decided his Russian was limited.

Back in the hotel room, they both watched TV, selecting an episode of The A-Team, followed by Bobby Davro on the Box. As the credits rolled up Christian said,

"Right then my lovely, time to get this show on the road. I am going to shower and then the bathroom is all yours, alright?" She was feeling nervous again.

"Oh god, you look gorgeous!" he exclaimed later as she materialised from the bathroom. She had been longer than necessary in there, fiddling about, too anxious to come out. She was bitterly regretting her decision to do this, realising she would be putting herself in the very position she hated - a social party. She had been concentrating on the listening part, but it occurred to her, she would have to converse and act as a legitimate member of the social party to overhear the chatter around her. She was a complete idiot, she told herself.

Christian was dashing in his dark suit, increasing her shyness. He closed the gap between them, sweeping her into his arms, and kissed her on the lips, first gently, then more passionately, softly flicking his tongue against her teeth. She pulled back sharply. He laughed at her.

"There, I thought that might take your mind off things, trying to keep me in order!" She unhooked herself from him to put on her coat and collected her bag. "Come on business partner, ready to go into role? Let's go." They left the hotel, taxiing across town to disembark at the bottom of the steps of a nondescript grey stone building. It was a blind building with no windows and an unimpressive front door - passing by you wouldn't notice it was there. They went up a few steps and Christian tapped a code into a number pad on the side of the door to make it swing open at his touch to reveal a surprising interior.

They were in a large palatial hallway. Clara handed her coat into the reception. Together they made their way past alcoves with small gatherings, dinner parties, and drinking groups, to a wide sweep of stairs curving down into a huge subterranean ballroom.

The whole environment was alien to Clara. It felt as if the world had become polished and soft, with wealth, glamour, deep plush carpets, dark reds, crystal, velvet, uniformed waiters, diamonds, fur, black suits, shiny shoes, perfume, and gold. She allowed the awe and wonder to reveal themselves on her face as she held Christian's hand and stuck close to his side.

To her surprise, she realised the other half of her brain was kicking into life, as if by an instinct she didn't know she had. She started scanning faces, taking in postures, body language, looks, and glances; she let the voices reach her and penetrate, discerning meaning, snatched greetings, and introductions as they ebbed and flowed around her: Her months of research into culture and language, of trying to mimic the posture and hunt out the meaning behind non-verbal expressions had become an automatic reflex.

They were about to reach the large ballroom, when she suddenly turned into Christian, reversing him out, pulling him back the way they had come against the flow of people to the foyer.

"I can't go in there Christian; we haven't thought this through. I know too many people. How do I explain being with you? I've changed my mind - I can't do this!"

CHAPTER 12

Chain Reaction: Diana Ross

"What? How can you know people? We haven't entered yet - who do you know?"

"Greg is here, he was ahead of us going down the stairs, didn't you see him? How can I be with you?!"

"Greg will be fine. Just stick to your story."

"Oh god," Clara moaned, "I have been stupid, I hadn't foreseen this." Christian tipped her chin to recapture her attention: He kissed her to ensure he had her back. The flare in her eyes reassured him.

"It's alright, it will be alright. Who else do you know in there?"

"I thought I saw Alec, Luke's boss, head of me - why would he be here?"

Chris ran his fingers through his hair and frowned at her words.

"He wouldn't be, don't be daft. You are letting your imagination run away with you." he scolded her. "It is crowded down there; you will find you are mistaken. But if you do meet people you know, you can explain you are helping Luke's cousin out with some translation for his business visitors. If we need to tell Luke about you doing this, we will, alright? It's not a problem. We can discuss it later at the end of the evening. We are not doing anything wrong - a little unscrupulous if you like, but not illegal." He studied her. "Shall we try that grand entrance again?"

They made their way across the ballroom, towards a group of people around a set of tables. A waiter furnished them with a glass of white bubbly stuff Clara thought was disgusting, reminding her of medicine her mother used to give her when she was 'under the weather'. She shook hands during the introductions. Christian was in full charm offensive. Clara found it interesting to see how he managed to have something to say to everyone

There were three English men, who smirked when Christian introduced her, giving her the once over as if she were a ripe fruit. She managed to smile shyly at them but was seething inside. There were also three Russian men, looking slightly older than their English counterparts, clearly enjoying their evening. They smiled and bowed a lot at Clara; although she had to listen to a long discussion between them as to whether she was a prostitute, and if they could buy her off Christian by the end of the evening. 'God help humanity if this was the level of debate within the wealthy elite,' thought Clara, disheartened by it all. She sat at the table, trying not to sip her drink, watching people mill around the room.

It was as the sea of people parted and she could see across the floor she noticed him for the first time. Their eyes met and locked. People surged back, closing the gap, hiding him from sight. She registered surprise at the jolt the look had caused. It was strange, as if she had been looking for someone her whole life and had found him. It was nothing more than that. A calm acceptance, as if her whole being had breathed a sigh of relief and her soul had said, 'Oh! There you are!'

She shook her head to clear the sensation: How can you see a stranger and feel as if you know him better than you know yourself? No, she thought, it was her emotions getting overwrought by the situation, and she was deluded, or the drink had been stronger than she thought, and she was drunk. Such a thing is not possible, all her psychology studying had told her that much. 'Keep a handle on some level of reality, for goodness' sake.' she berated herself.

A little later an orchestra struck up and Christian, making a big show of it, swept her towards the dance floor, and spun her around.

"Alright now?" he asked her as they twirled.

"Okay," she replied non-committedly. They were about to re-join the group when someone cut in on Christian with a quick triumphant glance at him, and she now spun away with the new partner. This was one of the Russians from the party called, Sergei. She chatted to him about where in Russia he came from, what he thought of London, and if he had a family. A slight change in music to another waltz, (seemed the standard tempo) and a change in partner. This time she found herself dancing with Harry, his soft American drawl in her ear.

"Well, aren't you a sight for sore eyes! Change of boyfriend - I liked the last one." His voice suggested he didn't think much of the new one.

"No, still with Luke. Christian is his cousin, and I am helping him with some Russian business visitors for an evening." Another twirl.

"Waste that story on someone else, honey." A change in direction, a twirl, and then he held her close.

"All I am doing is listening and reporting on what I hear," she replied.

"You can give me the report too then." A further twirl, and twist.

"All it will consist of is a debate on whether or not I'm a prostitute and whether Christian will sell me to them later on: Not sure it is what you are looking for," she commented bitterly. As they spun and then held each other close again he said,

"The night is young. I want the report too and will collect. And a heads up, he will sell you on by the end of the evening, you have my word. I know young Chris. In my opinion, he has cast you in the wrong role tonight. I am sure time will tell, and you are well able to look after yourself." A new partner cut Harry out and she saw him take up with another twirling skirt to disappear across the sea of dancers.

In his place was Greg. Clara groaned inwardly. They danced silently for a turn of the floor. He danced well for a heavy-set man, surprisingly light on his feet. He led with control, she had barely to think where to step he steered her so forcefully. She was expecting some admonishment for being with Christian, but his words surprised her in tone and content. "Clara, it's not right for you to be Chris' agent. Do it tonight, but don't work with him again in this role." Following another spin, he came in again. "Can you please tell me now which language besides Italian and presumably Russian, you are conversant in?" A spin.

"French, German, Spanish, Greek, Turkish, Urdu and Hindi - mainly." Twist and a tight grip around the waist. His hold on her made her feel safe and she considered she may have misjudged him up to now. His gruff exterior and blunt, humourless countenance made him hard to like, but she was beginning to appreciate and respect him.

"Thank you. Honest answer appreciated. From now on, be honest with no one, trust no one, and expect everyone to double-cross you, and you will be fine." With what she thought was a sad smile, he twirled himself off the dance floor, where Christian who had been hovering, now stepped in, yanking her off the floor roughly.

"What are you playing at?" he said crossly, giving her a little shake, "You are supposed to be smooching with my business friends, not spending all night making eyes at everyone and anyone!" She shook herself free and she headed back to their table, ignoring him. But he caught up with her and reached out to hold her by the wrist.

"Behave yourself, you are working for me tonight, remember? Come and get on with it."

But it wasn't long before she was back on the dance floor. Sergei had taken a shine to her, and no sooner had she sat down than he was asking if she would dance again with him. She glanced at Christian, and he nodded, waving his hand expansively as if giving his permission as a great favour. 'Git,' she muttered under her breath, but smiled at Sergei and they returned to dance yet another waltz. They danced in silence to get into a rhythm of their own and then he became quite chatty, telling her in broken English of his home in the Ukrainian countryside of sunflowers and wheat fields. But now and then he dropped in a Russian word.

At first, Clara thought it was because he didn't know the equivalent in English. But as the conversation went on, she realised he was also trying to communicate on a different level. He was not good at the waltz, they swayed haphazardly around the floor. She was quiet, trying to concentrate on the Russian words randomly dropped into English sentences. He repeated them over again, so she managed to pick up the pattern: "... - drop - changed - tailed - if - something - happens - information - is - under - red - lion-" She wasn't sure about 'lion' - could be 'dog' or 'monster'. She didn't know what to do. She dared not risk her cover, so smiled at him, thanking him for the dance, and they made their way back to the table.

To Clara's surprise the others all seemed to be getting up to leave. She looked at her watch to see it was eleven, but she had expected it to be a much longer night. However, she learnt they were relocating to a side room, and she followed along meekly. They went through to a large smoky room, divided at one end with a series of roulette tables and at the other end, clusters of armchairs. An archway led through to an even smokier, dark room where shadowy figures could be discerned, sitting and standing around a large oak table. It was through there they went, and Christian indicated she should go and join other women gathered around a cocktail cabinet, like brightly painted boats tethered in a harbour, waiting for the return of their sailors.

In the pretence of wanting a drink, Clara eased her way into their midst, receiving some smiles, and nods. Looking back, she noticed her party had joined the men at the table, and all were talking in low tones within the rifts of tobacco smoke. Christian seemed all puffed up and self-important.

Clara sipped a sweet drink she could not identify and tuned in to the women gathered around her, all frequent visitors and familiar with the evening. It was strange to be surrounded by boring conversations about the cost of a cup of tea at Selfridges compared to Harrods, and the fact the price of having a perm in Toni's had gone up in the last few months. She smiled inanely, totally unable to speak this language. Time ticked slowly by. Bored and restless she took a seat. The last dance with Sergei played on her mind and she wondered what to do about it. Suddenly one of the girls bent over to her.

"Chris wants you," she said, nodding towards the large table. Clara pulled herself out of her reverie and followed the 'nod'. He didn't get up as she went to him but swivelled around to enable him to put his arm around her waist, his hand lingering across her backside as he did so.

"Honey, Alexei, and Leonid would like to get a bite to eat and a change of scenery. I said I would ask if you would mind going along to make sure they have everything they need. Darling, do you mind?"

'My god!' she thought, 'He truly would share me around as if I am some object!' It was like a kick to her stomach: All the feelings from 'the cupboard' flooded back to take her breath away. A flare of anger came to her rescue. She remembered her resolution after the opera. She looked down at his upturned face, smiling at her with open, innocent-looking eyes while his arm encircled her waist: She saw him for who he was - a heartless, immoral almost sociopathic individual. At that moment she felt a sense of power over him instead: He was so transparent in who he was, but blind to who she was.

She couldn't however work out how to extract herself from the situation she was in, unsure who the other people in the room were, and how dangerous it would be to throw her drink in Christian's face this time.

"Not at all my love," she said brightly, bending over to kiss him on the cheek and at the same time pinching him as hard as she could, using her nails with all her strength on the flesh around his waist. To his credit, his eyes narrowed slightly, but he did not flinch.

With Alexei on one side and Leonid on the other, they retraced their steps towards the dance hall, but then veered off to a small alcove with a table and low lighting, open to the corridor through an archway. As soon as they stepped inside, a waiter appeared and they ordered food and drink in broken English, ignoring her - presumably, she was deemed too insignificant to feed.

Along the back of the room ran an upholstered long seat, which was clearly where she was to sit between them. The drinks appeared, and while they waited for the food, they seemed to think it was fine to fondle her absent-mindedly as they chatted over her head. Hands brushed along her arms, clutching at her breasts. Then each had a hand moving up and down each thigh, slowly tugging up the hem of her dress to allow access for their pudgy, probing fingers.

She felt rising panic. Not at their physical assault, but at their words. Their conversation terrified her. 'Ubiystvo'? Wasn't that the word for 'kill'?' and 'segodnya noch'yu' - 'tonight' or 'this evening'? Her mind tried feverishly to process the Russian she was hearing.

She pretended to be aroused as their hands fidgeted with her suspender belt. Then one of them unzipped the back of her dress to thrust a stubby fingered hand around her ribs to pinch her nipple, while the other pushed his hand between her legs, fingers clawing. But she was barely aware of their plundering. She felt numb, her brain full of sea mist. Luckily the food arrived, and they pulled away, releasing her so they could eat.

While they were eating, she succeeded in making them understand she needed to go to the toilet, and tried to slide out, going under the table if necessary. They weren't too sure about that and had a conversation on whether she should be allowed to wander off. They had paid handsomely for her time and hadn't finished with her. But she managed to make it clear she needed to go to the toilet, and could she leave her bag with them until she returned: Would they look after it for her? She wouldn't be long. Innocent eyes, simpering smile. This seemed to reassure them, and Alexei even stood up to let her out, although couldn't resist a final grope as she passed him. She giggled coquettishly and gave him a deep, alluring stare from under her fringe. He slapped her hard on the bottom as she left. 'Yuk! Gross,' she muttered under her breath.

As soon as she was free of the alcove she rushed to the dance floor, scanning it to see if she could find Greg or Harry - but they all seemed to have vanished. She tentatively ventured back towards the roulette tables and smoking dens but did not want to go in as far as the 'Big Table' as she didn't think Christian would be in a listening mood if he saw her short-changing his 'business cronies'. Yet she lingered a few moments more, as the content of her message should surely overcome his annoyance at her leaving her 'customers'. But listening to her intuition, she wandered away.

She asked a passer-by if they knew where the toilets were. May as well go while she thought about what to do next. Following their directions, she turned a corner and right into the 'mystery man'. They were both momentarily startled. After hesitating before him she made to move past, but he stopped her, blocking her path.

"You alright? What's the matter?" he asked her. His voice echoed in her head, jangling bells - she'd heard his voice before ... shaking herself she looked at him.

"I'm looking for someone - "

"Can I help?" She shook her head at him. Despite feelings to the contrary, she didn't know him. She couldn't tell him anything, even though he was waiting for an answer to his question.

"Do you know Greg Holcombe? I need to give him a message. I need to stop, um ... something ... urgently, tonight," she said instead. She was trying to link him to someone - where did he exist in the pattern of events? Who was he? If he knew Greg, then maybe he was alright to talk to.

"Your job is to listen and report, not act. It's alright: I'll take it from here. Go home - do you want money for a taxi?" His voice was reassuring, and she felt she believed him - and she desperately wanted to go home.

"Um, no, I'm okay, thanks." And he was gone, back in the direction he was coming when she bumped into him. 'What the hell was that conversation supposed to have been about?' she wondered, feeling more and more like Alice in Wonderland.

She found the toilets, went in, and spent some time in a cubicle trying to regain some sense of calm and clear thought. 'If I were swimming,' Clara decided, 'I would be seeking something to hold onto at this point because I am about to drown.' One minute she was listening to businessmen considering a vodka business deal and the next minute she was listening to calm discussions about plans to assassinate someone. Was this all real, or some elaborate joke Christian was playing on her? 'I am supposed to listen and report, not act,' she muttered under her breath - 'who are these people?'

Clara made a plan to return undetected by lecherous Russians to the reception area, collect her coat and leave. She would go to Paddington, where she could get the first train out of London and away from this madhouse. But that plan was followed by shame; how could she run away given what she had heard? She could go to the police and tell them? They could be trusted, couldn't they? They could get hold of Greg for her, and he would know what to do. She revised her plan; she would leave this place and find the nearest police station and make her report there.

Reassured, she emerged from the toilets and saw Sergei disappearing around the end of the corridor. Change of plan. She hurried after him. By the time she turned the corner, he was leaving the building. She dashed forward as fast as her shoes and dress could take her in time for her to join him on the pavement. As a taxi drew up, Sergei held the door open for her to slide in and together they sped off into the dark streets of London.

CHAPTER 13

News headlines: March 1986
The 'Today' newspapers is launched, a new broadsheet from Wapping.

Clara went with Sergei into a hotel room. He took off his jacket and tie, loosened his collar, and fixed himself a drink. He offered her one, but she shook her head.

"You are in danger," she blurted out in English. "You shouldn't be here, you should get out, leave this place." He glanced at her, downed his drink, and went to pour himself another. Then he came to her. He ran a finger around her face, across her lips, down her neck, and along the ridge of her collarbone to unzip her dress, so it fell to the floor. He stood back to survey her, taking another sip of his drink.

"And you come to give me comfort before I die," he said matter of factly. He took another swig of his drink. "I am mistaken," he said sadly, "You are a, how you say, 'hooker' - not Russe eh?" Putting down his drink he pulled her onto the bed.

"No," she tried to say, attempting to disentangle herself. But he clung on, now murmuring into her hair in soft Russian which she couldn't quite decipher - a poem? A nursery rhyme? Sergei was much more drunk than he had first seemed. After a half-hearted fondle of her breasts as he lay on top of her, he dozed. But as she was starting to ease herself out from under him, he jerked himself awake. Trying to focus, he gripped her shoulders, and shaking her with urgency, begged her in Russian to 'find his drop under the red lion'. Struggling for breath under his weight, she managed to reply.

"Lev? Lev - is that lion? You know - roar!" she tried to imitate a lion but sounded more like a sick cat. He stared at her for a moment, then his face split with a grin. He looked relieved to be understood and about to say something else when the door burst open with a startling explosion. There was a sound like the fart of a wet firework and Sergei's head sledgehammered into Clara's. A sting streaked across her cheek like a flame. For some confusing reason, she felt soaking wet, as if a bucket of warm water had been thrown over their heads. Footsteps retreated out and along the corridor, fading into silence.

She was pinned where she was under his inert body. She tried to wriggle out but Sergei, unresponsive on top of her, could not be shifted. The pain she felt to her face was worse when she moved, so she decided not to. The door flew open again. This time there was noise, voices - English she noted - lights were flashing, more clatter and Sergei was lifted off her.

As they lifted him, she was flooded with understanding - Sergei was dead. She was covered with his blood and brains, ejected through a gaping hole in the top of his head ... she promptly threw up. Hands came to her. Good guys, or not? Who knew?

Someone pulled her to standing and took her to the bathroom, a young girl, about the same age as Clara. She stripped Clara out of her underwear, pushed her gently into the shower, and turned on the water encouraging Clara to wash. Her hands felt as if they belonged to someone else, her fingers were all rubbery and uncooperative, but she attempted to shampoo and rinse her hair. When she stepped out of the shower the 'friendly unidentified girl' handed her a towel and presented her with a grey pair of tracksuit bottoms and a matching sweatshirt, which Clara obediently put on. Then her companion applied a plaster to her cheek and another to the side of her head, where a bullet had grazed her - ah! That explains the sting!

When she emerged from the bathroom, she found a new group of people had materialised: Now there was a gathering of men in suits, with notepads, who told Clara to sit and answer their questions. She told them what they wanted to know: She had returned to the room with Sergei to keep him company for the evening, then he was shot. No, she didn't see who burst through the door. No, she didn't know Sergei's other name. No, she hadn't met him before this evening. These questions seemed to be on a never-ending loop, and she kept answering them, hoping, they would stop. Then they did. There was a new wave of people in and out of the door, whispering, hushed conversations and then she was being taken out of the room, a firm hand on her upper arm. As if in a dream, she went where bidden.

The air outside was a smack in the face but before she had time to gulp a few lungsful, she was pushed into a car and driven away. Then she was being hustled into another building, long bleak corridors, and into a room - bare and cell-like, one Formica-topped table, and three hard wooden chairs, on one of which she was told to sit. New faces, same questions, over and over again. As she spoke others scribbled notes and a tape recorder whirred on the table. Then she was left alone for a long time. She sat and tried to concentrate on her breathing, let her mind go - it was a struggle as it wanted to revisit the horror and gore of the broken head and its spilled contents in lurid colour. Each time the image landed, she allowed it a second to settle and then batted it away. It returned, and she repeated the process. By the time she was joined by more people, she was exhausted and ready to put her head down on the table and sleep. This time she was introduced to a large rotund man. He had grey wires for hair sprouting densely at his eyebrows, ears, and nostrils but avoiding the head, which was polished and shiny. He introduced himself as Fergal and had a faint Scottish twang to his voice - he settled opposite and pushed a cup of tea across to her. She hugged it to herself and took a reviving sip.

"What time is it?" she asked him to try and get some bearings.

"Just gone seven in the morning," he told her. "Are you hungry?" She wasn't.

"Can I go home now?" she asked.

"When you have given me your report of the evening. I'm sorry," he added when he saw her face crumple, "You can do this: You're a tough cookie. Come on, let's have your report then I promise you, I will personally put you on a train back home. Deal? Take me through the evening from the beginning, and you can stop before we get to the end - we know that bit, alright?"

Taking a deep breath and another sip of tea she gave a full account of the event. Once or twice she was stopped to explain something, or to check a fact, but she kept going right up to the point where she met Sergei in the corridor after going to the toilet and he asked her to accompany her to his hotel room.

"And you know the rest," she finished. There was a long silence, and Fergal regarded her seriously. She held his gaze.

"Okay. Let's have it all again, one more time." She had no choice but to give the whole account again. At the end of the second telling, she rested her head on the table, then looked up at him.

"I swear, if you say you want it for the third time, I will cry and you won't be able to understand a word, so don't even think about it!" Again, he stared at her steadily, but he said finally.

"I am going to put you on a train so you can go home now as I promised. Come on."

Drained, she slumped in her seat as the train pulled out of Paddington staring into nothingness. She dozed off, lulled by the movement of the train. Someone walking along the aisle tripped and fell into her. She jolted awake. He hurried on but had left a folded note in her lap. She was tempted to screw it up and not even read it. It lay for some minutes untouched on her lap. Then with a sigh, she read it: 'Get off at the next stop'. Shit, she'd had enough. She wouldn't do any more bidding for others. So as the train slowed down, she made no move, until on the platform she caught a glimpse of a familiar face. So, changing her mind, she heaved her aching body out of her seat and clambered off.

He stayed a few yards ahead of her, leading her away from the station, down the street, into a hotel lobby, then into a lift. The doors closed, and they were alone, but in silence they watched the numbers rising to floor 6. Then she followed him to the room. Once inside, she sighed and turned to him.

"I am too tired to talk anymore."

"I know," he answered, guiding her to the bed. He pulled down the covers, levered her in, tucked her in, kissed her forehead and she fell into a deep sleep. When she woke, she lay for quite a while, awake but keeping her eyes closed. She didn't want reality to come back into her waking mind, she wanted to keep the last few hours away. Then she heard a faint rustle and snapped her eyes open, remembering that she wasn't alone. He was silhouetted against the window, his back to her, looking out into the darkening late afternoon city.

She slid out of bed and went to the bathroom. When she came out he turned from his vigil at the window and smiling at her, came across the room. He was in a suit but had taken off his tie, and his shirt was open at the neck, revealing a slightly hairy chest.

"Refreshed, Clara?" he asked her.

"Yes, thank you, much better," she answered as she realised how gorgeous this stranger was in daylight. Tall, slight of build, but with a strength suggesting real flexibility and wiry stamina.

"Good. I am afraid I have a couple of questions I need to ask you."

"But-" she started to say. He came even closer, placing his finger on her lips, hushing her. She nearly folded at his touch, her knees about to give way. With a hand placed lightly on her back he guided her gently over to a sofa. But she didn't sit. She remained standing so close to him she could feel the heat from his body against her arm. She wanted more than anything to hold on to him, and never let go. She felt as if she was in one of her nightmares and he was the stable rock in stormy seas to cling to. They both remained poised for a few seconds, both seemingly struggling with battles of their own, frozen in the pose.

Clara broke the silence and the tableau.

"Before you ask your questions, please may I know your name? You know mine I see." He smiled at this, and stepping back from her, he took a bow and said,

"Let me introduce myself, my name is Captain Ricardo De Burgh - but most people call me Rick." She inclined her head.

"Please to meet you - what are you Captain of? An army? Are you a military man?" Clara asked, finally taking a seat.

"Kind of. I have come up through the army, served for the United Nations, have worked for the Peace Keeping Force, but also the UN Security Force." He sat on the opposite end of the sofa, facing her.

"Don't you work for the secret service or anything?"

"Let's say our paths cross, but mainly I am with the UN."

"That's what I would like," she said wistfully.

"It would be a sensible goal," he stated simply. But before this line of conversation could go any further, he diverted it back to focus on Saturday evening. "I gather you have not done any work as an agent before last night?"

"What exactly is an agent, people keep saying that?"

"An agent is someone hired by an operator, someone working for the secret service, to gather information for them."

"Oh, I was an agent then but was told I was working for my boyfriend's cousin and his uncle's business, helping smooth a business deal."

"And did you believe him?"

"Christian? No, not really. I don't believe anything he says. It was just an opportunity to see, dip my toe in a world hinted at - others had suggested I could work in. I also love to use my languages. I suppose I was seduced by the thought of being able to listen to Russian if the truth is told - what an idiot!"

"You don't make a good agent," he said gently. He stood and poured two whiskies, handing one to her.

"Oh?" she answered mildly, "Why not?"

"Too much integrity to be 'used' and ordered around - and too much desire to solve problems and take responsibility for what you do - from evidence based on last evening anyway," he added. His words were like a balm to a wound, and she savoured them.

"I couldn't work at all for the Secret Service - too brutal in their games, too many twists and turns with no trust, loyalty, or the normal civilised 'law of society' to contain their activities, from what I witnessed. It may be all for the 'greater good' but it's not for me."

"May not be quite so easy to walk away, you know."

"I was thinking more of using the experience as a learning opportunity, but I will work for myself and not in the dark, for others, for reasons I don't understand," she said, hearing her own words with surprise.

Rick nodded and refilled their glasses. He then phoned down to order an omelette and chips. Once it had arrived and they had eaten, Rick sat back in his chair and considered Clara carefully.

"I have listened to the tapes of your interview last night with Greg," Rick spoke calmly but, in a tone, laced now with authority. He paused making sure he had her attention. "Greg is certain that although you did not once change your story, however many questions were fired at you, you have nonetheless adapted the truth for some reason. Others argued a young naive girl, thrown in the deep end, shocked by being nearly killed and seeing a murder close up, could not lie when questioned relentlessly for five hours. But some instinct has made you, nonetheless, leave something out of your record, hasn't it? I agree with Greg - something is missing, isn't it?" He held her stare for a moment, expression passive but his eyes seemed to reach right inside to her soul. She shivered, and broke the stare, wrapping her arms around herself. "Do you think you could now tell me the information you left out from the version you gave at the GCHQ last night? We do need to know if there is anything Sergei left us. He reached out to you at the end, what did he tell you?" Clara had to decide: 'trust no one' - but the information had to go somewhere, should it go to the person who paid for it, or not?

"I tried to tell you last night Sergei was in danger, but no one stepped in to help him."

"If you think again, you will remember you didn't tell me anything so concrete."

"Okay. I will rephrase it if you are going to split 'semantic hairs'. I communicated to you last night there was danger, and you told me to go home, and would look after it - but you didn't."

"And you didn't go home. Did you go to warn him yourself?"

"Yes, but he already knew. I think he knew he was about to die."

"He was willing to take you with him though, wasn't he?"

"No. He thought he had the night left to himself. He was in the middle of telling me something when they burst in. He was speaking heavily accented Russian and I was being squashed beneath him; hard to understand. Then he was dead."

"Who are you willing to give the message to, if it isn't me?" he asked quietly.

"I haven't ruled you out. I'm buying time while I am thinking."

"Can I help you decide in any way?"

"Well, it's like this: 'Trust no one' says Greg. But someone has to collect the information. Last night lots of people wanted it. Christian paid me for it. Now you want it. Now all of you might be leading to the same place, or all different - who knows? I could give it to all. Or just you?"

"How about we go and see Greg? And you tell him?" The thought of having to go back to London at this stage made her shudder. She looked again at Rick staring at her calmly with his large grey eyes.

"But you have come to get the message on his behalf," she stated as realisation dawned on her. It wasn't a question, she now understood.

"I volunteered to do so," he answered. She thought about it for a moment longer. Then she told him.

"The drop is under the red lion. Not 100% sure of the 'lion', but pretty sure."

"Thank you." He crossed swiftly to the telephone, dialled, then repeated the message she had given to whoever was on the other end. She realised he must have been desperately trying to be patient as she had hummed and 'ha-ed'. Once the call was made, his shoulders relaxed, and she could tell by looking at him he had achieved what he set out to do. His mind had now turned to other matters. She stood up.

"I have to go now," she said.

"Yes, so have I. Look, there's a car at the front of the hotel. Sam is the driver, he will take you home, just give him the address - alright?"

At the door, she turned.

"Rick? In your 'line of work', how do you, um, reconcile two extremely different worlds of work and home?" The question had been buzzing around her subconscious for some time now and as she thought of the car waiting to take her home, the question came almost unbidden to her lips. How on earth would she reconcile what she had done this weekend, with her life at home? He considered her question and gave it serious thought, crossing to her, standing close.

"It is not easy. The bridge between the two is narrow and can easily snap if you take burdens from one to the other. You need to be able to resolve the emotional impact while at work so when you cross the bridge to the other side, you leave everything behind. Unless you have worked in this environment you do not understand the pressures, and it is unfair to ask those you love at home to do so. You need to find a 'space of safety' within the world of work to 'cure yourself/mend'. Does this make any sense?" His eyes seemed to penetrate to her very core. Before she knew what she was doing, she reached up and stroked the side of his face.

"Yes. It does. Thank you." She went out, closing the door as he stared at the space where she had stood, deep in thought.

CHAPTER 14

Radioactive Russian dust cloud escapes from Chernobyl.

Waking up in her narrow bed at university on Monday morning Clara was besieged with memories leaving her breathless. She let herself out of the ground floor flat with her yoga mat, into the still dark of pre-dawn. She found a space, beneath one of her favourite chestnut trees, her back to the university looking out over the games fields becoming visible as the grey March dawn broke. She unrolled her mat and settled cross-legged, head over heart, heart over pelvis, pulling herself up tall, imagining she was a tree growing up to the top branches of the one at her back. She rested her hands on her knees, palms upward facing the wide skies.

She visualised the energy flowing up through the ground into her with every intake of breath through the nose. She exhaled, back into the earth below, every memory of the weekend - the fear, the sense of violation, of being a worthless pawn, a 'belonging' of someone's to 'own.' She let the hurt, pain, anger, and sadness envelope her, wash over her and drain into the soil. She relived the shock of meeting people who planned to kill; of meeting for the first time, death itself in such a violent way. She tried to allow these feelings to flow away from her, to shake herself free of their touch.

She did understand Rick's 'bridge'. But what at some point you must accept, she decided, was whichever side of that bridge you are on, the common denominator is 'self'. Although the 'rules' may be different on each side, the bridge itself was significant, and it had to span the gap. In full daylight, she made her way back to the flat for some breakfast and was munching her way through a bowl of Cornflakes when Reeta and Judy joined her.

Clara thought she would struggle to settle back into her dissertation work, but she was wrong. It became compulsive, to focus entirely on the work so all other thoughts were crowded out of her brain. It provided her with a satisfying sense of control and helped to restore her sense of purpose. She came at it with fresh eyes and ended up rewriting the structure and starting all over again, re-organising her research. Later she wandered over in search of Tony. He was where she hoped he would be, crowned in his usual halo of smoke. She made herself at home and he swung his chair round to face her, pushing the door shut with his foot in one practised movement.

"I know the theory of Communism, but can you tell me how this relates to cultural expression? For example, what is it like to be living in the Soviet Bloc? Would living conditions be problematic - harsh even? Because the true interpretation of Communism would suggest everyone is cared for; so, is it different in practice?" she asked, looking for all the world as if she had asked him to recite his favourite nursery rhyme. It was her attempt to understand some more about Sergei, what his life in Russia would have been like, and which was the 'good' side - if there was one at all.

"For the love of god, Clara! You are going to have to start giving me a warning of the questions you want answers for!" Tony exclaimed, searching for his matches to re-light his pipe. But she had faith in one of her favourite lecturers and knew after a few puffs she would be able to draw the answers out of him. She settled down for a long discussion.

Finally, as it grew dark outside, she uncurled herself to go, summing up the tutorial.

"So, political systems are all well and good - Communism or Capitalism - however, it's all about the people administering the political systems and controlling them - their sense of power. Power corrupts, either obviously in demi-gods and dictators or subtly but no less corrosively, through unfair trade deals and 'aid with strings'?" Tony nodded.

"Good summary of the last two hours. Definitely the problem, isn't it? We are all essentially a lot of self-centred people running around pretending to be altruistic. A rather sobering conclusion for an afternoon's work - see if you could come up with a more cheerful question next time, can you?"

It was as the darkness fell on the day and the world shrank down to her small bedroom, when what she came to think of, as the 'ghost of Sergei' came back to visit her. He hovered at the edge of her consciousness, haunting her thoughts and lurking in dark corners and under her bed. When she slept, he took centre stage, looming large and clear in lurid multi colour as he died over, over and over. She would wake up, drenched in sweat, feeling the weight of him on top of her and seeing again his destroyed head. He had told her he had two children, a boy of seven and a girl of nine - about the same ages as Bryn's children, Jenny, and Ewan. Where were his children now? What had they been told of their father? What had he died for? The questions circled, like bands of elastic drawing tighter and tighter around her chest, until she felt she couldn't breathe. She would lie, heart pulsing, lacking the will to calm herself, watching for the dawn to bring fingers of light, to chase Sergei back into the shadows.

Saanvi also lay awake with her heart hammering against her ribs. As she tossed and turned to try to settle, the blood pounded so loudly in her ears she sat up, hugging her knees miserably. She stared around the dark bedroom wishing Aarif, her husband would come back to bed. Above the sound of her heart, she could hear the rumble of men's voices coming from downstairs in the restaurant; what was going on?

It had all started earlier that afternoon when Jorwain had erupted in through the back kitchen door, striking his chest and wailing in anger.

"The Indian climbers are at the top and claimed Siachen! They have beaten our team and raised the Indian flag on our glacier! How can they? This is a terrible day - they have been helped - we have been betrayed! The British declared to be neutral, to oversee fair play, but you cannot trust a colonising power! Our course is now clear, and we must make plans!" He had ordered the women out of the way, roughly hauling grandmother to her feet and shoving her into Saanvi arms.

"Take her with you! Out! All of you, get out!"

Later Aarif looked pale and drawn but would only shake his head when Saanvi tried to discover what was going on.

"We must do what Jorwain says, it is what Allah wants. It is our land; we must fight to get it back."

"Are you having to go to Kashmir? To fight?" gasped Saanvi, horrified. But Aarif shook his head and would say no more.

Then in the early hours of the morning, the bedroom door had crashed open and Neref, the head chef had called Aarif to come. Jorwain wanted everyone down to the kitchen, they were to help. Saanvi sat up and reached for something to cover her shoulders.

"Not you. Stay here," muttered Aarif as he pulled on trousers and a sweater over his pyjamas. Shuffling his feet rapidly into some trainers he followed Neref. Knots wriggled in Saanvi's stomach as she listened to the muffled shouts, bangs, and crashes downstairs.

The sounds of Russian struck Clara like a thump in the back as she stood in the queue of a small cafe on Birmingham university campus. Sergei's ghost ambushed her, blurring her vision, and she was so disconcerted she dropped her coins and had to scrabble under the counter to retrieve them. 'Who is speaking Russian in this cafe?' she wondered, turning to scan the room as the waitress counted the change for her sandwich and a hot drink. In the far corner, she spotted Alec and Simeon. Their heads together, chatting earnestly. They were speaking Russian with a heavy accent, urgent sentences reached her ear, so fast and fluent she found it hard to make sense of it. She wove her way over.

"Can I sit with you to eat?"

They both made room for her while Simeon explained to Alec how the two of them had done a language exchange over the summer and how Clara had picked up some Russian. But Clara played down her ability, wary Luke would not be pleased if she was talking about her 'crazy language obsession' to his boss.

"So, you are a Russian speaker as well?" she asked Alec, "I heard you speaking Russian when I came into the cafe," she added in response to their blank looks. Alec shrugged,

"A few odd words," he said. Clara was puzzled by this but was distracted as Simeon started talking.

"I was keen to hear how the research was going from the summer," Simeon said eagerly. "I am doing a master's in politics and business this term, so I have lost track of the summer work."

Clara was impressed. He was more interested than she was; she rarely asked Luke how the research was going and wondered whether she should take a keener interest. However, implying to Alec she had indeed stayed up to date with the research advances, she listened with interest as Alec updated Simeon as she ate.

As she finished eating and made a move to go and return to Luke, Simeon also rose and offered to walk her across the campus. Charmed to be asked, she accepted, and they left together, leaving Alec ordering himself another coffee. They walked slowly, chatting. Simeon told Clara all about his master's research, which was a thinly disguised critique of communism.

"Doesn't that somewhat limit your chances when you return to your own country?" asked Clara, unsure how such a non-self-critical political system within the Soviet bloc, would view such a study.

"I believe there are changes coming from within the communist bloc signalling a shift on the horizon. If I am lucky, I will be there to greet a new kind of politics and possible business opportunities, and then my studies will prove useful."

"But I thought we were kind of at war with you - the 'Cold War' and the fact we have nuclear weapons trained on each other - how come you are allowed to study here? Do you feel safe?" But he laughed at her questions.

"I believe I am watched closely to make sure I am not causing trouble - but the ability to pay foreign fees to universities makes me desirable - even if, as you point out, we are kind of at war with each other."

"Fascinating!" replied Clara, and he laughed again, wishing her a good night as she left him to go into the bar to find Luke.

In the bar, Clara refreshed Luke's pint while he finished his diatribe on colonialism and neo-colonialism to his usual fan club, and then left him to it, taking her usual seat propped at the bar.

"Can I refill that for you, Clara?"

"Um, okay, yes please Christian."

"Why do you always insist on calling me Christian when everyone else calls me Chris?" he asked as his order was being taken.

"I like the irony."

"Bitch," he replied conversationally, "Here you are, one pint - are you going to drink it, or pour it over my head?"

"Oh, don't tempt me!" But she took the pint and sipped at it.

"I suppose you are looking to collect the rest of your payment?" He asked neutrally, also taking a sip of his pint.

"Well, no actually. I rather thought you would be looking to collect the first half back. I didn't after all fulfil your requirements, did I?"

"No, and yes. It's complicated and well, to be honest with you, Clara, it may have been a rather ill-advised idea in the first place - or so I have been led to believe." He took a long draft of beer. He seemed rather subdued, not his usual chipper self. She didn't know quite what to say, as she imagined he had not come away covered in glory that evening. However, if he was attempting an apology, she wasn't going to help out. Any further conversation on the subject however was then closed because, earlier than usual, Luke had dismissed his eager learners and joined them. He wasn't sure having Clara and Chris as friends was any better than having them at each other's throats.

CHAPTER 15

News headlines: May 1986
"Radiation high over Europe after Chernobyl disaster."

Clara and Luke clambered out of a taxi outside Swallow's Swoop on a sunny day in late May. She felt confident, in a thin blue and white summer dress floating around her legs, making her feel as if she could be blown away on a light breeze. Her spirits were also as light as her skirt at the thought that she had finished her dissertation. Luke had read it, and said it should get a First, praise indeed. She was looking forward to an afternoon of intelligent debate interspersed with hugs from her two favourite children.

As they approached the house hand in hand, two burrs of black wild hair hurtled towards them, pulling them both into the party. Bryn was pontificating on something to a group, waving a spatula in the air to stress his point, by a BBQ. Lin came up and kissed them, handing them glasses of celery sticks in wine glasses of Pimm's. Then she bustled away again. Luke and Clara sauntered around the lovely garden, struggling to drink from their glasses without getting a celery stick in their eyes or up their noses. They giggled conspiratorially and when they thought no one was looking, tossed the celery into a bush. They then went over to Bryn, Clara giving him a big hug.

"You look delightfully summery this afternoon Clara," he commented, "the sun seems to be shining for you again," he observed, "Glad to see."

"No one could be miserable on a day like this, in this garden!" she exclaimed. They both laughed. Others wandered over, allured by the smell of gently roasting sausages and burgers. A group formed, tossing conversational gambits back and forth lazily, as the buzz of bumble bees and high-pitched screech of early swifts accompanied them.

Linda also joined them, refreshing their drinks from a large pitcher, which she then proceeded to hug to her ample chest, while they talked. The conversation turned to world affairs and the issue of Ethiopia and the worsening famine. Clara became more immersed in the conversation, eventually holding court, on a passion close to her heart. She eloquently expanded for her audience on the hidden causes of power in providing the conditions for environmental disaster; the hollow echoes of help from organisations as corrupt and as nepotistic as some of the African governments directly responsible for the plight of their poor.

"The UN is doing their best," said someone innocently enough. But Clara was on a roll, even though Luke tried to shush her, and change the subject.

"The UN! Don't get me started! They are as nepotistic as all the others," she exclaimed. People around her expressed disagreement with this and a livelier discourse took place, but Lin suddenly rose above the din of their voices.

"My! Isn't that Rick over there?" She turned to Bryn, "I didn't know you had invited him. We haven't seen him for a few years! How lovely! Yoo hoo!"

"I didn't," replied Bryn, looking in the direction she was waving.

"Rick works in the UN," Lin told the group, "Let's see what he has to say about it." She called out to him. Everyone glanced around briefly, but since no one knew who he was, the debate continued. Clara struggled to hold on to her argument quite as well as before. As he joined them, she finished up out of politeness more than anything else and stepped aside to make room for him.

"Rick!" Linda cried, "How lovely to see you! Everyone, this is Captain Ricardo De Burgh, high up in the United Nations, based usually in Lucerne I believe?" She introduced the tall distinguished young man to the group.

Luke was thoroughly fed up with Clara ranting and raging on her favourite topic. He felt she was embarrassing him at the dominant pursuit of her convictions, at what was essentially a social gathering, not a political rally. He saw his chance to shut her down.

"Pleased to meet you, Sir," Luke said to the newcomer, "Perhaps as an undisputed expert, (he stressed the word 'expert', glancing at Clara meaningfully) on the United Nations, you would care to discuss the issue of nepotism and sexism with this young lady, so the rest of us can return to discussing less contentious issues?" Bryn made an involuntary move as if to discourage the idea, but Rick had inclined his head towards Luke, turned to Clara, and replied.

"Certainly, my pleasure. Shall we talk and walk this way?" Taking her by the elbow he steered her out of the group and down a path leading to the large ornamental pond at the bottom of the garden.

"I only caught the last of what you were saying I'm afraid," he said, "Would you mind taking it from the top, and then we can see where that leads us as far as a decent debate of the issues are concerned?"

"Not on your life: Me, argue against the expert - have a heart!" she smiled at him, and he smiled back, and they reconnected as if walking through an invisible doorway from the garden party to the workplace. "I was just showing off," she admitted. "I have finally completed my dissertation, feels good."

"You look pretty," he commented, melting her to the core. She was disconcerted and could only mumble a shy, "Thanks."

"How have you been coping since I last saw you? You are allowed not to be able to cope, you know? Most people would be deeply affected by what you went through," Rick asked her.

"Would you be?" she asked; she couldn't imagine him afraid of the ghosts in the dark, but he turned to look at her directly, and she saw the ghosts in his eyes looking back. She answered her own question, "Oh, I see you would." He continued to look at her intently for a few moments, then said.

"I see you are struggling at the moment but getting there." Then added quietly, as if to himself, "How do I know this?"

"Rick? Have we ever met before?"

"Not that I am aware; perhaps in a previous life maybe?" Then in a brisk tone he told her, "It will get easier, the clarity fades and the memories stop recurring, but be patient, don't rush it, don't bury them, let them breathe and then they die in their own time. Allow them to make you stronger and wiser, not cowed and a slave to them." She nodded. There was silence as they navigated the narrow path between Linda's rose beds, then as they reached the bridge over the pond, they stopped. Clara asked tentatively,

"I have lots of questions buzzing around my head: Am I allowed to ask any of them?" Rick stared down into the depths of the pond and Clara wasn't sure he had heard her, but then he said.

"I won't be able to answer them, I am not part of that operation. I just muscled in, to help and see who you were after I spotted you across the dance floor. And, you do have to appreciate in this business, often it is safer not to know things than to do so ..."

"Mmm. I would prefer to work in a business where I own the facts and can make decisions accordingly," she mused, "It is like having to work with my hands tied behind my back when I would be more effective with both hands at my disposal." Again silence, a comfortable one, as they stood in the warm air and felt the breeze against their skin, living in the moment. "There is one general question I would like to ask you though, and you can answer, or not, as you like," she said hesitantly, glancing up at his profile for a moment. "In my limited experience I seem to have been assigned a certain role, just, I presume because I am a woman, the 'sex card' to collect information. Is there any room, anywhere I can work, where I will be considered for my thoughts, ideas and well 'brain' rather than always being asked to employ my rather limited skills with my body?" He glanced at her with raised eyebrows and a slight twist to his lips in a half smile. "You know what I mean!" she added hastily, blushing.

He chuckled. It was a lovely sound, a deep rich chortle softening his features, making him look much younger.

"You want to play a man's role, in a man's world, where women, as you have correctly pointed out, are seen as nothing more than intelligent prostitutes at the best? No, is the short answer to your question, not in the line of work you have been involved in - but," he added quickly as he sensed the reaction of his words on her, "Don't let that stop you. There are others like you, quietly working their way up within male-dominated institutions to start the turning of the tide - you don't seem one to be put off because there is no path already created for you. What will your first steps be along your journey? What are you planning to do next after your degree?"

"Master's, maybe ..."

"But?"

"Not sure what other options are out there, it's hard to find out. I was going to ask Greg. Is that a good idea? Or, I did pick up a leaflet on VSO ..."

"Talk to Greg, that's the best thing to do, alright?" She was about to thank him when something in the way he said 'alright' caught her attention. He noticed.

"What?" he asked.

She looked at him closely.

"It's nothing, for a moment then, you sounded Danish." She watched out of the corner of her eye for his reaction, not expecting one but was surprised. He tensed, a slight quiver as of a taught bow string she felt rather than saw. He flashed her a look of shock, suspicion, worry, and anger all rolled into one: The wave of them crashed over her, leaving her gasping.

"It's okay," she tried to soothe, "A Danish friend of my parents told me how to spot a Danish accent. Danes, he told me, are private people and don't expect to be spotted as few people bother to learn their language. I don't know much Danish, just a few phrases." She knew she was waffling, but she was giving him time to recover. "I'm sorry." There was a long silence, she could feel Rick thinking of how to respond. She waited.

"I am proud to be Danish but prefer it is not known."

"Of course."

They stood looking out over the pond, shoulder to shoulder. Clara sensed steel, a cold steel as their shoulders touched - she realised in an instant she wanted to be recognised as an equal beside him, to work with him as a colleague - this was who she was going to save lives with. She needed some of that cold steel to keep her ghosts at bay. All this she realised in seconds, it soaked through from him to her as water through a sponge, faster than rational thought.

Jenny came running and shouting Clara's name across the lawn towards the pond, and the rest of the world came flooding back into their existence. She could see Bryn up at the top of the lawn looking across at them as if he had sent Jenny down. Sure enough, bending over and panting dramatically for a few seconds as she caught up to them, she said,

"Daddy says if you don't come soon all the BBQ will be eaten." She grabbed Clara by the hand and dragged her off the bridge, along the path, and back up to the rest of the party at the top of the garden.

Rick remained, staring at the fish in the pond, on the bridge. He later meandered his way from the pond up towards the BBQ, and eventually came beside Bryn. Bryn had been watching him approach.

"Rick. Good to see you. What brings you to these parts?"

"You know, just passing by, thought I would drop in, say hi. Didn't know you were having a bash - sorry to gate crash." Bryn didn't believe a word.

"No problem, the more the merrier."

"What is the story with Clara, who is she to you?"

"Out of bounds to you Rick, leave her be. She's not one for your lot and can do without your shenanigans messing up her life."

"I beg to differ. She's no wilting violet, despite her apparent shy innocence. No, I am very interested." They were chatting conversationally but tension underlaid outward appearances.

"Leave her be, I tell you. You have her wrong - she's smart but essentially a home bird, family centred, focussed on a research-based career."

"I am not so sure about that. What does she mean to you? Why are you protecting her?"

"I know her, you don't. She is my tutee, I feel responsible for her, and am telling you, she is not for you."

"Well, she has a mind of her own. Let's see, shall we?" And he looked as if he was going to walk away, but he hesitated and turned back towards Bryn. "With your professional psychologist hat on: Is there such a thing as telepathy?"

"Definitely not. Hokam," said Bryn brusquely, "Why?" Rick shrugged.

"Just wondered." Then he sauntered away. That was the last anyone saw of him at the party.

Bryn paced around his small office, agitated, and worried. He was keeping an eye on the stairs trying to intercept Clara who was upstairs reading to Jenny and Ewan and tucking them into bed. As he saw her coming downstairs, he appeared from the door across the hall and he called out to her.

"Clara, do you have a minute?" As soon as the door was closed, he turned to her. "What did Rick want?" he asked bluntly. She raised her eyebrows at him.

"What do you mean? Luke made him take me away as 'I was making an idiot of myself', - Luke's words. He had no choice but to talk to me, did he?" Her answer was sharp, and she flushed as she spoke, looking uncomfortable by the question.

'Rick is up to his old tricks, weaving his charm for his own ends,' Bryn thought to himself, glad he had decided to have this conversation.

"Sit down a minute, will you? I have known Rick for years. Our paths have crossed in our lines of work occasionally, and he makes a good house guest, but he is a dangerous man, Clara. Do not get tied up with him, will you?"

"Why do you think he is dangerous?" she asked, looking genuinely curious.

"Some people can come across as charming but inside they have no emotion. It makes them dangerous; they blur the distinctions between 'right and 'wrong': Very dangerous."

"Are you saying he is a sociopath?" she asked surprised. Then added, "No, you're wrong, he has feelings, just under lock and key." As soon as the words had escaped her mouth, she clamped her hand over her mouth looking as if she wished she could scoup them back.

"What the hell went on between the two of you this afternoon!" Bryn was angry and scared. He had seen them on the bridge and the picture had filled his heart with ice. There was something about the way they were standing shoulder to shoulder - he had wanted to run over and drag Clara away. What was he more afraid of, that Clara, whom he regarded as a surrogate daughter of his, had anything in common with that monster of a man; or that she had been snatched away, right from under his nose and protection, to be pulled into a world he did not want her to know about? "I mean it more than anything else I have ever said to you. You have to listen to this one. Please stay away from him." He felt distraught in his helplessness as she regarded him calmly, unconcerned. He was at a loss on how to explain to her the dangers this man posed to her.

Clara touched him lightly on his arm and gave him a reassuring smile, "It'll be alright Bryn, when will I ever come across him again? Don't look so worried." And with another smile at him over her shoulder, she went to join the rest of the party on the veranda.

CHAPTER 16

News headlines: August 1986
*Manchester United and West Ham United football fans
clash on ferry bound for friendly match in Amsterdam.*

Clara persuaded herself life was wonderful as she and Luke walked arm in arm one Sunday afternoon under the weeping willow fronds, in the park. She was back in Birmingham with him for the summer, working as a researcher once more. She was also visiting her foreign restaurants, and working on perfecting her languages, as she was continuing with the language and cultural studies for her master's. She pushed aside, as they did the weeping willow branches, the undercurrents of friction between her and Luke; like a chain coming off a bicycle, somehow things didn't work as they had before. She felt restless and caged, Luke was tense and withdrawn, but there was nothing tangibly wrong. Clara didn't know what to do about it. Luke pulled her down with him to the grass under one of the huge trees. They lay in a world of their own, a curtain of yellow-leaved branches drawn right around them.

"Fancy a weekend away?" she asked him as she nestled into him, "I could take you to visit my parents? Good long walks, local pub, and... well, not much else!" she laughed. He tightened his arm around her briefly.

"Goodness, I am to be introduced to 'the parents'? I am honoured." he commented lightly. "Shouldn't you learn to stop screaming at night before we go and stay? I don't feel we can go anywhere until you can stop," he added in the same light tone. She sat up to look at him.

"What? What screaming?" He wasn't looking at her but was staring up into their leafy bower.

"Most nights you have nightmares, you thrash about, scream and shout. I try to wake you, but it is hard to snap you out. Last night I had to shake you quite hard to make you stop and I felt bad about that. You did settle eventually though. Don't you remember?" He glanced across at her and her blank face answered him.

"I shout? What do I shout?" Again, Luke addressed the tree.

"Oh, lots of stuff. Doesn't make much sense, especially when most of it is in what sounds like Russian ... but generally, you seem to think you are being shot at, or about to be killed, or someone else is because you are trying to save them but can't. Then lions are chasing you and ghosts are trying to drown you, that is the general gist from the pieces I can gather from your nightly rants."

"Why didn't you tell me?" Clara was amazed by both the nightmares she didn't know she had and the fact he hadn't mentioned it before.

"I suppose," said Luke slowly. "I was hoping they would just stop and go away. Then I wouldn't have to ask you about them. People don't have recurring nightmares for no reason, do they?"

"Of course, they do. They can be caused by lots of things. What are you imagining - I am afraid of lions? It can be caused by eating too much near bedtime, or, my birth control drugs may be affecting my sleep, I don't know, perhaps I should see a doctor ... I can't sort it if I don't know about it. I have always talked in my sleep and had nightmares, so it must just be something triggering them - sorry, annoying for you." He seemed to be considering this and didn't reply for a while, but then sighed deeply and pulled her to him.

"As long as I am not the lion, and you are not afraid of me!" He joked in a different tone of voice altogether, switching the mood. "Go see the doctor about it this week, and then we will take it from there." Suddenly the enclosed space of yellow fronds seemed claustrophobic, full of ghosts and fears; Clara felt the walls she had set up between one world and another start to crumble.

The following week Clara came home from a visit to the Blue Tiger to find Charlie and Greg installed in the flat, a drink balanced on their knees, chatting with Luke. They were on their way to Scotland for a week's holiday and were stopping by overnight. Luke had booked a restaurant, one of their favourites, overlooking a large park, and so they planned to walk as it was such a balmy summer's evening. As they set off, Luke and Charlie set the pace, soon disappearing as they talked and walked, heads close together marching on ahead. Clara walked in companionable but cautious silence beside Greg. As they passed a bench overlooking the boating lake, Greg indicated they should sit. He then turned to her.

"Are you alright? I am a busy person you know, and can't traipse all over the country checking up on daft idiots who get themselves tangled up in events they have no business being tied up in. You understand? You have to look after yourself." Clara smiled. Despite the brusque tone and his words, he had just crossed the country to check up on her well-being - whether on her behalf or Luke's, who could tell.

"Thanks, Greg. I appreciate the visit. I feel okay, but Luke tells me I scream in my sleep and speak Russian. I have been to the doctors to get sleeping tablets to try and stop this from happening. I didn't even realise. What can I do about it? I am worried if I talk in my sleep - what I say ..."

"I figured it was something like that. Charlie said Luke seemed tense and worried, he wouldn't say directly, but those two are close and have radars to detect things others don't due to their upbringing. It is a danger; he may talk to others ..."

"Greg. Explain from the beginning, please. What do you mean by 'special radars'? Do I know my boyfriend at all?"

"Does he ever speak of his parents, upbringing, and home?"

"No, it never comes up in conversation. Christian has asked me this question before. In fact, Christian has told me more about Luke's parents and background than Luke."

"Christian Marsdon?"

"Yes, that's the one."

"Keep him close. You need him on your side. Play along, okay?"

"Oh! Bloody hell!" Greg frowned at her.

"Come on, it could be worse. He is quite dashing and has a good taste in fast cars and expensive wines. Don't underestimate him. He is intelligent, smart, and well connected. No, keep him close, Clara, you need him."

"Like the mess he involved me in, in London a while back you mean?" she asked bitterly.

"It was foolhardy of him. Which is why he needs you as much as you need him. You need to keep him in check, he can be short-sighted and get himself in too deep - He is always trying to impress his uncle." Clara did not want to talk about Christian and the assumption underlying Greg's words she would 'work' with Christian again in the future scared her.

"Let's get back to Charlie and Luke's parents. How are they impacting things?"

"Their father worked in Intelligence for the British Government. He was one of the best, which means he was operational more than usual. He worked throughout the 1960s and 1970s. He has been part of a history unreported and has seen things to make him scream in his sleep forever. He was away from home, an absent parent. When he was home, he would have suffered from post-stress disorder, and was a thoroughly horrible individual. At least three times I am aware of his poor wife had to prepare for his death only for him to limp home after all hope of this happening had been lost. The kids grew up amid this. Charlie never talks directly of it, but throwaway comments and some behaviours display their trauma of growing up under such conditions. They both crave 'normality' and 'routine' and both block out any reference to the concept of 'spying' and 'national security'. Deep down I think they resent other people gaining security and being saved at their expense.

"I thought Mr Marsdon senior worked in international drink purchasing," said Clara confused, remembering the vodka deal Christian had supposed to have been undertaking at the behest of his uncle, Luke's father.

"He does now, yes. His brother, Chris' father, died, and he took over the company."

"But how do you two manage to be a couple under such circumstances?" Clara asked. She was aware Greg was highlighting problems with the relationship between Luke and herself, she genuinely wanted to know how to overcome, although realised at the same time, it was rather a personal question. She held her breath, waiting for the brush-off she expected. But he accepted her question with good grace.

"We agreed I would promise not to work away from home; in 'the foreign field'. She wants me close by, and to be honest, I want to be always close to her. I work mainly for the Foreign Office and in Intelligence, to share experience and knowledge. But I don't work on the front line often, certainly not abroad. I work from a desk. Beyond that, she ignores what I do, and blocks it out. She can, as I don't scream at night." He concluded pointedly.

"So, what do I do?" Clara asked bluntly.

"Have you told Luke about London?"

"I was going to, but then decided if I never did that kind of work again, if it was a 'one off' I wouldn't need to, so no, I didn't. If I told him anything it would be about Christian asking me to attend a party and translate Russian for him. It would upset him as he tries to keep Christian and myself apart."

"Hmm. He is sensing it though. Have you discussed long-term plans?" Clara was nettled, but given the nature of their conversation, calmed herself and considered an answer.

"Not directly. He wants to gain tenure at a university lecturing that much I know. Presumably, from what you are saying, he will be expecting me to settle beside him. Currently,

I am going to do my master's, but was then hoping you might find me a way into the Foreign Office, or Intelligence or something like you, an office job to keep Luke happy."

"Ah, won't keep others happy though I'm afraid, nor yourself, will it?" he barked, returning to his gruff voice. Clara was startled by the sudden switch in tone and what he was saying. She didn't know how to respond. She returned to what had become her mantra over the last few months, ignoring the little voice in her head agreeing with Greg.

"I don't want anything else Greg, I don't know what you are talking about. I want to stay with Luke, in his 'normality', if you like. I have done my bit for my country: I retire. I will see how far research can take me in bringing about some change and a desk job in the Foreign Office maybe," She petered out, scared of pushing too hard against the thin veneer she was trying to keep in place. "I need you to report back to Charlotte, who will tell Luke exactly that please," she added with firmness. Silence reigned for a couple of minutes as her last words drifted out across the pond, which was vanishing from sight in the gathering darkness. Greg stood and held out his hand to help her up, smiling at her.

"Come on young lady, let's catch up with the others. Let the future take care of itself, eh?" Side by side in silence they followed on to the restaurant.

CHAPTER 17

News headlines: August 1986
*Government reveals that a record of nearly 3,100,000
people claimed unemployment Benefit last month.*

"How was your day Saanvi? It's busy here tonight, are you going to be on chopping duty all night to help out?" Saanvi rolled her eyes and peered at the list Clara was holding.

"What are you up to? Is it going to be an intimate meal for two very hungry people, or are you holding a party?" They both laughed.

"Trivial Pursuit Game evening. Luke still had some work to do so I said to fetch the food order, then when I get back, we will go on to the party together. I will soon have everyone on campus ordering food from this restaurant!"

"Oh no!" moaned Saanvi dramatically, "Even more vegetables to prep!" The grandmother and aunt were hovering close by, tutting as the girls laughed loudly.

"What's up with those two this evening, they are looking grim. Why aren't they in the kitchen if you are so busy?" Saavi looked worried and absent-mindedly plucked at a loose thread in her sari.

"Jorwain is in a strange mood, scheming and plotting in the kitchen and we are not allowed to hear what is going on," she explained, "'Not for women's ears'" she mimicked Jorwain, and although Clara smiled, she was perturbed at Saanvi's distressed expression. "I'm afraid, Clara," Saanvi confided, "Something bad is happening, I don't know what, but I am afraid."

"Do you have any idea what it is? Can I help in any way?" Clara asked, "We have wondered before what Jorwain is up to with all his plotting, and us being banned from the cellar for long periods - what do you think it is all about?" But Saanvi just shook her head miserably,

"I don't know, but there is a lot of talk about us having to make a stand and be prepared to die for our cause."

"Yes, Jorwain is often saying that, but I didn't think he meant - it was just his rant when he felt persecuted by racism - what cause? Is it related to the Siachen Glacier dispute?" Again, Saanvi shook her head.

Two tall men wearing long gowns or thawbs, and heads covered with white keffiyeh came to the counter to ask for a table. The girls heard them speaking in Hindi, with terrible English accents, which distracted Clara and Saanvi from their conversation and despite themselves, making them snigger. Why speak Hindi anyway if you were English Clara wondered out loud in Urdu? The aunt and grandmother waggled fingers at them and told them to be more respectful, the two were known to the family and they were important business associates here to talk with Jorwain. It would be safer if the young women shut up and stopped making irresponsible comments. Suitably chastised, the two stopped talking and stood silent for a moment.

But, then the two men turned round to follow their waiter to a free table, and Clara came face to face with Rick.

"Rick!" exclaimed Clara in surprise before she could stop herself. Thoughts flashed across her mind so fast she felt dizzy - delight, annoyance, consternation, suspicion, then dread as her mouth went dry and she knew she should not have said anything. After a fraction of a pause, he frowned at her muttering, "bloody women!" in Hindi to his partner and pushed roughly past her without a backward glance. She spun back to Saanvi, but her friend looked worried, and the aunt after a look of mingled fear and accusation, disappeared towards the kitchen. The grandmother tugged at Saanvi's arm.

"Come away Saanvi now, get back to your work in the kitchen," she ordered.

"I thought I knew him, but I was mistaken," Clara said quickly, turning to the grandmother as Saanvi fended off the old woman's clawing fingers to stay where she was. The grandmother's tone was fierce, and her eyes were small black bullets as she spoke in low tones to Clara.

"How do you know that man? What do you know about it all? We took you in as a friend. You, a woman! What would you know of the business of men?" Jorwain appeared from the kitchen, frowning at Clara, signalling for the grandmother and Saanvi to go to him. The grandmother pulled her khimar more tightly around her head and withdrew. Clara turned to her friend anxiously to be met with an equal level of fear mirrored in the face of Saanvi.

"You should go," Saanvi said urgently. Clara cast a glance at the older women, and she faced a wall of glares and folded arms. What was going on? But Saanvi kept shaking her head, "I'm not sure what's happening, but how come you know that man? It is not good you know him, Jorwain will think bad things about it - it means trouble - we will all be in danger. You need to go quickly ... wait out of sight and I will get your order ..." she pushed Clara from the premises.

As Clara hovered on the doorstep. Jorwain appeared by her side. She was startled to see him there, as one second earlier she had seen him with the women by the kitchens. He must have rushed round the side, although he did not seem to be out of breath. She was almost tempted to go back in, to see if she had been mistaken about him being at the kitchen door and see who it was instead. But Jorwain took her elbow and directed her into the narrow alleyway running along the side of the restaurant. She resisted but he held her more firmly and told her he just wanted a little chat while her order was being prepared. Although he guided her forcefully, he spoke pleasantly enough, even with a trace of apology in his voice. She took a few hesitant steps into the passageway with him towards the kitchen door.

As they passed open doors to the wooden shed-like building storing the drums of oil, he shoved her inside. She tripped and fell to the floor. The door slammed closed behind her. She was in the pitch dark. She was not alone.

As she staggered to her feet rubbing her grazed palms she was grabbed from behind. Rough hands squeezed around her throat. Clara dug both elbows sharply into her attacker. The grip on her weakened momentarily. She twisted and managed to break free, kicking out in the dark. He caught her ankle and slammed her onto the ground. He stamped on her as she lay on the floor, smashing her ribs with his boot. She screamed. The attacker launched himself, pinning her to the ground and shouting into her face. His hot angry breath blew straight into her mouth as she gasped for air.

"You traitor! You whore!" he spat. It was Jorwain's voice. "What do you know of the business of men? They used you as a mole A spy. What affairs of ours have you reported to them? What have you said, in all your notes and recordings? Learning our language has been a lie!" The blade of a knife caught a tiny raft of light in front of Clara's eyes. She felt the cold edge against her cheek.

"I'll teach you a lesson you won't forget in a hurry - not to interfere with us again! Go back to Them. Show Them what we do to spies and traitors! You thought you could pull one over on us? Let's see about that, shall we?" His voice was hoarse with intended violence and ice slid into Clara's stomach at his tone. He held her head down in a vice grip by her hair. With the blade of the knife, he lifted the skirt of her summer dress. The sharp cold prickled her knee, then higher along her thigh, scratching cruelly at the skin, immobilising Clara with horror. She felt as if her body had turned to jelly, the sense of powerlessness overwhelming her in waves of panic as she felt the knife graze upwards over her hips and against her stomach, then circle slowly before descending back down. She struggled to get away, but the knife point pierced her inner thigh with a teeth-jarring stab.

"Be still!" he hissed. Then he continued to rove the knife across her body.

"Come on. Tell me what you know before I slice you into little pieces" threatened Jorwain with calm malice, clearly enjoying his sense of power and what he was doing. His tone triggered a release for Clara from helplessness to anger. Her brain kicked into action: 'Think your way out of this girl' she thought grimly, clearing her mind of all the expletives towards her aggressor flooding her brain.

"I came to introduce you to an important businessman who can help your cause," she tried, dragging her breath painfully, "But I was pushed out of the restaurant. He will be wondering where I am, and where you are. Can we go back in so we can meet him?"

"You are lying," he replied lazily, moving the knife now back between her legs, nudging her thighs to get her to open her legs for him. "I will carve my name in your flesh here for that lie." He jabbed her in the top of the thigh, breaking the skin again and making her flinch and squeal.

"Hold yourself still or this knife will take your leg off!" he hissed at her, as he dragged on the knife scouring a line in the flesh. Clara screamed and jerked her legs away from the source of the pain. She received a fierce tug on her hair as a result and a renewed threat.

"Keep still I tell you. I am branding you a traitor, a scar forever to remind everyone of what you are." Again, the knife stabbed, drawing across her inner thigh. She couldn't help screaming again, her back arching as she tried not to move the leg being mutilated and incur further wrath. The pain cut through her, more severely than her ribs, and threatened to block out clear thought. She needed to stop this, and now: Clara took a risk.

"He knows what you have in your cellar so we should go and meet him," she told him. She had been hoping to momentarily distract him with her words. It was like lighting a fuse to a rocket. Jorwain shocked at her words, exploded with a cry and raised his arm high, the knife poised to strike. In that instance, she kicked out, and her foot struck his throat. Jorwain released his hold on her and lurched back, winded. She sprung to her feet, but he snatched at her ankle, and she toppled once more, this time against the wall of the shed. With a splintering crash, the wall gave way under her fall, and she spewed out into the alleyway in a shower of jagged timber.

Before she could escape Jorwain was after her. He lunged forwards. She grabbed blindly. Her fingers closed around a splintered plank from the destroyed shed wall. She held it up to protect herself as he closed on her. Jorwain met the post with full force to the groin. With a shriek he folded in half. Clara scrambled away, hurtling towards streetlights and noise onto the High Street, with him yelling behind her. As she reached the end of the alleyway she came face to face with Saanvi, who was looking around puzzled, holding the takeaway. Saanvi thrust it into her arms.

"Here is your order. What's going on? Where were you? You have blood all over you!" Her words tumbled out, relieved to see her friend but worried about what had happened to her.

"Quick! We must get away from here!" urged Clara. "It isn't safe. Come with me." But Saanvi had pulled off her scarf and was trying to stem the blood gushing down Clara's leg. She mopped up the flow and tied the scarf tightly around her thigh, as Clara twitched impatiently, keen to get them both away. But before Saanvi could stand upright from administering her first aid, the head chef Naveed and Saanvi's husband Aarif came up to them. Aarif grabbed Saanvi and tugged her back towards the shop. Jorwain was lurching down the alley and Naveed moved to hold Clara at Jorwain's command, but she pushed him roughly aside and fled up the street, calling back after the retreating Saanvi. "I will come back for you. I will come and get you to safety!"

Clara was surprised to find the takeaway bag still warm as she clutched it to her chest. Had all that happened in such a short space of time? On the main road, people were cycling past, groups of glittery girls tottering to go nightclubbing, others less glittery, off to pubs in groups laughing and joking, it all seemed impossible. For her, time had stopped, her life ripped from the fabric of her being. She was floating, disconnected, and alone - seeing everything from a long way off, as if from the wrong end of a telescope.

She watched herself enter the flat and Luke get up from the sofa, greet her and grab his coat to accompany her to the party. He commented on how pale she looked and whether she was okay. She said she had a bad headache coming on, and would he mind if she didn't come after all. He was worried but she assured him she would be alright, just take some painkillers, go to bed early, and phone him if she felt worse. Reassured, although looking back at her frowning, he left with the Indian takeaway.

As soon as he was gone, she stripped off. She examined her wounds. She could see the bruises on her ribs, a nasty red-blue, and she had a deep cut in the shape of a six-pronged star chiselled into her inner thigh, angry and still bleeding profusely. "Bastard!" she muttered as she found some TCP, screaming as it cleansed the wound. She then stepped into a hot shower to try and relieve her ribs as well as mentally wash away the pain and shock.

As the pain subsided slightly with the hot water, her brain began to thaw. Previously unrelated facts and incidents shuffled in her memory to be seen in a new light after this evening. She had detailed the lives of this family for over a year. As the water flowed, she realised what she knew may be of interest to Greg and his team in a way she had never considered before. Then she realised what she knew and had recorded would be of interest to many people. The resulting sense of impending danger prompted her out of the shower. She dressed her wound with bandages, and then hastily pulled on jogging bottoms, a t-shirt, and a warm jumper. She got busy.

Breathing with difficulty, her heart pumping loudly in her ears, she pulled her large box of cassette tapes out from under the bed, tipping them all into a suitcase. Her ribs were proving a hurdle to her movement and breathing, so she swallowed down some strong painkillers. She tied a label onto the handle of the suitcase; 'For safe Keeping - Christian from Clara. You owe me.' Luke had a key to Christian's flat. He was still living there, supposedly doing a Ph.D., but away with a girlfriend. She took the key off the hook and with effort, cautiously opened the flat door and listened for sound: There was none. She dragged the suitcase across the corridor, and let herself in, parking the suitcase behind the sofa.

Back in her flat Clara grabbed her dissertation off the bookshelf and gathered up all the rough notes and diaries she had kept relating to the Blue Tiger. Next, she rummaged through the desk drawer pulling out some large envelopes. She shoved the dissertation and notebooks into them, addressed the envelopes, and found a book of stamps, dividing them all onto the envelopes, hoping the postage cost was covered. All she needed to do now was get them to a post box before someone else intervened.

Clara listened again along the corridor. All was silent so she headed out. As she reached the top of the stairs however, she heard the front door open and a slight sound on the steps below as if being stealthily climbed. She backed away and went out instead through the fire escape. She had just made it to the cover of the shrubbery when the fire door burst open and two men hurtled out, looking around and running off in different directions as if searching for someone. Once it all sounded quiet again, she emerged from the shrubs, making her way towards the main university building where there was a post box. Every shadow made her heart thump, and every whisper of the wind made her jump.

Finally, with great relief she made it. Hugging close to the post box she rammed the large envelopes inside. At first, they refused to bend and drop down because they were long and bulky. But she kept pushing and, in the end, they fell to the bottom with a thankful thud. Keeping her eyes and ears strained for sounds or movement, she made her way off campus, towards the restaurant to go and rescue Saanvi. She turned into the main road with the restaurant in her sight. She sighed with relief and quickened her pace. But a black car sped alongside her, the doors sprung open, and she was bundled unceremoniously inside.

Pain shot through her taking her breath away. She was in a car with black-suited men with no expressions. The car accelerated and she was thrown back against the seat, then just as suddenly it stopped, throwing her forwards, making her gasp. She was pulled roughly back out. They had stopped on what looked, in the dark, to be a construction site, and as they stood by the car, figures materialised around her; one in particular.

"What the hell are you doing? Are you going to try and tell me you just happened to stroll into the middle of another key operation by accident? I don't think so. Tell me this minute, or by god, I shall - " Rick was towering above her in full rage, his fury so intense the expressionless men from the car pushed her within his range and stepped back. "What did you say? What did you do? Who in god's name are you!" He demanded. Clara struggled to be able to respond against the flood of accusations and ended up opening and closing her mouth several times before she could loosen her dry tongue enough to croak an answer of any kind.

"I wasn't - Just getting a takeaway - It's in my neighbourhood - don't know anything about your operation." But it was no good, he had made up his mind and was not to be pacified or appeased. He grabbed her by the arm and shoved her back towards the men from the car.

"Take her to GCHQ, pump her for every scrap of information she has, and I don't care what you have to do to get it out of her, but make her talk! She lies. Deal with it." She found herself being seized on either side. But she struggled and yelled at Rick's retreating back.

"No, don't do this. You are making a huge mistake. They are dangerous - I have to get Saanvi out of there - she's my friend. Rick, please get her out! - " But he was gone, and she was yelling into the dark. They put her back in the car which sped through the night, a silent guard to each side of her.

CHAPTER 18

News headlines: August 1986
MORI poll showed that the Conservatives had eliminated Labour's nine-point lead and drawn even with them gaining 37% in the latest opinion poll, in the space of just over two weeks.

"Something's going on, on campus. The place is crawling with police and plains clothes. Anyone know anything?" said Tristan as he came in late to join the Trivial Pursuit party. They didn't and decided it must be a drug raid or something when the doorbell rang. Police were on the doorstep asking for Luke Marsdon.

"You may wish to come with us sir, there has been a break-in, in your flat I believe," he informed the group.

"Clara!" exclaimed Luke to the policeman, "Is she alright? Who broke in? My girlfriend's in the flat!" The policeman didn't know anything about anyone being in the flat and so Luke hurried off with him in a panic.

The front door lock had been smashed and the flat was in turmoil. Books had been pulled from bookcases, clothes ejected from all the drawers, tables knocked over, and wine glasses from the previous evening lazily abandoned on the floor, smashed. But Luke ignored the mess and rushed around the flat frantically. He found her discarded clothes in the bathroom, soaked in blood. The police tried to calm him. When they realised the issue, they began to take a statement and radio in that it also looked like a kidnap. Luke produced a photo of her from his wallet and begged them to do something! More police arrived, asked more questions, and carried out another search of the flat themselves. Luke was beside himself, "You are not going to bloody find her in here! It is a small flat and I have already looked - you need to concentrate on finding her outside!"

A pin thin detective arrived. Once more Luke was made to describe the evening and what had happened. He was also asked if he could tell, apart from Clara, whether anything else was missing. He cast a half-hearted glance around the chaos but couldn't tell. No, his money and anything worth anything, was still here. He was pressed many times to try and be more specific, but he just couldn't spot anything different. The phone rang making them all jump, and a policeman answered it, then turned to the detective, it was for him. With a half-apologetic glance at Luke, who was helping himself to a stiff whisky, he took the call. Then he reassured Luke the phone call had been to inform him Clara was safe, so he needn't worry anymore. Luke was confused, where was she? The detective scratched his head and took a seat on the sofa indicating to Luke he should do the same. Some of the policemen left leaving only one, who stood silently making notes.

"Apparently your girlfriend was here when the burglars arrived but escaped. The police have found her. The robbery is connected to some illegal smuggling centred around some characters from the Blue Tiger - do you know it, the Indian takeaway on Main Street?" Luke groaned in response. The detective took that as an affirmative. "Your girlfriend has been taken in for questioning, apparently she knew the people from the restaurant. She will be home safe and sound when they are done," he finished reassuringly as if he was describing her on a holiday and would be home with a souvenir for him shortly. Although the detective seemed to have finished his explanation, he made no move to leave. If anything, he rooted himself more securely into the sofa. He then began an endless ribbon of questions for Luke about Clara's association with the Blue Tiger.

Luke answered the questions as fully as he could but was lacking in detail. He hadn't in truth ever listened attentively to her descriptions of her friends there. He always tried to erase that part of her life. He was able to describe the fact she knew them all quite well, visited regularly, and was particularly keen on a girl her age, but couldn't quite remember her name. When asked how she came to know them well, he told the detective about her dissertation and her investigation into language and culture. That gave him an idea. He pushed himself wearily up, sifting through the books on the floor.

"Her dissertation is here somewhere, perhaps that would help you?" But he couldn't find it. The policeman in the corner continued to make notes. "She had tapes too," he suddenly remembered, "In here, under the bed -" But the box was gone. The policeman made a note of this too. Finally, the detective unfolded himself out of the sofa and sweeping the scribe along in his wake, left Luke with the mess, a vague promise someone would be along to fix the lock and another reassurance Clara would be back soon.

Once alone, Luke collapsed on the sofa, head in hands. He was reeling, the rug of security pulled from under his feet. He couldn't go through another evening like this! And why did he feel as if Clara would put him through this again? Lately, he reflected as he flopped back into the cushions, she felt to him insubstantial, like a shadow of herself, only partly with him. She was like smoke, evaporating when you reached out to touch. Even when she was physically present, he felt if he held her too tightly, she would vanish. He wanted her to always be around and when she wasn't, to know where she was and when she would be back, - and that she would be back.

Luke felt history was repeating itself. He remembered, with a shudder, his long-buried memories of himself as a 6-year-old, listening at night to dark-suited grey men coming to the house and explaining to his mother that once again his father had been in 'a bit of bother' in Congo, or Vienna, or another nameless mysterious place. They told her he had 'given his life for his country'. Her wails had chilled his blood. He had wanted to rush downstairs to comfort her. But he hadn't done that, he remembered with shame. He had curled into a ball in his bed and his sister had crept in, and they had huddled together listening. In the morning they would be greeted with hugs and kisses from a falsely cheerful mother, who would suggest as a special treat they could take a picnic tea into the orchard as it was such lovely weather.

Luke swore to himself as he played 'catch the apple' in the orchard with Charlie, he would live a boring life and would not be so selfish as his father. He would have kids and be with them. He would always be home on time, and he would always stay at his wife's side. Clara challenged that whole idea, making him

194

feel selfish for wanting it. He so admired her energy and desire to overcome, to fix and mend, solve and repair, whatever the cost, wherever it led. But he wasn't sure he could walk by her side, or even follow.

Luke was also aware he had turned a blind eye to things his upbringing should have alerted him to and suspected the detective had not been entirely truthful with him. Or maybe he was, he was just saying what he had been told, sitting a long way down the chain of command. Did Clara know more than she had let on about the people in the Blue Tiger, or had she just been in the way? He should have listened more closely. Pakistan and India were at loggerheads over a land dispute along the northern border, hadn't Clara said that was where the family originated? She was a smart one, had she worked out what was going on, or had she somehow crossed paths with his father's kind? Was she really ok? He refilled his whisky glass and wondered whether to phone Christian to see what he knew. But he shied away from that, the less he involved Chris where Clara was concerned the better.

There was a timid tap on his door, and a small curly redhead appeared. Her eyes widened as she stepped more fully into the room and saw the level of destruction. She looked at him in dismay.

"Want a shoulder to cry on?" she asked. And he thought, everything considered, he did.

Chapter 19

Top UK chart hit: August 1986
Fight for Ourselves: Spandau Ballet

Clara nodded off in the car, lolling beside first one of her guards and then the other until eventually, they came to what could only be London. They swept along the empty, rain-washed streets to come to a stop outside a tall ugly tower block. Clara was ushered into the reception area. It was familiar to her. She was fairly sure this was the same building she had been brought to, the night of the party with Christian.

She was led along a maze of corridors, up twisting flights of stairs, until she was pushed into a room, of which she instantly tried to back out. At one end was a whole wall of switches and electrical computing-like gadgetry, along another wall was a two-way mirror, and in the middle of the room loomed a large black chair with straps for wrists and ankles, and wires poking out in different places. She felt the panic rise, and bile collect in her throat. Her guards, however, just held her firmly and levered her into the chair, fixing the straps to her ankles and wrists. She had never been so frightened in her whole life, and fear loomed before her eyes like a black cloud threatening to suffocate her.

"Would you like a sip of water?" a kind voice came from her side. Clara, forcing her head to look in that direction, noticed a young woman holding out a cup of water to her. "It's ok," she reassured, "it looks far scarier than it is. It is a lie detector. We have been asked to strap you up to it before they ask you questions. At least you get the comfy chair!" She smiled. Clara relaxed slightly and returned a weak smile. She also felt a surge of anger, which served to dispel some of the clouds of fear. Noticing this, Clara tried to fan the flames of her anger to give her courage - how dare they treat her like this! Why assume she would lie? She wanted to tell them what they needed to know and then get back as quickly as possible to Saanvi.

Electrodes were to be fixed on her. The woman with the water, rolled back Clara's jumper sleeves to fix a couple to her wrists, and then, gently lifted her jumper to fix some to her chest, just below her heart. She gasped when she saw the injuries. She looked up at Clara, who looked blankly back shrugging as much as she could in the trapped position.

"Fell," she said. Carefully, and tenderly the woman fixed the electrodes, and lowered her jumper again.

"You should get a doctor to look at that," she suggested.

"No," Clara answered shortly. But the woman went out of the room at that moment, to be replaced by two suited men who took up positions on the wooden chairs. A third man fiddled with the wall of switches. While they sorted themselves out, Clara did as well, stilling her inner voices of fear, relaxing against the tension in her body, and emptying her mind of everything except the version of truth she was prepared to tell. Once everyone seemed ready, Clara was asked to say her full name. A needle on the wall juddered along a paper turning automatically with a slight whir. The line the needle drew met with everyone's approval apparently, so the questions began. Clara was patient for a while, answering them all in a monotone, as well as she could. But after a couple of hours, going over and over the same things, she began to get less cooperative and suggested it would be more productive if they just asked her what she knew, then she could tell them, instead of playing this guessing game.

"You only get answers to the questions you ask," she pointed out with exasperation. "So, you only cover the ground you already know about, merely confirming your original suspicions. It is a limited process. I would have thought you guys would have more sense and a more creative approach to getting information from people!" She was genuinely disappointed and tired of their bungling. But they were relentless. Clara slid her mind into neutral, and answered automatically, sticking to her original script, refusing to vary her answers to the same questions, asked over and over again. 'This is a waste of time!' She fumed.

The interviewers had breaks, but she didn't as they just switched to a fresh set of interrogators. Time lost any meaning, the needle continued to flicker across the paper, and the circular conversation went round and round. At one point there was a variation. She was asked where her dissertation had gone from the bookcase, had she taken it? The thought of her flat reminded her of Luke. She wanted to know if Luke knew where she was. But they wouldn't answer her questions. So, she wouldn't answer theirs and went silent on them. Lots of comings and goings, and hushed conversations in corridors ensued. She was then told Luke had been informed she was safe, currently with the police 'helping with their enquiries.' So, bad temperedly she told them she had no idea where her dissertation was now, it had been there earlier on in the evening. The needle kept to its steady scratching across the paper with no variation in rhythm Clara noticed with sly appreciation.

Just as Clara thought she could not go on any longer, a short man in a white coat with a stethoscope came into the room. He took her pulse, removed the electrodes, tutted over the state of her ribs, and ordered her to be taken down to the medical room. She wasn't keen on this but had little fight left in her. Having been strapped so long in one position, she found she couldn't walk, her legs had gone numb and useless. One of the larger silent guards scooped her up and carried her down another maze of corridors like a baby, setting her on a doctor's couch in a small dispensary.

Left with the doctor, he bathed the ribs in antiseptic and strapped them up with white tape.

"Might sting a little when you come to pull it off again, but I think you will find it more comfortable. These are painkillers, you need to swallow them now," he added, handing her two small white tablets and a glass of water.

There was a knock on the door. Yet another new face emerged, a broad-shouldered suited man, with hair reminding Clara of shiny conkers, and a friendly expression on his lightly freckled face. He smiled at her and held her hand as she gingerly climbed down off the couch.

"Hi, I have a wordy title, but why don't you just call me Barney, as I understand you have had a bit of a night of it?" he said pleasantly. "I am going to take you to a 'safe house' where you can get some much-earned sleep." He guided her out of the building and into a car, then out again at a nondescript residential street, up a garden path to a small, terraced house. All the time, he kept up a constant chatter of small talk, which although she couldn't return, was grateful for, nonetheless. She was asked if she wanted any food but dumbly shook her head, so he took her upstairs to a bedroom, where he went briskly to the windows drawing the curtains against the light of dawn. "The bathroom is along the landing, then hop into bed and get some sleep," he advised, "I will be downstairs if you need anything."

Once left alone, she made use of the bathroom, flushing the sleeping tablets (so-called painkillers) the doctor had given her down the toilet, then came back to the bedroom. Instead of getting into bed, she sat cross-legged in the middle of the floor, assumed an active position with head over heart, over pelvis, drawing herself up tall, and imagining herself reaching out to the wider universe. It was agony for her ribs, but she allowed the pain to wash over her. There she stayed, in the silence and stillness. She slowed her breathing and let the last few hours drain through her into the ground with each outward, albeit shallow, breath, while drawing in fresh air, clarity, and focus for the future with every return breath: She needed to prepare herself to go and rescue Saanvi.

Finally, she was ready. Very quietly she opened the bedroom door, listening carefully. She could dimly hear voices downstairs coming from a TV. She crept down the stairs testing each step for creaks, holding in check her urge to rush. Slowly and gently, she unlocked the door, releasing the various chains, and deadlock (the keys were left in the locks on the inside, presumably no one had considered her going out.). She trembled with the desire to hurry but forced herself to let the locks click gently and the chains loose link, by link. Once the door was open, she pulled it to, but not closed, in case it made a noise. She desperately wanted to run, her heart beating loud and furiously, but walked slowly, with outward calm down the path to the street. As she reached the pavement, she met Rick climbing out of a car. They came face to face and both froze.

"What are you doing out here?" asked Rick, with false calm laced with menacing anger.

"Leaving. Going home," she said bluntly.

"I thought you would be asleep," he said grimly, grabbing her arm, spinning her about, and marching her back inside.

"Yeh, well, the doctor lied to you about me taking those."

"Did he lie to me about you having three broken ribs?"

"Yep." she bluffed as Rick opened the door and shoved her inside.

At the sound of the door slam, Barney came out of the living room in time to see Rick pushing Clara to the wall and pulling up her top to reveal taped ribs, with ugly red angry bruises showing between.

"Jesus," Rick said softly as he gently lowered her top. Then he spun round to Barney, who was looking somewhat mystified by the situation. "I found her outside. I told you to watch her and keep her safe until I came." He spoke with shards of ice spitting towards Barney at each syllable, and Clara could see him wilt under the torrent.

"It's not his fault," she said, stepping forward, "Leave him be. Am I a prisoner here?" she said, sounding far braver than she felt, "Because I can't wait around while you two fight. I have to be going." Again, she made for the door, although not imagining for a moment they would let her, but at the same time so desperate to be on her way. Rick blocked her path. Their eyes locked. "Please. I need to go," she said quietly but with an urgent edge to her voice.

"You can't until we have talked," he answered. Without looking around, he barked out to Barney, "Barney. Go away." The poor man melted out of sight.

They stood in the hallway, eye to eye, each daring the other one to make the first move. Seconds ticked by, but both were as spiked as hedgehogs, ragged and battered by their day. Suspicion, anger, and confusion chased each other across the space between them, both wary and scared of making a critical error that would cost so much to so many people. Were they on the same side or not? Finally, Rick said,

"I need answers. I will get them. I will resort to every measure at my disposal to get them - do you understand?" His voice was icy and sharp.

"We don't have time!" retorted Clara, the stress breaking through her walls and barriers. But Rick grimly set his jaw, seized her by the arm, and pushed her to sit down on the stairs.

"I need answers," he repeated.

"Well, the questions had better be the right ones then," she snapped, nervous now she knew she was about to have to share with him the experience in the alleyway.

"Yes, I heard you have a view on our questioning technique. Well, go on then, have it your way. I won't ask you any questions at all. But I would like you to take me through Friday from the time you entered the Blue Tiger to the time we picked you up in the car, unedited - the truthful version, and by god, if you try to lie to me - I will know!" Silence.

"I don't think I am strong enough to give you the unedited version," she answered truthfully, her voice trembling.

"It's crucial you do tell it to me though. Listen, try this, it works for me: Imagine all your feelings, fear, shock, revulsion ... whatever. Pull them from you and throw them into say, the sky or an ocean. This leaves you without them, and able to look at a situation as an objective audience. Mind you, you have to retrieve them from wherever you have put them later, so don't forget. But for now, try that, so we can go over your experience and see if we can learn anything to get a grip on the situation we have."

She breathed deeply despite protests from her ribs, stilling her mind, then imagined twisting her emotions all into a thread and casting them into a deep black lake. In her mind she watched them spit and sparkle on the surface before sinking, down to the hidden depths of the lake. Then she brought the early evening to mind, seeming so long ago now, and watched it replay as an old cine film, crackly and without sound. She narrated for Rick's benefit, in a toneless voice, keeping in time with the action as it rolled in front of her on her 'big screen'. Her voice broke when she reached the alleyway, as she did not have the vocabulary to describe what was happening, but Rick stopped her.

"Think of it as not you. Describe it in the third person. Look at it again, see if you can remember anything said during it, anything you remember seeing that can help us." But she was stuck, she couldn't keep the walls up against the shock of her attack. Without realising what she was doing, she grabbed Rick's arm, clinging to his sleeve. He shook her off.

"Clara," His tone was severe and threatening in its seriousness and she met his eyes. "Sit up straight," he ordered her, "Tall and straight. On your own. You didn't need me earlier when you were yelling at me about what to do. You don't need me now. You are the same strong person. Someone attacked your body, but not you, you are still here. Are you listening to me?" She nodded. She was trying to follow but still trembling.

"The pain ..." she whispered. "I thought I was going to die with the pain," she whimpered, looking down at her feet. Rick leaned over her and spoke into her ear in a hushed tone,

"The pain is good. It lets you know you are still alive. That is what I used to tell myself." The understanding of what he said only half registered, the empathy of his words however washed over her, and the intimacy of the connection was so unexpected, after a moment or two she sat up straight, regaining her composure.

"What is it you are looking for exactly?" she asked, taking a deep shuddering breath.

"To be honest, I don't know. But something is wrong, doesn't work. We have the family wrong, someone is not as they seem, with all our surveillance - you might fill the gap. Come on, give it another go, back to the beginning."

So, she forced herself to replay the scene in the alleyway again, this time trying to think of the exact activity, who said what, and how the action changed from the pleasant walk along the shortcut, to the brutal, sadistic attack. Rick waited beside her, willing her to be able to do it one more time.

"I left the restaurant to find Jorwain outside -"

"Are you sure? Did you not go down the alleyway and then come across Jorwain? I was in the restaurant remember; I saw him in the kitchen."

"No, I wouldn't have gone down the alleyway if Jorwain had not persuaded me to; but I was surprised to see him there as I thought I had just seen him in the kitchen in a bullish mood and here he was being as nice as pie ..." Her narrative dwindled as thoughts clicked and flickered into a dawning picture and she looked up at Rick who seemed to be merely one pace behind her.

"Jorwain in Urdu means twin," Clara stated simply and they both knew the missing link.

"Makes sense. They have been sharing a passport. So, when we thought he had left the country, he probably hadn't. He could pop up where we didn't expect him. Well done, Clara." But she was looking deathly pale, a hand to her mouth.

"What is it?" he asked.

"Is this all about a land dispute, a war between Pakistan and India over some land?" she asked.

"Well, yes, in a nutshell. The Foreign Office had been helping to mediate a peaceful process. But India jumped the gun and took possession. Then the Pakistanis found out and say we betrayed them because a British business provided India with the resources they needed to climb the glacier - the centre of the disputed land - and stake a claim," he told her. Clara groaned.

"I have to get Saanvi out of there - it's not safe. The family is from the glacier region, they feel betrayed by the British. They are making a protest, a terrorist act, to force everyone to go back around the table to talk and negotiate a deal over the land. Is there an important meeting taking place to discuss the issue? Did they negotiate for it to be held at the restaurant?" Rick nodded.

"Yes, the main meeting is tonight: What do you know?" His voice was rough, urgent.

"How is the meeting going? Because if it fails, they are planning something, I don't know exactly; would they have guns hidden in the cellar? They are planning some 'retribution'".

"How do you know all this? Who are you working for - the Americans? I can't act without more information; you must realise that?" She didn't have the patience to explain as it came from snippets of conversation over the past year; twists of vocabulary taking a long time for a person new to the language to spot, especially when they switch back and forth between two, Urdu and Hindi. She tried to think about how to communicate it quickly.

"I don't work for anyone: This family was the focus of my dissertation. There is something important in the cellar, which had repairmen in and out, a 'special' delivery Jorwain Bad Twin oversaw, with lots of reference to 'forcing the hand'. Everyone was forbidden to go there, although the big freezer is there so it was inconvenient. Jorwain is the only one who was allowed." She could see she had not fully convinced Rick, although he knew about the focus on the cellar. "I have a written record of all activity and taped conversations from the past two years, but I don't think we have time to analyse them now."

"I don't think we have. We went to your flat to search it for information - on you and how you were involved. We were beaten to it by someone else and that is how we discovered the break-in."

"The dissertation won't help you. Anyway, there is a copy in the university library, so feel free to read it any time. No, it is the rough notes and tapes you need."

"They weren't there either."

"Naturally. They weren't left lying around for anyone to take as they felt fit - the tapes are in a suitcase behind the sofa in Christian's flat across the hall. The notes should be landing on Greg and Charlotte's doorstep any moment now - depending on what day it is, I have lost track." They stared at each other for an intense moment as Rick had to acknowledge he had underestimated her, and she was silently waiting for acknowledgment. He gave her a slight twitch of the lip and an almost imperceptible nod of the head. Then without breaking their stare, he called out loudly.

"Barney?" The reply from somewhere close by came instantly,

"On it sir!" Barney's reply broke the spell. The need for action, not talking took priority. They all dashed to the door.

"Whoa there! You are staying here!" Rick told Clara firmly.

"No way, I have things to do." She pushed him out of the way. But he grabbed her, both of their tempers flaring.

"Stop it. I can't waste any more time, step aside and let me get on with the job now."

"I need to come too. I want to get Saanvi out of there, then you can do what you have to do."

"No! You can't do that - I will make sure she is safe. Stay here."

"You won't. You are about to go into 'operation mode', you will be objectively managing the situation, and individuals are collateral. You do your job, leave me to mine - I want one individual out of there, once I have her, I will get out of your way."

"The women will all be gotten safely out of the way," he snapped at her trying to free himself and not let her out at the same time.

"Then you need me at your side if you think that! The women will be used as shields, not let go - how can you go into a situation like this without knowing the culture? Let me come with you, you aren't safe - you are all too ethnocentric!" They were both extremely angry, physically tussling at the door, but Clara's injured ribs and Rick's strength meant he overpowered her quickly.

"Sorry to do this to you. You can yell at me later, but I can't have you near the place, you've done your bit. You have been through enough already - Barney?" As if waiting for his cue, Barney stepped forward and forcibly took Clara from Rick's grip. She was unceremoniously handcuffed to the bannisters, and without a backward look the two men hurtled out of the front door, slamming it behind them.

CHAPTER 20

News headlines: August 1986
Pickets gather outside Rupert Murdoch's newspaper plant at Wapping.

In their haste, Clara had both hands handcuffed around the banister at an awkward angle, arms pulled above her head unable to even stand properly. She cursed them loudly in the now silent house. She had no option but to stay where she was, impatiently worrying about her friend.

After what seemed like forever the door opened behind her. She was unhooked from her uncomfortable position by two cheerful policewomen. Her arms were dead, she couldn't feel them, and they hung limply by her side. She could do nothing more than be led, unresisting to the back of the house. In the kitchen one of the ladies sat Clara at the table and rubbed her arms, helping to get the blood flowing again, while the other made tea and toast. Clara couldn't remember the last time she had eaten.

"What day is it?" she asked with mild curiosity. She was informed with some amusement it was Saturday afternoon. After eating she was guided through to the living room. The two women, Grace and Hilary, settled down on either side of her on the sofa. They wanted to watch 'Grandstand' as they were both Tottenham supporters. It was clear they were appointed to guard her, ' keep her safe' was how they put it. For a while Clara settled down between them, glad to catch some rest. Then after about half an hour, refreshed from a little catnap, she asked to go to the toilet, and they surprised her by not coming with her. One went to the kitchen, calling after her whether she wanted coffee or tea. They seemed quite relaxed, but Clara was taking no chances this time. After having a quick look around the house on her way back to the living room for her coffee, she had a plan. She suffered through an episode of 'Bob's Full House' playing along with the women. As the globe revolved on the screen to announce the next BBC programme, Clara stretched cautiously, wincing as her ribs protested. She asked her companions.

"Is it possible for me to have a bath to ease my ribs? They're throbbing." Hilary leapt up from the sofa.

"Of course!" she exclaimed, "We should have thought of offering you that. I will fetch some towels for you". Grace had also risen and led the way upstairs, where she helped by putting the plug into the bath and turning on the taps.

"Here you go," said Hilary entering the crowded bathroom, "Put some salt in too, my mum always swears it is brilliant at healing wounds." As she spoke, she laid a pile of towels on the toilet seat and poured some 'Saxa' salt under the stream of hot water.

"Thank you," said Clara sincerely, wishing for nothing more than to be able to sink into the glorious hot water and stay there forever. Grace stood, hands on hips eyeing their charge.

"Look, ducky, if I were you, I would have a nice long soak and then climb into bed, see if you can't recover some colour in those cheeks. You don't look too good to me."

"You've had a tough time of it," agreed Hilary, "Get some sleep and we will be downstairs when you want us." And with backward glances at the pale, dark-eyed waif, they reversed out of the bathroom and went downstairs. Despite their helpfulness Clara heard them double-check all the locks on the doors as they returned to the living room, propping the door open so they could listen out for her - the message about her will to escape had obviously been communicated to them.

Clara closed the bathroom door firmly upstairs, although she was on the outside of the door. Moving slowly, holding her emotions in firm check (she had hurled them all into her lake so she could concentrate on the next little while with a clear mind: She liked Rick's trick.) she eased her way downstairs. She knew if she moved sooner rather than later it would be less expected. She could hear the women still rearranging themselves, discussing the channel selection and how long they would wait before checking on her. They decided to go up every 15 minutes. 'Shit!' thought Clara, 'doesn't give me long!'

With forced patience, she crept past the living room doorway and the backs of their heads as they started to watch an episode of Home and Away. She scuttled along the passageway into the kitchen, where she closed the kitchen door behind her with velvet softness. She cleared the draining board of the clutter of dirty dishes from their toast. Wincing with the pain it caused, she climbed up, opened the window and half tumbled, half jumped out. She pushed the window to behind her and scurried along the back garden to the neighbour's fence. 'Sorry about this' she muttered under her breath as she gave the rotten part along the bottom a firm kick, breaking a gap she could roll under. Then she gave up on going slowly and pelted down the neighbour's garden path, out onto the residential street, and along towards what she hoped was a main road.

She followed street signs towards the town centre. As the roads became more traffic-heavy, she started to hitch. She was picked up almost immediately by a lorry, setting off from the depot heading for Merseyside. Pleased, Clara settled down happily beside him to entertain with funny stories she invented as London retreated in the rear-view mirror.

Fred, her friendly lorry driver, dropped her on the main ring road outside Birmingham, so she could hitch her way into the city. As he drew away, and she resumed her stance with her thumb out, a dark van slewed to a stop beside her. Before she could react, the back doors opened, and she was bundled inside. The back of the van was surprising. There were machines, like giant tape recorders all around the walls and seats looking like swivel office chairs, fixed to the floor. There were six men, each on a chair, all looking down at her as she sat where she fell, on the floor by the door. The van started up again and sped off, throwing her back against the doors.

"Shit, girl, you are in so much trouble," said one, looking at her with a mixture of fear and awe.

"You are so dead!" agreed another.

'Unfortunate choice of word', thought Clara wryly. "What is this place?" She asked.

"Can't tell you," said another. A partition window from the front of the van snapped open.

"Don't talk to her!" came the order. "I've radioed in that we have her. I am supposed to keep her up here with me, but I haven't time to stop to do that now. So, she is not to move an inch from that spot. That's an order!" The window snapped shut again.

"Rude," commented Clara, and the others exchanged a grin despite themselves.

They eventually came to a stop. The men immediately took up their positions. The tapes whirred round, and they all bent over notepads listening with big Mickey Mouse headphones clasped to their heads. Clara heard people get out of the front and expected the back door to open and someone to haul her off. But the sound of voices receded, and she was left with the backs of the men and the whirring of the tapes. She tried moving, tentatively putting out a hand to open the van door herself, but without even looking around, the man nearest her thrust out a foot, kicked her on the leg, and barked.

"Don't even try it." She retreated. After a few minutes, there was a buzz of muttering between the men. One of them said,

"Play it back aloud so we can all hear." With a click, Clara heard Saanvi crying and begging someone,

"Oh no oh no." Then, what sounded like a slap against flesh, then Naveed's voice.

"Get on with it. We are all fighting for our homeland, we are family, and we stick together. For the love of Allah, we need to do what Jorwain says. Put it on."

"Now look here Naveed, we don't want this, it is not the way – all this violence, it is unnecessary and we want no part in it -" Aarif's voice pleaded. Clara made an involuntary movement, but this time no one noticed, they were all trying to check the stream of Urdu against a set of keywords they had on a written list. Clara crept closer peering over their shoulder. They had a list of words and were trying to decide if one of them had just been used.

"Can't any of you speak Urdu? What a crazy process ... I can translate what was just said if you like," she offered. They jumped, startled, and tried to push her back. But she was angry. "Look, this is stupid! I know what they said. They are planning to kill or die or both, we haven't time for this slow process. Do something!" They looked at each other and then one of them grabbed a walker-talkie and jabbered into it. They left the tape to run out loud for Clara to translate as they scribbled in their notebooks. One of them repeated a summary to someone else listening to the walkie talkie. It sounded as if the family was gathered, making plans to initiate violence on those in the restaurant and passers-by as talks were breaking down. It was not entirely clear how, but it sounded organised. Clara heard the wails of the women. It sounded as if one of them had fallen or was unwell. It was chaos and hard to pick out one voice from another panic-stricken voice.

The team worked in this way for about half an hour. Then they all heard at the same time the strident, icy tone outside, scalding someone so severely they all shrunk down, their shoulders hunched. It was clear Rick had learnt who was acting as translator and knew his previous order to keep her out of the way had been ignored.

"Shit!" said Clara. Looks of sympathy were shot in her direction although fear of their resilience under such a dressing down made them hunch even further down on their chairs. The back of the van was violently jerked open crashing back with a thunderous roar making everyone flinch. The whole van swayed with the force. Clara was unceremoniously hauled out and the door slammed shut again. Without making eye contact, Rick pulled her to the front of the van, handcuffed her to the door handle, and marched away.

Frustration threatened to overwhelm her at this point. For a moment she sank with despair onto her haunches - as far as she could fall with one wrist bolted to the door handle. However, as she sank low, she glanced down. There lying abandoned on the ground, was what looked like a discarded rusty part of bike, a part of a peddle or handlebar. She used her toe to inch it painfully slowly towards her. Then, using it as a crowbar, she put one end in a small gap between her wrist and the bracelet. Using the side of the van for leverage ('Sorry van owner' she muttered), she succeeded in distorting the handcuff enough to wriggle her wrist out, although it cost her a nasty gash which started to bleed heavily. She yanked open the van door, and rummaged round, finding an old rag, perhaps used to clean the windscreen, and tied it tight around the wound to stem the blood. While finding the rag she also spied a walkie talkie concealed in a side pocket and snatched it up. Then looking around to get her bearings she realised she had finally reached her destination. The restaurant lay across the patch of wasteland, along the High Street. What now?

She knew the place was under surveillance and did not want to impede the operation. So, she decided to creep close along the alleyway for now and watch to see what was going on. It would all have been a lot better if she had been allowed to go along with the investigation instead of risking getting in the way. But she was driven on by her concern for Saanvi. The taped

215

voices suggested the whole family was being incorporated into the activity. But what form was it taking and what was Saanvi being asked to wear to make her cry out in such anguish? She double backed, down the High Street and then into the top end of the alley. Keeping to the edges, she moved cautiously, reaching the splintered wreck of the shed from a lifetime ago. She stepped over the timbers to reach the kitchen entrance, and scuttled down behind some bins to listen. All was deathly silent. She crept up to the back door trying to listen. But her heart was thumping so loudly it deafened her, so she retreated behind the bin. This would not do. Get a grip. She forced herself to relax, let her mind slip out of focus, and breathed in, out, in, out. At the edge of her consciousness, she was aware of her feelings screaming at her, fear looming over her shoulder. The urge to run away threatened to disable clear thought. With a huge effort, she hurled them all into the black lake holding them under the water until they stopped struggling and went still. She completed one round of breathing and then before impatience rose back out of the water, releasing all the other feelings as well, she retraced her steps back to the door.

She crouched down behind the prep tables and benches where she had spent so many hours chopping vegetables and mixing spices with Saanvi. Her target was the cellar. Keeping ears and eyes scanning she crossed to the door leading to the steep stairs. All was still and silent. She tiptoed down. It was pitch dark as she descended. She dared not put on a light. Suddenly she realised someone was there. She could sense them and hear their ragged breathing. She stopped stock still on the stairs and waited. There was no movement, but someone was there definitely below her in the dark.

CHAPTER 21

Top UK chart hit: August 1986
Camouflage: Stan Ridgway

At the bottom of the stairs was, she remembered, a large room with shelves built into the walls where tins and cans were stored. Leading off the room, a series of other storage rooms including the cold storage room, spanned the length of the building. She was halfway across the room, feeling her way in the blackness, when the cold storage door opened, casting a flash of light across the room, highlighting Clara. She came face to face with a grim-faced Naveed, the head chef. He wasn't his usual smiling self, dressed in his whites today. With a sneer and a look of pure hatred, he grabbed her, pulling her into the cold storage room. He forced what seemed like a life jacket on her, then pushed her hard in the back, catapulting her across into a pile of sacks of flour before going out. The door slammed shut.

Clara had understood everything in the blinding flash of light. She had seen the discarded dying heap of the grandmother at the foot of the stairs. She had seen Saanvi and Aarif wearing a jacket of wires. She had seen a large barrel spitting more wires with a menacing ticking sound and rapidly flicking numbers in decreasing order. Clara didn't know much about bombs, but this barrel looked to her as if it could do a lot of damage.

Saanvi! She had found her! They hugged briefly. But Saanvi was distraught at seeing her. What was she doing here? She had no business being here. This was not her fight.

"But I came back for you, and you Aarif, to safety – this is all crazy – but why are you locked in here?"

"Aarif and I tried to argue with Jorwain, to persuade him return to the talks –" Aarif snatched Saanvi away from Clara, pulling her into a firm hug by his side.

"Saanvi, you have said enough – you are doing it again, involving this foreigner with our affairs, that is what has got us locked up in here! Her! " Aarif spat at Clara, terror and anger mixed to twist his face into a wild grimace.

"We all want peace Aarif," argued Saanvi, "all three of us here are on the same side."

"No Saanvi, she is not of us, I don't think we should be killing people over this, but we do at least feel the depth of despair Jorwain does, after all these years – generations and generations of our people trying to secure our land; when will it stop, when will people listen and help?"\

"I can help," said Clara, "There must be another way – not this way-"

"Too late, it is all too late," whispered Aarif, the energy draining out of him as he shivered and tugged Saanvi closer. "You have sentenced us to death." He told Clara, "Jorwain says we deserve to die as traitors, and cowards…is that your way of helping?" Aarif looked so young at that moment, big eyes round with terror and loss of hope; no anger now, just stunned emptiness. He started to mumble in rapid Urdu to Saanvi. "We are defeated Saanvi, crushed by shame at being branded a traitor by my own family... how did we go from happy family to 'call to arms' so quickly? I am caught by so many conflicting values; it is tugging me in so many directions I feel dizzy." He glanced at the flashing numbers. "I wish those numbers would speed up, get this over and done with so I don't have to think or feel any more..." Saanvi made reassuring noises to calm him as he slumped back on the flour sacks.

But Clara was not accepting they were about to die, refusing to consider the odds stacked against them.

"No," she told the couple, "This is all about Jorwain, not you – you have done nothing wrong. We will get out of this, all of us. " But Saanvi shook her head dumbly and Aarif stared at her in silence.

Clara examined the jacket she had on; a fuse across the clasp, no doubt set to blow if the clasp was opened. There was a detonator switch, presumably for her to activate. Why had Naveed had one in his hand when he came out of the cold room?

"Was this jacket meant for Grandmother?" she asked Saanvi, who nodded.

Clara examined the barrel. The timer was clicking relentlessly. 43 minutes left with rapidly dismissing seconds. Did seconds pass that quickly? A cold fog of sheer terror enveloped her as she watched the seconds flicker past. The rest of her life in lurid red neon. She tried to breathe the terror away, but couldn't draw the breath, she seemed to have forgotten how to - was there no air left in this cell? Her eyesight blurred, her knees gave way and she fell to a heap on the floor. Saanvi let out a gasp but did not come near. Clara knew the only thing to make her fear to diminish was for her brain to take over, be fully occupied with thinking, as in a game of chess, an intellectual discussion, working out how to escape letchy Russians, getting out from under a dead body or knife-wielding angry Pakistanis, or ... Clara laughed hysterically, 'I may have lived a short life', she thought, 'but it had at least been quite eventful'.

As she raised her hands to her face in her foetal huddle on the floor, she felt the radio in her pocket. Her brain clicked into action. She gave it full reign; she would die thinking, not feeling. She stood up and peered at the clock, 37 minutes. 'Okay, okay, steady girl, think, think. It's a game, a twisted three-dimensional game of chess and it is your move - concentrate.' She examined the radio, tweaked some buttons, and tried to talk. But her voice was gone, her mouth dry. She bit her lip, sucked on the blood, and tried again.

"Hello, hello, anyone there?" Just crackles. Perhaps there was no reception down here? The black dog of terror pounced, kicking her in the chest and sitting on her shoulders. She tried again, twiddling the knobs. "Hello! hello!" More crackle, then a voice.

"Hello? Who are you and what are you doing on this frequency? It is an illegal offence, and you need to report your name and address this instant."

"I am in the cellar of the Blue Tiger. My name is Clara Day. The bomb is set to go off in 36 minutes. You need to clear the area as it's enormous. If you can tell me how to diffuse it, that would be helpful. Um, over." She felt silly, not knowing how to use the contraption, not even sure her message could be heard. There was silence, more crackle, then the voice again.

"Repeat please."

"No, I bloody won't! You heard. Give me directions on what to do. Now!" She tried to mimic Rick's icy ordering voice. Again, more crackle.

"We have bomb squad already on their way. Repeat your location."

"I am locked with the bomb in the cold storage room in the cellar under the Blue Tiger. A bomb squad will not get in. Tell me how to defuse this bomb."

"We are getting bomb squad to talk to you. Hold in there, kiddo. Are you the escapee from the van?"

"Yes. How long will they be?"

"Any minute, honey. It's alright, my name is George, saw you earlier in the van. I am in the van now talking to you."

"Do people know to clear the building? Are they taking notice?"

"Yes, Clara. Everyone is taking notice. I am going to pass you on to Bill, okay? He is from bomb squad alright?" But as George passed over to Bill, Clara was thrown to the floor with force. Aarif had launched himself on top of her, punching and kicking her. The radio flew out of her hands and shot under the door of one of the freezers.

"No, no, you don't destroy the bomb! I won't sit here and let you! You are in the wrong place at the wrong time. This is our battle. We will control what goes on. We are ready to die for our cause, so our children will have the land they deserve!"

Clara had never been so angry and terrified at the same time. She heaved herself away from him, ignoring her screaming ribs hit hard under the assault.

"Stop being duped by Jorwain! Where is he at this moment? Dying alongside you? No! How can your children enjoy the land if you are both dead, you haven't had time to have any yet! You are pawns in a game, victims, help me defuse the bomb! This is going to kill hundreds of innocent people and I know you don't want that!"

Clara was scrabbling under the freezer door as she spoke, desperately trying to get hold of the radio, as it chatted and crackled out of reach. But Aarif drew himself up to a great height. Out of the corner of her eye, she saw, in an instant realising what he was about to do - she had incited him, not calmed! She just had time to stagger to her feet and throw herself physically on top of Saanvi to shield her when there was an almighty deafening blast. It was as if they had all exploded. The blast seemed to rip them from the inside out, breath torn from their chests. An invisible weight stormed into them, suffocating, and thumping them with such force they smashed together as one body: Saanvi and Clara pummelled and broken in a pile of blood, body parts, flour, ghee, pickled limes, and plaster from the roof.

Clara could hear screaming that wouldn't stop until she realised it was herself making the noise. Even then it took some time for it to fade. When the screaming had ceased the ringing in her ears continued to deafen her. Saanvi shifted, sobbing, and clawing at Clara in frantic movements. Clara was afraid she would also press her detonator button by mistake as much as anything, so took some time to try and calm her. Slowly Saanvi subsided in shock; she slid, unresponsive back onto the mangled pile of flour, staring at nothing, whimpering like a sad puppy.

Clara shifted the large freezer door that had nearly squashed them to death. What she could see as a result was so horrific, she could barely sustain her view. She was violently sick, retching over her shoes until she had nothing more to bring up. Aarif's head stared up at her in disapproval. Severed from the shoulders, his spinal column a snake of glaring white bone, glistening with beads of blood and trails of nerves and sinew. Hopelessness swept towards her like a tidal wave, and she had a fleeting memory of her recurring dream of her drowning, trying to reach out for Luke on a raft. Luke! Another life, another plane of existence. But the thought of him gave her strength as she remembered life behind the cell of horror she was in. She remembered Ewan and Jenny, Linda, and Bryn. Bryn! Suddenly she heard Bryn saying as loud as if he was standing beside her, 'call when you need me.'

"I need you now Bryn," she said aloud to the room.

"Hello? Come in, please. Hello? Come in please." The radio! Since the freezer door had been blown off by the blast, the radio was now accessible. Amazingly it was still cackling to itself. With shaking hands and an equally shaky voice, she spoke.

"Hello. Please tell me what to do." A relieved sounding voice came back.

"Hello, is that Clara?"

"Yes. Are you Bill? Can you tell me what to do?"

"Pleased to meet you, Clara. Yes, I am Bill. let's get to work, shall we?" he said as if they were planning to assemble a garden shed on a sunny day together.

Clara looked to find the barrel. It had fallen over in the blast and rolled into the corner. She told Bill this and asked if she should try and stand it up again. He thought not if she could still see well enough all the wires and detonator. Holding her breath, and her nerve she carefully followed Bill's calm and patient instructions, loosening one wire, then disconnecting another.

Still the clock flashed. The numbers receded. There were now 12 minutes left and decreasing. At one point she faltered, unable to follow any more instructions as her brain fogged over. Tears blurred her vision, and she couldn't control her shaking. Her chattering teeth stopped her speaking. But Bill remained calm, talking to her the whole time.

"Hang in there Clara, you are doing an amazing job. Listen to my voice, concentrate on me, nothing else. We are the only two people in the world at the moment. You are nearly there. Take it easy, we have plenty of time, take it steady." And with a final tug of a wire, the flashing stopped at 9.32 minutes. Clara melted to the ground.

"Clara? Clara?" The radio was still talking to her, wanting more from her. Reluctantly she said into the mouthpiece.

"What?"

"We have a saying in this job; 'we are not home safe until we are home safely'. You are not yet out. Are there any other incendiary devices left? Can you see any more wires?"

"Oh, I am wearing a vest with lots of wires on, I can't get off. Saanvi is wearing one too."

"Calm, calm, it can all be dealt with. We will get you out and then get them off for you. The bomb squad is now outside the cold storage room, but will have to blow the door off to get in. Can you take cover?"

"Um, maybe. Hang on. Okay. They can come in."

Saanvi cried out as Clara curled with her into a foetal position on the bloody flour pile. She held the refrigerator door to shield them. Another painfully loud explosion blew the outside door inwards smashing up against the far wall and causing more plaster to fall. Heroes strode through the falling dust and flour. Clara wept, allowing herself to be helped up, and out of the room. With a glance over her shoulder, she saw Saanvi was following behind with a hero holding her up on either side. Clara was nearing the top of the stairs when she heard Saanvi's voice penetrating the air from below.

"No! I can't come with you. I love my husband. Without him I am nothing. Without family you are nothing!" Clara paused at the desperation and distress, yet iron-strong conviction in the declaration. She turned back towards her friend, but a blinding flash and deafening roar blasted her across the kitchen and into the prep table. For weeks, that was where Clara's memory of the evening stopped.

CHAPTER 22

Top UK chart hit: August 1986
Madonna: Papa Don't Preach

Bryn had just settled down with Linda to a post-gardening drink on the veranda when his bleeper sounded. It was getting dark, that gorgeous half dimpsy between evening and nightfall, when bats flitted out of the corner of your eye and the roses wafted their heady perfume into the still air. It was hard to believe anything other than stillness and calm existed anywhere. He levered himself up out of the chair and with a sympathetic look from Linda went through to phone in.

A pleasant young voice informed him he would be required at headquarters at 0700 tomorrow; there had been a 'major incident' in Birmingham. But also, she had been asked to let him know three of the casualties of the 'incident' were currently in Birmingham Royal Hospital. She could not provide details over the phone, but he was required there this evening. She had no further information to provide. He returned to the veranda, to tell Linda he had to go and kissed her. She squeezed his hand in reply and with an effort, he dragged himself away from the calm beauty of a late summer evening and the dusky delights of his wife's company.

At the hospital reception, he identified himself as the psychiatric officer with National Security and was directed to a wing where heavy security was in evidence. There he met Ronnie, an MI5 officer he had worked with many times before. They went into a small waiting room where they could have a private conversation.

"Sorry to drag you out tonight, Bryn. I know you usually put their minds back together once the hospital has finished with them, but this is rather different. Clara is floating in and out of consciousness but keeps calling out your name - "

"Clara!"

"Good, you know her. Her parents have been informed and will come up to see her tomorrow, but she is agitated and hard to settle, which stands to reason, but with her saying your name we thought it might be worth calling you in."

"What happened? How injured is she?" Bryn was at a total loss. If asked he would say Clara would be at home enjoying a lazy Saturday evening in with Luke - how is she in hospital under police protection?

"You will be fully briefed tomorrow. But she has five stitches in her wrist, a messy slash wound to her thigh, three broken ribs, and a grazed left lung from a gunshot wound." Bryn sat down heavily in one of the chairs.

"Who else do you have here? I was told there were three I know."

"Oh yes, we have Ricardo De Burgh with a broken leg, and a gunshot wound to the upper arm, and Barnabas Mitchell in with a gunshot wound to the leg."

"Sweet Jesus!"

"They are the lucky ones. We have eight in body bags; four of them are our bomb squad guys blown up by a suicide bomber. I have just returned from informing loved ones and next of kin."

"Is this all one incident?"

Ronnie rubbed his head as if to polish it and subsided beside Bryn.

"Yeh, hence the heavy security. Something went wrong and still doesn't feel right. Let's just say we need to closely analyse what went on and spot any suspicious activity - we are straddling too many departments, foreign office, MI5, you know the score ..."

"But, Clara, how is she in the middle of this?"

"It is not entirely clear at this stage. It was thought at first, she was an innocent bystander who happened to be buying an Indian takeaway at the wrong time. But since the reports have started coming in, it seems she was arrested the night before for being in the Indian - who then for some reason, returned this evening, discovered a bomb. She tried to save her friend who blew herself up, then diffused an even bigger bomb that would have sent the whole block sky high and all the nightclubbers around the city on a Saturday night with it - " He spread his hands expansively "- Would likely have been hundreds of casualties right? Then she shows up in the middle of a gunfight between MI6 cronies and goodness knows who else, saves Rick's life by pushing him out of the way of a bullet with his name on, he didn't see coming. She took the bullet herself and went down. There are clearly pieces to add. Been speaking to Bill, bomb squad who talked her through the diffusing of the bomb - did I say she was locked in a room with it at the time? -

And he says he has never met such a cool head in the time of chaos." Bryn didn't know what to make of the strange account.

"Can I see them?" Ronnie heaved himself out of the chair.

"Sure, I'll take you along." They walked along the corridor, meeting the nurse on the way. Each door to the hospital rooms was heavily guarded. Bryn went to see Rick first. He was propped up with his shoulder taped up and arm in a sling, his leg elevated in a pulley system, staring into space, looking grey and drawn. They eyed each other warily.

"I'll go again if I am not welcome," Bryn said lightly. "It is a social call only." Rick looked at him through half-closed eyes.

"You are saving your wrath for when I am stronger, are you?"

"That's not my usual counselling style as you well know. What are you feeling guilty about?"

"Nothing. I did everything I could to keep the minx away. I had her arrested, locked up in a safe house, and even handcuffed her to a banister and a car door for god's sake! So, don't come back to me about why she was where she was." Bryn, unable to understand what he was saying at this point, accepted his story with a nod, realising 'the minx' was Clara. The details were lost on him, but he heard loud and clear the message Rick was not to blame.

"Ronnie says she saved your life, took a bullet for you," he said gently. Rick frowned and fidgeted as if he wanted to be pacing the room.

"Something is not right. It is plaguing me to death! It is all I keep going over in my mind. How did she see what I didn't? Have you been briefed on the whole operation?"

"No, coming at it cold. I am due in London first thing tomorrow morning, they called me in tonight to check up on you, Clara, and Barney."

"Okay, I have been spouting gibberish to you up until now then. Sorry. But I tell you, something was amiss. We did not expect that shootout at the end. The whole place was crumbling after being pummelled by the explosions, everyone was trying to get out before it fell on our heads. Then suddenly everyone was firing. I keep going over it. Clara walked or rather staggered from the kitchen. I saw her arrive. I told her to get down, but she had seen the shooter over my shoulder and told me to move. But I had seen another shooter coming from the left, and had already committed to that shot, so she had no choice but to push me. The one from the left hit me in the shoulder and she took the one from the right. But what I can't work out is who was firing from behind me. Everyone is accounted for. We think Clara saw who it was, but she apparently can't remember that part of the evening, having just witnessed her friend being blown up. But she is under strong security until we find out or her memory returns."

"She saw her friend being blown up!"

"Yes, apparently they had strapped them up with explosive vests. Clara escaped but her friend and her husband were not so lucky."

"Shit!"

Rick grinned, a flicker of his old self.

"You have your work cut out for you this time eh old man?" Then the grin faded back to grey tension. "It was horrific. The ones not hospitalised are all down the local station chucking up as they give their stories; blown up body parts are grim."

"I am going to suggest you are sedated for tonight, to try and stop the circular thinking, would you cooperate with that?"

"Yes, thanks. I need rest to be able to think afresh tomorrow." Bryn turned to go, but at the door, he stopped.

"In your account you made it sound as if you and Clara had a conversation. You said, 'I told her to get down' and then 'she told you about the shooter'. Are you sure that happened? Were words actually exchanged?" Rick looked at him, then away across the room as he revisited the scene.

"No," he said slowly, "There was no time to say anything, it all happened too quickly. In fact, now you mention it, there was barely time for rational thought, we were acting on instinct only at that stage. "But," he held up his good hand, stressing the word, "Communication did occur, maybe by a look or body language, I don't know - you're the psychologist - but I was aware of her arrival on the scene, despite the chaos. I would not have known there were two shooters without her. Does it matter?"

"It does if the fact there were two shooters is based upon it."

"For god's sake get me those sedatives, I am done in for now," he said, lying back and closing his eyes. Bryn left him to go and find the nurse.

Clara was in a darkened room with a light over the bed. A nurse was sitting by the bed but stood up when Bryn crept in. Clara appeared to be asleep.

"She may look asleep, but she isn't," the nurse whispered, " She is floating in and out of consciousness. We are considering taking her deeper into a coma, to give her mind time to repair itself. She has been through hell and back again and is in deep shock. You sit with her for a moment and then let us know what you think?" She tiptoed out. Bryn took the vacated seat, aghast at the tiny face on the pillow. There were ugly bruises on her face, a big lump on her forehead, a bandaged wrist lay over the covers, and she whistled and wheezed as she took shallow breaths, like small gasps. Machines pinged, whirred, and bleeped around the bed. He reached out and took her hand in his. Her eyes fluttered open, fixing on his face as if trying to focus. He smiled and said 'hello', so she could hear his voice. She smiled then and croaked.

"You came. See, I knew when to call for you." As she spoke tears streamed down her face. He slid his arm under her shoulders into a clumsy embrace so he could hold her while she cried. After a little while, she exhausted herself and Bryn eased himself out and back into his chair.

"I'm stuck in hell. Please make it go away," she said in a small plaintive voice, ripping at his heart. He patted her arm softly.

"I can make it go away for you tonight, but we have to conquer the demons, you know that. We will do it together when you are stronger, alright?" But she just stared at him beseechingly. He kissed her on the forehead and told her he would make it go away, leaving the room quickly to find a nurse to say yes, put her out for 48 hours, please.

Barney was more chipper and upbeat, sitting up in bed with his wife at his side. When Bryn entered, his wife made an excuse to leave, and he took her seat. It was clear the cheerfulness had been a facade. As his wife closed the door, Barney sank back on the pillows with a haunted look in his eyes.

"I suggest you say goodnight to your wife in a minute, Barney. You need a good night's sleep." Barney laughed bitterly.

"The time to sleep is what I am putting off," he admitted sheepishly.

"I can prescribe some sleeping tablets if you like. Just for tonight, give you a fresh start tomorrow." Barney grimaced knowing what that 'fresh start' would involve - yet another reviewing of the day he was trying to forget. However, he gratefully accepted Bryn's offer.

"How are the others doing?" he asked.

"Both will be alright but are also accepting drug-induced oblivion for tonight," he said. Barney nodded.

"I keep seeing Clara's expression when that young lass blew herself up … the horror in her eyes … we huddled under a table in the kitchen while the building fell on top of us … she dragged me there, goodness knows how, I'm not a lightweight … there we lay covered in blood and guts and God knows what else, and all the time … Clara's look, haunted she is, poor lass. I tried to comfort her, but it was the other way round really … what with my leg all shot up. She seemed to be operating on automatic pilot; nothing in her eyes; no one home but doing everything right at the same time. She found the shelter, she bound my leg with tea towels … god the pain - found it hard to concentrate on anything else ... " Bryn let the verbal torrent subside, then patted his arm.

"Sleep!" he commanded, "Let me sort that out for you, then we will work through the rest together?" Red-eyed, and exhausted Barney lay back.

"Aye aye Captain," he replied, staring once more off into a tortured replay of the evening. Bryn hurried away to intercept Belinda, Barney's wife, and send her home for the night and dispatch the nurse in to provide some relief for the 'Government Official'.

CHAPTER 23

Top UK chart hit: August 1986
I wanna wake up with you: Boris Gardiner

"Hello?"

"Hello, Luke?"

"Yeh."

"Linda here. Glad I caught you before you went to work. Bryn asked me to give you a call."

"Oh, hi Linda, everything alright?"

"Um, no, not really. Bryn asked me to phone you, to let you know Clara is in hospital -"

"What?! Where? What's wrong -"

"It's okay. She's okay - or will be. She is currently in an induced coma, also under heavy police guard so you can't see her for now - but he is happy for you to phone him later if you want more information. He saw her late last night, but is in London today, and couldn't get to phone you in time. He said you should know in case you heard from other sources. He says you are not to worry - easier said than done, isn't it? Look, you can come over if you like?"

"Right," came the icy reply, "well, thank you for letting me know. If Bryn says she will be alright I will have to believe him, won't I? And if I can't see her ... well, I will just wait until someone lets me know what the bloody hell is going on!" Luke's voice rose with fury. "Sorry, Linda, shouldn't shoot the messenger and all that, but shit! I would have been better off not knowing anything than just this little scrap; obviously you now have me worried sick! You don't put someone in an induced coma lightly - what are her injuries, am I allowed to know that much? Have her parents been informed? What cock and bull story did they get told?"

"She was caught up in the gas explosion at the Blue Tiger last night - is what her parents have been told."

"Bloody hell! What was she doing there last night? What are her injuries? And don't bloody tell me they are classified, or by god, I will drive over to the hospital right now and -"

"Calm down Luke. She is in good hands. She has some broken ribs, and a wound to her wrist - she was put in a coma because she was in mental trauma as her friend was killed in the explosion which by all accounts Clara witnessed. I am sorry, that is all I know ..."

"I just hope against hope that is all there is to know!" The line went dead.

CHAPTER 24

Top UK chart hit: August 1986
A Question of Time: Depeche Mode

Clara's first conscious thought was of being thirsty. She opened her eyes in search of a drink to find herself looking into the distressed faces of her parents. Her throat was so dry she couldn't speak, so waved weakly towards the jug of water by her bed. Her mother rushed to hold a cup to her lips.

"How are you feeling darling?" asked her mother. Her father leaned over her mother's shoulder, worry etched deeply into his face.

"Um, I don't know, what day is it? What time is it?"

"Hush, don't you worry, you need to rest. The doctor said when you gained consciousness, we were to call them - Arthur, would you mind?" Her father obediently disappeared. Clara sank back and felt herself drifting back off to sleep as her mother's chatter receded into silence.

The next time Clara opened her eyes, it was dark outside, and a low light was on by her bed. She thought it was quite cosy, lying there in the stillness and quiet, glad no one this time was by her bed. She didn't want to see or talk to anyone. After a while of her lying there, a ray of light flashed across the room as someone quietly crept in. Clara gasped, her heart suddenly hammering with fear. It was a nurse. Smiling, she checked her pulse, tweaked the machines, asked if she wanted anything (Clara shook her head), and then left.

Clara lay there checking herself out, wiggling her toes, moving about her legs, - all seemed good. She examined her bound wrist frowning, unable to fathom what it was binding. She considered unwinding the bandage to have a look but decided it was too much effort. It was, she concluded, her chest area that was damaged in some way. It hurt to breathe. As if remembering a book, she had once read, or a film watched many years ago, she thought it may be her ribs were broken, but didn't want to answer why they were. Well, people could walk about with broken ribs, couldn't they? She was just entertaining the thought of disconnecting herself from the wires and tubes - they made her afraid for some unknown reason - when she fell asleep again.

Voices woke her. She snapped her eyes open in annoyance. The light in the room was bright with the sun streaming in. She quickly shut her eyes again, but her companions had seen her movement.

"Clara? Your injuries are healing well. How do you feel?" She kept her eyes closed tight and willed them to go away, refusing an answer. After a minute or two, the voice told her.

"Alright, go back to sleep now if you wish, but tomorrow we will get you up and about. You must start re-joining us in the waking world. You have been warned, so you can prepare yourself."

It was late but she was not asleep. Lying in the dark she was unable to get back to sleep after dozing all day. The click of the door made her jump. She watched as the door fell open. She thought for a moment it had sprung open of its own volition, but a second later a hunched figure eased itself into the room, silhouetted with light from the corridor outside. Whoever it was, closed the door behind them quietly. Clara's heart started to pound inside her chest. Her mouth went dry. She struggled to a sitting position and was about to push her alarm button when she realised who it was. She fell back against her pillow in surprise - and relief.

"Shove over. Give me some room here, and a hand, will you? It is not easy with one arm and one leg out of action." She shifted and helped him get up beside her. Once, they were in, side by side, with the blanket drawn over them, they lay panting for a moment, out of breath from the sudden exertion. He slipped his good arm under her and drew her near. They lay curled together, her head on his chest, her arm across him. They both relaxed for the first time since they had been admitted to the hospital. The healing silence wrapped them up..

Eventually Rick sat up, clearing his throat. Clara made an involuntary movement, but he stilled her.

"Our time is nearly up - the guard will be waking up from his 'little nap'." He said softly with a chuckle. She lay back on her pillow to release him, to show she understood. As he painfully and awkwardly clambered back off the bed, he talked.

"I am being discharged tomorrow. Going to get some TLC from the fiancée, save the nurses. Barney went earlier into the tender care of his wife. I expect they will suggest it, but if given a choice, go to Bryn's okay, to recuperate? And Clara? You once said you would like to work alongside me. Well, so you know, while you are considering your options after this, I would be honoured to have you beside me in the field. But you need to know; each time can be as brutal as the experience we have just been through. If you couldn't do what we did again, see what you saw, or couldn't shoulder the responsibility for the outcomes of your actions, then you need to get out and find another line of work, right? If you can find the strength to embrace them, learn from them, and still have fire in your belly to continue to 'save lives' - as you would say - then go and see Greg when you are ready - he will guide you." By now he was across the room, and about to open the door. Clara sat up suddenly.

"But I didn't save any lives! I caused death!" She wailed as if the deep subconscious thoughts had ripped through her conscious mind unbidden, to find a voice.

"Well for a start, you saved mine, and about a hundred others if the bomb you diffused had gone off - including Barney's and your own. Life is not tidy and not without pain, but you saved more lives than were lost. Hold that thought. Vi ses senere." With a flash of light and a soft click of the door closing again, he was gone.

The nurse was pleased to see her awake the next morning, willing to eat some breakfast and even get up to go to the bathroom. Clara then remained in the wheelchair looking out of the window, a blanket over her lap. Reg and Harold found her there when they arrived for the first tentative stages of interviewing her about her version of events. She was as cooperative as she could be, reciting events from her dispassionate view, having made great use of her black lake combined with deep breathing to keep the emotions separated from the factual description of events. Once she had finished, she expected them to leave, but they expected her to continue.

"That's it, then I was taken to hospital - I think," she said again. They shifted about, looking at each other.

"You were there for at least another half hour, you know. Can you not remember?" she looked at them blankly.

"Did I lose consciousness then?" she asked. Again, they exchanged looks. She was getting cross with them. "Stop with the meaningful glances! What happened then, as you seem to know? What are you asking me questions about what you already know anyway - "

"Sounds as if someone is on the mend." Bryn's voice came from the doorway. "Can I come in gentlemen? Sounds like you need a hand." He smiled at Clara, who scowled back at him. Reg and Harold looked relieved to see Bryn. Preparing to leave they said they would return another time, but for now they had received a detailed report.

Silence fell in the room, Clara resolutely stared out of the window while Bryn sat by her side, watching her. She knew he was looking at her and eventually she dragged her eyes away from the horizon and met his.

"When do I get out of here?" The way she said it, stressing the 'I', made Bryn raise his eyebrows at her.

"As opposed to who?" he asked. "How do you know there were others here, and they have been discharged?" She shrugged slightly and didn't reply.

"Clara," Anxiety etched across his face as he held her hand where it lay limply in her lap, "You do seem to have become mixed up with something beyond your experience. All these people, they should be asking nothing more of you, you have given them enough - more than enough. Do not let them near you again. I will help you as much as possible. We need to extract you, get you fighting fit and back on track." He held her gaze, a slight pleading in his voice. Again, she deigned to reply, returning to look out of the window. "As soon as you have clearance from the doctor on your gunshot wound, we will see if we can get you out of here, okay?" Now he had her full attention.

"Gunshot wound? What gunshot wound? Who shot me? When!" Her mind scrabbled around in the dark, unable to connect the fact she had been shot, with her memory. "Where was I shot?" Bryn laid a restraining arm on her.

"Hush, and I will tell you. You were shot in the chest; the bullet grazed your left lung. That is why your chest is all strapped up and you find it painful to breathe."

"I thought the bandages were all to do with my broken ribs..."

"Well, yes, that is what you were told earlier, and what your parents were told, and Luke ..."

At the mention of Luke's name, her mind jolted, she had forgotten all about him. Was she a terrible person? Why wasn't she asking for him all the time? Come to think of it, where was he? Why hadn't he been to see her? Bryn watched the thoughts flit across her face and waited to see what the next question would be.

"Bryn, is Luke allowed to visit me?"

"Yes," he answered slowly, somewhat reluctantly.

"Well, why hasn't he?" she asked, frowning.

"You would have to ask him that," he said non-committedly. Clara found it to be an unsatisfactory answer.

"I'm asking you. I can't ask him if he isn't here can I?" she snapped, "He's mad at me, isn't he?" she continued, not giving time for an answer, "He always said my language study would land me in trouble - am I in trouble by the way? Who with? Why exactly?" Bryn put his hands up in surrender.

"You have to choose which order you want all those questions answered." She glared at him. "Okay," he said in a resigned voice. "Yes, Luke is mad at you, mainly and on the surface, for the reason you have correctly identified. Yes, you are in trouble. You are under police guard because you have information everyone needs but you seem to have forgotten. You are also potentially in trouble for disobeying orders of an officer, escaping after you were arrested, and acting recklessly without due regard for your safety." He stared at her to watch the reaction. Unexpectedly she smiled at him.

"Thank you for good answers - they have obviously spawned a hundred more but thank you anyway." She sat back looking tired. He wheeled her to the bed and helped her back in. She was asleep before he had pulled the blanket up over her.

She was gently nudged awake by the nurse with her lunch, and to be informed she had a visitor if she felt up to it. It was Luke. She wasn't keen, but felt she couldn't say no, so nodded at the nurse who went to get him. Clara was left with a solid lead weight in the stomach, and a lost appetite. Luke appeared around the door. He looked shocked at her appearance, which did nothing to raise her confidence. She thought he might hug her, but he stood irresolute in the middle of the room. So, she pretended to be eating her dinner to keep her hands busy, moving the food around her plate. There was an awkward silence.

"You didn't have to come, you know? I know you are only here because Bryn has spoken to you," she said in a small, flat voice.

Luke perched on the edge of the bed, looking out of the window. He didn't know what to say to her. Every time he thought of something to say it sounded wrong, or inappropriate, or he knew she couldn't tell him - he knew about 'classified information'. She had secrets.

Clara watched him for a moment, aching for his arms to go around her. But with what felt like a freezing wind rush right through her, she realised he wasn't going to; didn't want to.

"I'll tell you what," she suggested, and he looked around at her, "Why don't you go away again? Tell Bryn we had a nice little chat. Then when I am out of here, have my strength back - it is disorientating falling asleep every two minutes - I will come and find you. After all, I know where you live don't I ... then we can talk?"

With tears in his eyes, he stood and kissed her lightly on the lips and nodded.

"I will always love you, Clara, you know that right?" he said hoarsely.

He crossed to the door, "For the record," she said to his back, "I love you too. And always will."

Luke blundered out of the door blinded by tears running down his face. Clara lay back and wept herself back to sleep, as the world where she loved Luke slipped from her grip and the shadows swallowed her.

CHAPTER 25

Economists warn that a global recession is imminent,
barely five years after the previous recession.

Two days later she was ensconced in a chair on the veranda at Bryn and Linda's, drinking in the beautiful garden in late August. Her soul reached out to the trees and skies, rejoicing in them. She was to stay on the condition she attended at least an hour's counselling with Bryn every day. She had to regain her memory of the missing part of the evening in the Blue Tiger, as well as recover sufficiently to be able to resume 'life as normal' (whatever that was, Clara thought with trepidation.).

Her parents had come along with her and stayed over for the night, happy then to leave her in Bryn and Linda's care. Jenny and Ewan were on holiday with cousins until the end of the week, so she had time to soak up the silence and rest before they came home. She liked sitting on the veranda but was also keen to get mobile again and had insisted on helping with the cooking and washing up. She had also resumed her yoga which made her feel more like her old self again, even if she could only manage a few moves for now. During the day, Linda was at work, but Bryn was home with her, on holiday - or working with her, depending on how you looked at it. It was agreed until the kids came back, they would have their hour together during the day, then move it to an evening session.

Bryn was now fully versed with the events surrounding the Blue Tiger having attended a series of meetings in London. He had read the reports of interviews carried out by everyone, including the transcripts of Clara's interview. He was also familiar with the report written by Barney documenting the evidence she had given at the safe house, describing her experience in the alleyway, and the discovery of the 'Jorwain twins', providing a big breakthrough in the investigation.

"Bryn?" she asked at the beginning of the first session together, "How come you are counselling me? I mean, are you an agent? Are you employed by the secret service? MI5? Who are you - I thought you were a lecturer."

"I am a lecturer - and a counsellor. I work freelance for the Government when they need my services, as I do for the military forces, the migrant centre Linda works at, and others who may need me."

"So, you work for the secret service and with agents - some of whom are your friends?" she persisted. He frowned at her.

"No, I don't. I am bound by the Secrets Act for the work I do, but beyond that, I don't 'work' in any other capacity with the secret service. I know some in a professional capacity, but I wouldn't call them friends. What have you heard? What are you basing your questions on? Does it bother you, the work I do?"

"Yes, no, um ...well. I would like to be certain who I can trust. I have always wanted to trust you. But I also know you surround yourself with agents and those who work within the shadows."

"The shadows? What do you mean by 'the shadows'? Who has been telling you about the agents?" But she remained quiet, surveying him with steady blue eyes. He tried again. "Clara, please know you can trust me. I feel as if you are a daughter to me, and I care for you. I honestly have no secret life other than counselling people who have experienced great trauma in their line of work. Only rarely are they from the shady world of espionage - is that what you mean by 'the shadows'? - it is not a world I have any enthusiasm for. I prefer to help those in the military if the truth is known. Even that is ruthless beyond belief and inflicts indescribable misery and trauma onto people. No one I am aware of from the Blue Tiger incident are agents or linked to the spy network. They are all linked to the Foreign Office and international diplomacy corps. There are no shadows near you Clara. You were just in the wrong place at the wrong time, just trying to do your best as you saw it ..."

Clara's gaze slid out over the trees, and she watched the swallows wheeling across the skies as she thought through Bryn's words. She would like to take his words at face value - something was nagging in the back of her mind about it though. If Bryn was telling the truth and did not know any spies, she did indeed feel she could trust him. He was however, perhaps not quite so aware of his friends as he should be. She tried once more to recall who was at the first dinner party she had been to at Swallow's Swoop when Harry had told her ' a wide range of operatives and officers known to us' had been present. She felt it was important to remember, but she couldn't. Bryn was waiting to start the session. 'Later, I will think about it later' she told herself, and turned back to Bryn, "Let's make a start then, shall we?"

The day the kids were due back from holiday Linda, looking a little embarrassed, suggested Clara may like to take some sleeping tablets to help her sleep. Clara was surprised and assured Lin she had no problem sleeping. But a meaningful glance exchanged between Lin and Bryn made her query what they meant. They told her every night so far, they had been into her to snap her out of nightmares, where she screamed and screamed. They were concerned about how this would disturb the kids. Clara could see their point and realised she was aware of the nightmares but didn't realise she was making so much noise. She agreed to take the sleeping tablets.

However, they didn't work well. In the early hours of the morning, the whole house was echoing with blood-curdling screams emanating from Clara's room. Linda and Bryn woke with a start and Linda pushed Bryn out to go and intercede before the kids were woken. However, as Bryn reached the bedroom, he realised he was too late. He saw the pyjama-clad duo scurry to Clara's bedside. Bryn was about to intervene when he heard Ewan's clear voice ring out, as Jenny shook Clara awake.

"Wake up! Wake up, you are screaming the house down! Are you having a bad dream?" Clara was slow to come around, but she did stop screaming as Ewan climbed up into bed beside her.

"I have bad dreams too sometimes, but I can't scream as loudly as you. That is very good screaming," he said, clearly impressed. Jenny had climbed into bed on the other side and was hugging Clara.

"Daddy can cure bad dreams, you know?" she told Clara seriously. " Is that why you are staying with us, so daddy can mend you and stop your bad dreams?" Clara hugged them.

"Yes," she said sleepily, "that is exactly right."

"In that case," said Jenny, "You must tell daddy the right things. He can't cure you if you don't tell him what is wrong, you know," she added severely. "And," she added helpfully, "I will sleep with you until you stop having them. I think that will help you, don't you?"

"You two are the best kids in the whole wide world," said Clara, and Bryn agreed, as he tiptoed back to bed.

But things were not going well. Clara simply could not recall the missing half hour or was unwilling to do so: Bryn couldn't decide which it was.

"I don't understand why I can't remember this part of the evening!" said Clara exasperated as Bryn's questions grated on her. "What I don't understand is why everyone is sure something did happen. I mean, who's to know I didn't spend the rest of the time under the table with Barney and was accidently shot with his gun? What does he say happened? Can't you get the answer from someone else?" Bryn studied her closely. She held his gaze but was clearly feeling upset, to the point where she could make something up if the questions didn't stop soon.

"We know what happened, but we want to hear your version of it," he informed her. She was furious! She stamped around Bryn's study where they conducted their evening sessions, now the kids were home.

"What! Well, why on earth are you grilling me about it then? How about you tell me what happened! Is this some form of torture: Some kind of punishment? What the hell?! I have been racking my brain when all along, you know!" She was incensed by the injustice of it all. Bryn let her rant and rave. In the end, she ran out of puff and came back to sit with Bryn. "Go on! Tell me. I insist on knowing what happened and what my brain is refusing to remember," she demanded, infuriated .

"Sorry, it doesn't work like that. Why do you think you have blocked it out?"

"I'm not playing anymore. You aren't being fair at all! I want to know what happened - please!"

"No, not happening. My rules, not yours," Before Clara leapt up again in fury, he added, "But you answer one question of mine - properly - and I will answer one question of yours. Deal?" Glaring furiously, she conceded. "Right, why do you think you have blocked out this part of the evening?" She sighed and fished around for an answer, about to say, 'a bump on the head caused concussion' when she caught his eye and thought about it properly. She badly wanted to be able to ask her question.

"Well, I have been thinking I have blocked it out as something terrible, more terrible than had already happened, occurred, and is too awful to recall ..." she spread her hands earnestly, hoping he believed her. He considered for a moment.

"If I were to tell you that, nothing as bad as what happened in the cold storage room happened later, does that help you to remember?" She had the grace to consider this for a moment, but she shook her head looking regretful. He held the silence for a few long minutes, then said.

"During the time you can't remember, there was a gunfight." Clara leapt up, totally infuriated now.

"I know that much! Otherwise, I wouldn't have a bullet hole in my chest, would I?" she screamed at him in rage. "That's not an answer, and I haven't asked a question yet, so you let me ask one!" He sat waiting for her to calm herself and frame a question. With an effort, she reigned in her emotions, eventually sat back down, and asked. "Who shot me?" Bryn smiled sadly.

"That, my dear, is the one question none of us can answer and are waiting for you to. I will give you another one." Clara was calm now, her mind racing, it was like a jigsaw puzzle. She needed to know what everyone else said happened, maybe she could then try and see it from her perspective. She thought about another question.

"Who was in the room when I was shot?" Bryn sighed, and walked over to his desk, returning with a report in his hands. "This is an account of what happened from witnesses who have reported what they remembered," he raised it high above his head as Clara eagerly reached for it, "Wait," he cautioned, "This has a high price, are you ready to pay?" Clara fell back into her chair.

"That's blackmail," she grumbled sulkily.

"Do you want to hear my theory on why you can't remember?" Clara looked at him, waiting for him to continue. "Well, I think the trauma of what you had been through was too much. You shut down, as a survival mechanism. It is not what happened afterwards that is the cause of the block. It is what happened just before: Between you leaving the cold storage and reaching the kitchen and Barney." She was watching him closely, guardedly, suddenly wary of where this was going; it had taken a bad turn. Bryn realised he was striking close to the source of the issue. Clara's face had drained of colour and small beads of sweat were forming on her lip. Her hands started to twist and turn in her lap.

"Yeah," said Clara jumping up "I don't need to read the report." and she headed towards the door.

"Open that door and walk out and I will recommend you are allocated a different counsellor, I promise you." His voice left Clara with no doubt he meant what he said. She rested her head against the door, trying to control her breathing. After a few moments, clearly, with great effort, she returned a little way, to stand behind the chair she had been sitting on before.

"When I am doing things that make me nervous or afraid, I pull my feelings and imagine casting them into a deep lake for safekeeping. I know I have to go back for them afterwards, but some I would rather leave where I put them - such as the ones you are now asking me to fetch." Now it was Bryn's turn to jump to his feet.

"Who told you to do that?" he demanded sharply.

"Told me what?" Clara asked, playing for time, sensing she had given something away - had Bryn taught someone else that trick? Rick? She shrugged, "I dunno, you, probably. It sounds like something you would recommend. What does it matter? It works for me anyway - up to a point."

"How many times have you worked for the Secret Service? None of your trick answers, I want to know the truth." She looked at him in amazement ('Does Rick work for them then?' she wondered).

"I never have! I don't. I am only tied up in this malarkey because I refused to leave my friend, you know that. Have you heard anything to the contrary with your level of security clearance?" She challenged him. He ran his hand through his hair and sighed deeply.

"Clara, these experiences are not adventures to be enjoyed as a career you know. Whoever is talking in your ear, don't listen to them. You do not want this kind of work and should not need to employ such tricks - it is emotional suicide! You do not need strategies to protect you, because you never need to be in such a position again. Let Luke love you. Finish your master's. Find a career where you can exercise your deep desire to 'make a difference' and 'help others' - there are so many ways you can do this - but not this way - stay away."

'I am not sure it is a choice ...' she thought. Out loud she said, "Bryn, it's okay, you know I don't want that kind of work."

There was silence while both tried hard to recompose themselves.

"Right then," said Bryn with effort, "let's go back to the feelings in your lake; which ones do you think you need to fish back out to relieve the mental block you have inadvertently created?" Clara stiffened. "I am going to have to insist you relive the, let's say, ten minutes before you ended up in the kitchen with Barney. Barney was already there, having crawled to safety after being shot in the thigh. You can stand, sit or even lie on that couch over there, but any which way, you are going to tell me - now."

He felt for her, but kept a neutral profile, as he watched her struggle. She seemed to know she was out of options, out of time, out of tricks; she stayed where she was, white, drawn, and clutching the back of the chair so her knuckles shone bloodlessly.

"What happens if I can't do what you say?" she said, her voice breaking. He ran his hands through his hair again and slouched forwards.

"I don't know, Clara, I don't. There are other methods we could try - hypnotism? Perhaps we are rushing things; how about we have another go tomorrow? And don't spend the intervening time worrying about it - or making up an alternative story," he added with a sharp look at her, "We will take it step by step; we'll get there." He thought grimly of the phone conversation he had had to endure earlier from Headquarters. Everyone was straining to get their hands on Clara, to extract the information they desperately wanted by methods they thought would work. He couldn't protect her for much longer.

CHAPTER 26

Top UK chart hit: August 1986
Lady in Red: Chris de Burg

Clara woke instantly, all her senses alert and alive. The window had been open to let in a cooling breeze, a sash window above the porch to the house. But someone had come in and was in the room. She lay frozen, the gut punch of cold terror stealing her ability to move or even breathe. But then she felt Jenny stir beside her, and adrenaline kicked in. She sat up to face whoever it was, to protect Jenny to death if need be.

"What are you doing here?" she whispered, getting out of bed carefully and going across the room to him. "I thought this house had been secured. How did you get in undetected?" she asked, panic rising as the implications of him standing in front of her coiled and twisted in her brain. 'Who are you?' she thought for the hundredth time. He put his fingers against her lips, and 'shushed' her.

"Who says I was undetected, and I wasn't given a leg up into here by the guard?" he whispered into her ear.

"Well, you can't stay here. I am not having a child mixed up with all this." she hissed back. At her words, he looked around at the bed. He went across, lifting the sleeping child into his arms. Jenny murmured and he turned to Clara, indicating with his head she was to show him Jenny's bed. She led the way across the landing and watched as he gently lowered her down. Clara pulled the duvet around Jenny and dropped a kiss on her forehead. Then she followed Rick back to her room.

As she eased the door closed, he was standing right before her, a blurred image in the night. She could see his outline, the white of a plaster cast on his leg, and the glimmer of his teeth when he spoke.

"You are still having nightmares too - Does the little girl stop them? I have been ejected from the marital bed and told to come back when I can stop thrashing about. I think we need to sort ourselves out, don't you?" Clara considered his words carefully.

"Yes but -"

"But? There's a but? Go on -"

"If I remember what I have forgotten, I will be in danger, won't I? Everyone is after it and won't move while I remain forgetful. Maybe I don't want to be healed this time. Maybe, I will walk away, with my memory loss intact - Rick, I don't want to remember."

"Let me reassure you my love, you are in mortal danger as you stand there in front of me. Has it occurred to you it may be in someone's interest to make sure you never remember? How would they be certain of that?" The seconds ticked by. An owl screeched outside, making them both jump. That in turn made them smile at each other. She made up her mind.

"Okay." He scooped her into his arms, as if she were no heavier than Jenny, and laid her on the bed, before climbing in beside her. He reached her to him, and they hugged each other, both drawing close and intertwining. Clara luxuriated in his strength and the feel of his iron-like girdle of arms braced around her. She felt safe and able to relax, letting the walls crumble, free to let them fall. Rick felt her determined reach around him and her hands massaging against his back, drawing him to her. She felt him relax into her side.

They talked in undertones, into each other's breath, as if one voice. They took each other through their own experiences of the evening, encouraging each other to interlace the emotions back into the accounting. The honesty they were able to articulate was more binding and more erotic than any physical touching could achieve. Clara experienced the sheer terror of connection between them as well the ecstasy of it. The rollercoaster ride took them to relive the cold monster of fear. Clara was able to let it engulf her, while she lay in his arms. Feeling safe and secure the horror lost its power; The ice cold turned lukewarm and slid off her back.

Rick shared his torment of having to make decisions that saw his good friend fall in front of him in the restaurant that night. He let in the grief as he saw once more the life in the eyes switch off like a light, blood drip from the mouth. The death stare eradicated the memories of a good man. Clara held him to her, stroking his hair and back in rhythmical caresses with complete understanding and empathy. Clara was seeing Saanvi again before her eyes. She heard once more her cry. Clara turned at the sound of her voice. Saanvi was alive, eyes wide, a pale face in the gloom. The next second she had gone, dissolved into splintered shards of flesh expelling Clara backwards at such force it was as if Saanvi's last breath had spat Clara out. A final rejection.

The two bodies clung to each other as the storm of retrieved emotions rode above them, tore through, and left them washed ashore, bedraggled and gasping. Then, tenderly, and deliberately they made love. Rick gently manoeuvred her on top, so she could stay in control and manage her mending ribs as they rode their passion to its climax, collapsing in a silent shuddering heap. After a moment while they steadied their breathing, Rick kissed her on the top of her head and swung his legs over the bed to sit up. Silently he dressed, and Clara pulled on her dressing gown.

"I will let you out the front door or you might break the other leg," she whispered, going over to the door. Before she could open it, he pulled her back, and in a firm embrace whispered to her.

"If you remember anything, tell Bryn first but stay with him and insist he phones what you remember through to Headquarters. This is important. Understand? I will send extra security in the meantime." He opened the door, and they crept downstairs. She let him out into the night.

Clara went back to bed and fell asleep immediately. She dreamed she was under the table taking shelter from the falling masonry, trembling. Her world literally in pieces. Barney was lying with his head in her lap. He had been shot in the thigh and she had tried to tie a tea towel around the wound to stem the blood. He was grey and ashen.

"Bloodbath out there!" he told her through gritted teeth. "They are trying to take out that Jorwain guy, but he is not alone and well-armed. I was trying to give our guys some cover to allow them to get out, but they are cornered. It is going to end badly ..." He seemed to lose consciousness for a moment. Clara let his head down gently on the floor and taking the gun from his grip crept out from under the table and approached the restaurant. She had lost Saanvi; she was not going to lose Rick as well all in one evening.

She had no fear, she was beyond that. She crept forward so she could view the room. Rick and two others she assumed were 'our guys' had their backs to the wall in one corner. There was shooting from other angles of the room. As she watched one of the three crumbled and fell at Rick's feet. Rick faltered and a bullet skimmed his ear. Rick glanced over at her, and she knew what to do. Sheltered partly behind the counter, she fired indiscriminately across the room, to surprise and disorientate the others for a moment. In that split second Rick and another flew across to an upturned trolley, diving for cover.

Clara huddled behind the counter; her job done. She was about to retreat to be with Barney in the kitchen when she caught movement at the door. Reinforcements had arrived. A swarm of flak-jacketed gunmen flooded the front of the restaurant. Even more shooting was ricocheting around the room. She ducked to avoid getting caught in the crossfire and peeked out, to watch. Navy blue-clad men fanned out across the room. She watched as the two behind the trolley shuffled it backwards, using it as a shield, intending to join Clara behind the shelter of the counter. She saw one of the navy-clad gunmen peel away from the others, dodge behind pillars, using falling rubble and plaster as cover, and aim at the trolley, now directly in her line of sight. Rick and his partner, looking towards the front of the restaurant where the battle was now going on, stood to dash the counter. Clara saw the lone gunman aim. If they ran now, the lone gunman would get at least one of them. She couldn't tell them in time what the problem was, as they had their guns trained in a different direction. So, screaming at them as she went, she ran full pelt at them to shove them as hard as she could from the line of fire. She felt the jolt of impact as she slammed into two grown men running, followed by a sharp sting in her chest that then seemed to explode, blowing the air out of her. She was falling down a rabbit hole, spinning faster and faster, feeling sick and dizzy. Then everything faded away and she woke up with a start.

CHAPTER 27

Top UK chart hit: August 1986
Calling All Heroes: It Bites

Clara was having breakfast when the others came down the following morning. As they started to get their breakfast, she suggested as lightly as she could that it might be a good idea if Linda dropped the kids off with Granny for the day on her way to work. Linda and Bryn exchanged glances, and then Clara exchanged a meaningful look with Bryn. After a moment of hesitation, he supported the idea. The kids were not pleased to be suddenly faced with a day with Granny, and Jenny wailed.

"I will only go if the handsome prince comes back tonight - will he Clara?"

"If you are good," Clara replied.

"What prince?" Ewan wanted to know.

"He was so handsome! He came and lifted me in the night and took me to my bed, he was lovely! Why did he do that Clara? I wanted to stay with you - don't you want me anymore? Is he your handsome prince?" Aware of Bryn's stare on her, she spoke to Jenny.

"Hush honey, he was a dream. I took you back to bed, it was too hot last night. I thought you would sleep better that way."

"No, he wasn't a dream!" Jenny protested, "I saw him - he had a bandaged leg, how did he hurt himself?" Her nerves already stretched to breaking point, Clara couldn't take anymore. Unable to come up with any further plausible responses, she ignored Jenny and wandered out of the kitchen, onto the veranda. She stayed resolutely out there until she heard the children's voices and the car engine die away in the distance; until she heard the heavy tread of Bryn come out to stand beside her.

"Join me in the den please." he said sternly. She followed in his wake. He launched at her even before the door was closed.

"What the hell is going on? Who was it in the house last night and who did you permit to go anywhere near my daughter? Don't deny it, none of your tricks now. Honestly Clara, I don't recognise you half the time these days. They are sending more security guards by this afternoon for all around the perimeter of the garden. But I suppose you know all about that, do you? I am not having my family put at risk! Do you hear me?" He yelled at her, fear and fury combined. It reminded her of her first-ever meeting with Bryn when he had yelled at her as a first year, for not caring about an essay she had written for him. She felt herself shrink back to that person she was then. Her heart starting to hammer, her tongue dry, her brain turning to mush. But then she thought of the issue she was trying to resolve, what she had to achieve. She stepped out of her old self to take command of the situation. She waited for him to finish yelling at her. "Now you answer me this minute because I will not have anyone in this house put in further danger"

She spoke softly but earnestly, looking him in the eye, willing him to be calm, and accept what she was saying.

"Bryn, I am so sorry. I will tell you everything you want to know, of course. I love Jenny and Ewan as much as I love anyone in this world. I would never do anything to put them at risk. You must believe me. I am tangled up in things I only partially understand. Distrust and mistrust seem to weave throughout everyone I meet. There are no rules to the games they play, and if I am bringing any danger to this family, then I will go and pack this minute and leave. Please," she finished, beseeching him to settle down a little, and be ready to listen. He had stopped pacing about in a rage, but was suspicious, eyeing her cautiously. She wasn't there yet. "I promise faithfully to answer every question you ask me if you do something first?" Still reluctant to bargain, he waited for her to continue. "I want to tell you what I have remembered, and I want you to immediately phone the number you usually ring to GCHQ and tell them too. Then I will sit here with you and answer every question you put to me, no games, just straight answers." She looked at him, holding her breath.

"I no longer know what to believe. How have you suddenly remembered when last night you were trembling at the thought; oh, your midnight visitor is a better counsellor than me, eh?" he spat bitterly. She winced, feeling his pain.

"No," she said quietly, "no one is better than you - he had, um, different methods, that's all. They are impatient with me." He went quiet at that, seeming to read something into it. Then he shrugged.

"Right, the sooner we get all the answers the sooner all this will be over. Life can go back to normal, and I will not be afraid for my children." He switched on the tape he always used in their session, took up a notepad and pen, and assumed his cross-legged position in his chair, while she obediently took hers. She told him about her dream. "Who shot at Rick then?" He asked when she had finished.

"Alec." She looked at Bryn's blank face. " Alec, Luke's project leader. I don't know his surname." Bryn was startled. He protested.

"Clara, surely not, rethink. You have made a mistake. The place was falling around you; how can you possibly be sure? Why would he turn up at the restaurant dressed like that, firing a gun, when he is a researcher and probably sharing the latest figures with Luke over a pint?" But Clara shook her head.

"You promised to phone it in when I had told you the account. I may be wrong, but that is my opinion and that is what everyone is waiting for. Please ring them now." He looked at her calm and determined expression, then went over to the phone. 'I know what's happening here,' he thought, 'she was so fed up, frightened by whoever was here last night, with everyone waiting for her memory to come back, she has dreamt up this elaborate story. I'll play along so she feels more relaxed, with no one hanging on for her recall, then she may truly remember'.

He dialled the number while she watched and waited. He told them who he was and what he wanted to report. He repeated her story, glancing over to her as she watched him. He said she wasn't 100% sure she recognised who it was and he would continue to work with her. He put the phone down. Clara settled back in the chair waiting for Bryn to join her to ask all his questions. He had just sat down when the phone rang. He answered and after a brief exchange turned to Clara.

"It's for you." He held out the receiver. On the end of the phone was a voice sounding as if it belonged to a substantial man.

"Clara? The report Bryn has just called in, well a couple of questions or follow-ups - you know the gun was pointed at you, not Rick, right?"

"Yes, I have figured that out, think everyone made the same mistake initially, didn't they?"

"Smart girl. So, I guess you have also worked out why?"

"Not really, but I need to get out of here now, I don't want to bring trouble to this family, can you get me out?" Bryn had come over and was hovering, a hand on her arm, trying to tell her not to worry.

"We need you to stay put for a minute, while we, um, look into it."

"Hey, no you don't! I wasn't born yesterday. I am not playing cat-and-mouse games. Come and get me out, or I will just leave. Now I think of it, that might be the best ..."

"No, stay there. We will be there as soon as we can." The line went dead.

"They are sending someone immediately, to get me out of here, to keep you safe," Clara told Bryn.

"Come on, let's go make a coffee and go outside, then you can tell me the answers to all my questions while we are waiting." Together they busied themselves in the kitchen making a pot of peppermint tea. Bryn was just pouring it out into mugs when the kitchen door opened, and Alec walked in. As he did so, Christian entered from the living room.

"What's going on?" said Bryn sharply, looking from one to the other.

"It's fine Bryn, thanks for keeping her. We'll take her to safety now. Luke is waiting for her." Alec moved in to take Clara's arm, nudging her out of the door. Christian wordlessly followed, leaving an uncertain Bryn, standing helplessly in the middle of the kitchen with a teapot in his hand. He knew Alec so well that despite the news Clara had provided earlier, Bryn still could not believe Alec was the one who had shot her. He didn't know who the other man was. Perhaps Clara had it wrong, as he had expected, and this was the rescue party; she had said they were due to arrive immediately. With the security man on the gate, they wouldn't have been able to get in anyway, if they were not meant to. He thought he would however just go and check. He wandered out to the gate. The friendly guard he had got to know over the past week or so, was slumped against the gate with a bullet through his head. In a panic, he rushed back through to his office to the phone. The phone line was dead. He raced to his car to go for help, but his tyres were slashed to ribbons. So, teapot still in one hand, he set off on foot across the fields to the neighbour's house, to break in, if necessary, but to seek help.

CHAPTER 28

Top UK chart hit: August 1986
Don't leave me this way: The Communards

The trio went down the garden, through a gap in the hedge
they had presumably found earlier, and up into the field
opposite the house. Alec looked grim and wild-eyed. He kept
one hand squeezing her upper arm. The other held a gun trained
on her. In such a fashion, they walked clumsily, constantly
tripping each other and knocking together as the path was
narrow and uneven. Clara kept casting glances at him, but his
jaw was set, and his eyes registered no recognition nor emotion.
She tried talking to him.

"What is happening, Alec? Alec? Where are you taking me?
Why?" She tried to get some reaction, but there was nothing in
return. They stumbled on. Clara knew the path, she had come
this way many times with the kids, picking blackberries in early
September. When they reached the top of the hill there was a
small coppice of scraggly looking trees. By this time Clara was
feeling angry more than anything else. It was a riddle seeming
to make no sense. Why couldn't she solve it? Why Alec? And
why was Christian here? He was 'trogging' along behind like

some obedient puppy, saying nothing. God, he drove her mad - couldn't he give her a clue, make a noise, a sign - anything to give her an idea of where he fit into things? What was the common link; Alex, Christian and herself?

Then suddenly she made the connection; they all spoke Russian. The clouds of mystery rolled back: This was nothing to do with the affair at the Blue Tiger, this was to do with Russia and Sergei in some way!

As Alec forced Clara to stop in a small clearing, making her kneel on the ground, she looked up at him and said,

"Pochemu ty eto delayesh? Chto on dob'yetsya?" (Why are you doing this? What will it achieve?") This time she hit home, although it was not a reaction she wanted - his face turned puce with anger, and he reared up above her. Brandishing the gun, he struck her with it across the face making her fall, sprawled to the ground.

Alec replied in Russian: "How dare you address me in Russian! You are not fit to speak to me in that tongue. If I could have found you earlier, or had more time, I would have made this a much more painful death for you than it will have to be!" he spat out.

The gun had given a glancing blow to the side of her face. Her face stung making her eyes water, and she felt the blood run down her cheek, dripping to the ground. Alec pushed her roughly back into a kneeling position, pleased to see the tears and blood everywhere. He ordered Christian to tie her hands behind her back. He peered into her face grimacing at her.

"They should have put a bullet in you at the same time they put one through Sergei," he told her, still speaking Russian. Then he stood back and aimed, pointing the gun at her chest, declaring loudly to the crows in the trees above them that she deserved to die. At that second Clara propelled herself forwards grabbing Alec around the ankles and toppling him backwards. The gun fired up into the rookery above and a cloud of rooks streamed up into the sky, wheeling and screaming above them. Their noise hid a second shot that rang out just after the first. As Clara raised herself from her rugby tackle it was to find Christian standing over Alec's body, a small gunshot wound in Alec's head, and a gun hanging loose in Christian's hand.

She staggered a little distance and collapsed onto the grass, searching in her pockets for a tissue to mop up the blood from her scratched face. Christian fell into a heap beside her, and they sat, looking out over the countryside, both breathing heavily. After a few moments, once the birds had settled again back into their messy lookouts, Clara glanced across at Christian. He looked white. She gently took the gun from his hand and put it in her lap.

"What the bloody hell was that all about then?" she demanded. Without looking away from the horizon he muttered.

"Classified." She lifted the gun from her lap, pulled back the clip at the top, making a reassuring clicking sound. She pointed the gun at Christian's head.

"Try that answer again," she said, in Rick's icy tone. Christian glanced across and with a start leaned away from her, alarmed.

"For god's sake Clara! What are you doing? I just bloody saved your life you know! Put the gun down!" But with steely resolve, Clara repeated her question, her arm steady and unwavering.

"Start talking Christian. I am a little beyond the 'classified' response, you should know." He looked at her with narrowed eyes, registering through his shock that things were different, she was different. He shifted uneasily.

"Put that thing down. It's rude to point it at people. I will tell you but play nicely," he said in his more normal tone. Clara sighed, released the spring on the gun and returned it to her lap.

"I wouldn't have shot you anyway, I suppose - even if I felt like it." They caught each other's eye and smiled, the tension leaving them. Chris put an arm around her shoulder.

"We don't have much time," Christian said, "Knowing you, you have pieced it all together by now anyway ..." Clara pulled out of his clumsy embrace and turned to face him.

"A few questions then," she said, "Alec wasn't even Russian, why was he so zealous about communism?"

"No, he was Russian. Well from Ukraine, anyway. He disguised it well: He was a double agent, working to help squash a potential nationalistic uprising in Ukraine for the Russians, as well as passing on information to the British."

"How can someone work for both? Why, it makes no sense?"

"He has a wife and kids being threatened, or they were. The Government there needs to. He was originally a 'nationalist' working to support the Ukrainian desire for independence, working for us. Sergei was getting information to him to pass on. But Sergei must have caught on before we did, that Alec had switched. That's why Sergei turned to you. Ever since then Alec has been incensed by the betrayal, and after you."

"Thanks for the warning," she told him bitterly, "But you are wrong. He had plenty of time to get to me before the other night. He works with Luke and has been in and out of our flat discussing research constantly. Why attempt to infiltrate a gunfight surrounded by all kinds of agents on the outside chance he could take a random pot-shot at me? No, not buying."

"Well, it's true. He wasn't after you until Luke, naturally, I guess, told him all about the break-in at the flat and you being involved with those linked to the Blue Tiger. Alec had an inside connection with a young naive lass on police radio (She's been 'alleviated' from her post now.) who regularly let him in on communication. So, he already knew there was surveillance focussed on The Blue Tiger and started to suspect you. On Saturday, your name cropped up many times in radio communication what with your idiotic disappearance from a safe house, then your reappearance in the back of a surveillance vehicle, and your request for the bomb squad's attention - you can't keep a low profile if you tried! - Ow! - He then put two and two together and made five, deciding you had duped him and were an operative! Really! You? I mean! - Okay, okay Clara, don't punch so hard! - It was opportunist: As he listened in on events unfolding Saturday night he preyed on the chaos, wove his way into the restaurant, hoping to find you already blown up; sorry - " Clara had flinched at the last words, and Chris, being uncharacteristically sensitive, rubbed her back briefly before continuing. "It wasn't until your report came in earlier, and different departments linked up across different operations that the penny dropped. I was already appointed to 'keep an eye on', and 'build a sympathetic relationship' with Alec, as he had triggered a few alarm bells due to the company he was keeping outside work, so he tasked me to help him today - and he led me to you."

"And so where does Simeon fit into this then?" Clara asked him, frowning.

"Who? The student from Russia at Birmingham Uni? I don't think he does - does he? How do you know so much?"

"I don't. It seems odd, to have someone from Russia in the same research team, who met Alec for coffees, and for there not to be a link." Chris was getting cross with her; she was supposed to be the thankful saved victim. He scowled at her and shrugged, pulling bad-temperedly at blades of grass at his feet. Silence fell once more as both were lost in their thoughts.

After a while Christian heaved himself up, and stood in front of Clara, to pull her to her feet too.

"Come on." She followed him back down the way they had come only a short while ago.

"Chris?"

"Mmm?"

"Thanks. Did it cost you a lot - to not tie my hands, and shoot him dead?" A long silence. He kept on walking, but then he stopped, turning to wait for her to catch up.

"Just between you, me, and this bramble, a lot. I have killed a key informant. He became side tracked by the desire to kill you. But you should have been collateral, we needed to keep him alive; he didn't know we were on to him."

"Had you intended to allow him to kill me then, up until the last moment?"

"Yep." He looked at her for a second but then his eyes slid away towards the hedge. She smiled to herself. Then he looked back at her, almost angry. "But I didn't think you would be so placid! Why no fight, no struggle? I thought it would be impossible to take you so easily."

"You need to learn telepathy then! I figured you would either rescue me or were now a double agent and in which case, there was no escape I could see."

"You could have jumped through the brambles or something as we went up the hill, that is half what I expected you to do."

"I had a gun trained on me! But, yes, I did consider that option. But I was curious as to where we were going."

"Bloody hell Clara! I have told you before; curiosity is dangerous, and in your case, life-threatening! Can't you take advice?"

"From you Chris? No. Anyway, you are lucky I didn't. You need to brush up on your powers of observation because by deciding to save me, you saved yourself." He frowned.

"How come?"

"I presume that 'execution' spot was preselected and you were there earlier today?" He nodded. "Well, the little grassy hillock you made me kneel on, ensured you were standing behind me, on lower ground. Alec barely waited for you to tie my hands together, let alone stand away. The bullet, which he looked as if he was going to put into my heart, was also going to go straight through yours too. Very tidy. Don't know much about guns, would the bullet have gone that far?" She didn't need him to answer verbally to know the answer. "I suggest your cover was indeed blown." She stated the obvious. He looked at her steadily for a long moment, then grabbed her to him and stole a kiss in his usual rough and impolite want of snatching affection from her. They were both aware of a team of uniformed men coming towards them.

"Catch up with you later kiddo." He tore into the brambles and vanished from sight. Clara could only be impressed by this ability to breach such a thorny barrier. She turned to meet the police coming her way.

It was mid-afternoon and the sunlight was catching the thistledown as it lazily floated over from the opposite field. There had been long and repetitive interviews on the events of the day with varying tiers of authority and 'men in suits'. The house had undergone a thorough invasion of police, and plains clothes 'engineers' fixing phone lines, checking for 'bugs', and any other evidence they needed. The garden had been closely inspected, and the two dead bodies had been tidied away in body bags. Even Bryn's car tyres had been replaced. As Bryn and Clara sat in the living room, the last of the retinue of workers packed up and left. There was no trace of anything untoward happening to rock the quiet and stillness of this tiny corner of rural tranquillity.

"You know, I have no real idea why what happened here today, did: But I have a feeling, you do," Bryn observed. Clara nodded.

"Wheels in wheels - things that don't seem connected one day are tied together the next."

"But how could Alec want to shoot you, shoot innocent people? He was such a nice guy. I thought I could assess people! I introduced him to Luke; is that how he crossed your path; I placed a killer in your way?"

"He was a nice guy, so you were not wrong. He happened to be a 'mole,' I think that is the term, as well as a researcher. He was being coerced. His family was being threatened, so a 'good guy' really. It was not your fault at all," she told him reassuringly, whilst recalling to her mind the demented red eyes staring at her as he attempted to kill her. There was no right or wrong, she thought, just grey.

They lapsed into silence.

A man came into the room, with a ready smile and a warm handshake. Clara recognised him as the man who had taken cover behind the trolley with Rick at the shootout in the Blue Tiger. He introduced himself as Matt and took a seat on the sofa between her and Bryn.

"We are nearly all done here now," he informed them, giving them a wide smile. "Sir," he addressed Bryn. "I must say it is good to meet you, you have a fantastic reputation. Um …" He hesitated, "would it be possible for you to 'take me on' or whatever the phrase is? Rick particularly speaks highly of you, and I know he came out the other night for counselling - he was struggling with Sam's death. It was amazing, the next day he was back to his usual self. Would you mind?" With a glance across at Clara, who was suddenly absorbed in plucking invisible fluff off her jumper, Bryn nodded his head.

"Sure, whatever Rick says though, I can't produce miracles; but you are more than welcome." Matt headed for the door, then remembered, patting his pocket.

"Oh, Clara, I promised to deliver this to you." He passed her an envelope. She thanked him. Shaking hands with them both once more, he left, shepherding anyone else still around with him, so in a further five minutes, the house settled quietly around Bryn and Clara. They were left alone together for the first time since their tea-making earlier that morning.

Clara took in Bryn's pale and tired face, the way he was slumped in his chair as if exhausted. She went over and sat on his lap, hugging him as he buried his face into her neck for a few moments. Then with a deep sigh, he pushed her off him and stood up, leading the way out onto the veranda.

"So, it was Rick you trusted to carry my daughter." he stated, an edge to his voice.

"I love Jenny. I did not let her out of my sight." Was her reply.

"Clara, be careful. This man: I warned you against him, remember? How did you heal him? How did he make you remember when I couldn't? Did he hurt you?" The tension in Bryn's voice rose with every new thought and question. He turned to face her, full of fear. But she refused to meet his eye and stood resolutely staring out over the valley. She shrugged.

"I heard your warning Bryn, so I am aware, but we have a 'connection'... I can't explain ... We work well together."

"Clara? Do you love this man?" he asked anxiously, "He's just getting married. Do you know?"

"Yes, I know. And no. Love? No. Not love." She thought of the power of emotion that bound them, how it seemed to frighten them both. "No. I trust him. That is what is important. Trust. Nothing is more important than that."

"I beg to differ. Love, love is the most important thing in all this world."

Clara thought about what she knew of love. The cosy feeling of being home when Luke scooped her to him in the night, the flutter of her heart when she heard him turn the key in the door at the end of the day, that glow of intensity when he gently crushed her lips against his velvet touch; it was also his silent corrosive disapproval of what she wanted to do and to be, it was the ironing out of interest into routine and it was the hunched back turned away from her on the end of her hospital bed. Love was friendship, laughter, giggles, and a place of safety to discuss life - and then suddenly it was nothing at all but horror and emptiness.

"Not for me; love seems to me like a gilded cage with no key. It comes with too many conditions, full of false promises leading down a cul de sac. I don't want it," she said with certainty, hearing Saanvi's heart-breaking cry before she dissolved into a million pieces and seeing again, Luke, blundering away from her when she needed him.

"Clara! You can't mean that! You are still healing after your experiences. Give it time. You still have a long recovery journey to make. You need to think about what you want to do, which paths to follow." They watched the swallows swoop.

"When I am fit again, I think I am going to go to the opera," said Clara thoughtfully watching the paths of the diving birds. She patted the envelope Matt had given her, now in her pocket. Inside was a ticket to see the opera Tosca, with a post-it note stuck to it that said 'G'. "Or," she said, "I might go and look for a lost cousin in America - I haven't quite decided which yet." They both stood to watch the swallows gathering along the power wires, preparing to leave to head South for the winter.

&&&&&&& THE END &&&&&&&

AUTHOR'S NOTE

This story is a product of the author's imagination. Places and characters have been inspired from the author's own experience but are totally fictional and bear no resemblance to them other than a source for creativity.

Clara's adventures relate to real historical events. The Cold War was at its height with tensions running high between the Soviet Union and the Western countries in 1984/5, fear of imminent nuclear annihilation far closer than any of us knew at the time – however, the world Clara was flirting with were aware of it at the time and the significance of being able to access the information Sergie was trying to transfer was urgent and crucial. The Pakistan-Indian land dispute was also pertinent at that time, and although the involvement of the Blue Tiger is fictional, the struggle between India and Pakistan over the Siachen glacier has been going on since the late 1970's. The incident that spurred Jorwain to fury was based on a true story. Pakistan purchased climbing equipment from a provider in London. India used the same provider and learned of the new order of climbing equipment by Pakistan, thus getting wind of Pakistan's plans. India raced them to the top. This is why Pakistan felt so betrayed by the British and suspected the Government of taking sides – the retailer unwittingly upsetting relations between everyone.

This is the first book in a series of Clara Day mysteries.

ACKNOWLEDGEMENTS

I acknowledge with gratitude all the help and encouragement I have received to bring this book into the daylight. To name but a few:

Firstly, thank you with all my heart to Linda Ellis, and Alison Humphries, the first to be introduced to Clara. Their sustained encouragement has made me brave.

Secondly, grateful love and thanks goes to my daughter, Hannah Munro O'Brien, whose combination of unvarnished criticism and timely encouragement has developed my ability to reflect, edit and re-write to improve the book from when she first read it; so be very grateful to her!

Thank you too, my daughter, Caitlin Munro-O'Brien, for your quiet certainty that the book will be good – I hope I haven't let you down.

My Beta-readers have been essential in their keen eye and combined positivity when doubts besieged me. Thank you to Suzanne Mitchell, Hannah Powell, Louise Rogers, Flo Kingfisher, Jane Parsons and Ginny Bridger.

Many thanks to Jane Tomlinson for her creative advice on cover design.

Thank you to Michael Heppell and his Write That Book Masterclass for providing the momentum to drive the book towards reality; and to Matt Bird for his skills and patience in typesetting and finalising the cover design.

ABOUT THE AUTHOR

I write what I like to read. Clara, the hero of the book, was born while I looked after my father in his last years. She was my alter-ego as she leapt from my imagination into a world away from quiet sickness into adventure, intrigue, and romantic excitement.

Unfortunately, unlike Clara, I didn't go into the spy world on leaving university, I went into teaching and then educational management. I have a degree in geography and psychology and a master's in environment and developmental education. I have taught in Zimbabwe and England.

In my spare time I have written articles for Country Life and Coast on environmental phenomena such as sand dunes, waves and the life of snakes found in our countryside. I also have a blog site about, the sea - shared! It aims to bring to as many people as possible, the deep soul-thumping drum of the waves and calming moments of reflection to improve mental health and a sense of well-being.

Let me know how you liked the book:
www.marinemoments.uk/fiction

Ideas for book club discussion on Into the Shadows

1. To what extent is this a book about the relationship between trust and love?
2. How does this book compare with your own experience of living through the late 1980's?
3. How does the author's belief in there being a deep connection between human emotion and the natural world manifest itself in the story? How does Clara use this connection to her own benefit?
4. What message does this story give those who feel crippled by being shy?